DO566316

8/23/11

MR. DARCY'S DREAM

MR. DARCY'S DREAM

ELIZABETH ASTON

THORNDIKE PRESS
A part of Gale, Cengage Learning

GALE
CENGAGE Learning™

Detroit • New York • San Francisco • New Haven, Conn • Waterville, Maine • London

GALE
CENGAGE Learning

LIBRARY OF CONGRESS CATALOGING-IN-PUBLICATION DATA

Aston, Elizabeth.
   Mr. Darcy's dream / by Elizabeth Aston.
      p. cm. — (Thorndike Press large print clean reads)
    ISBN-13: 978-1-4104-3974-1 (hardcover)
    ISBN-10: 1-4104-3974-7 (hardcover)
   1. Darcy, Fitzwilliam (Fictitious character)—Fiction. 2. Young women—England—London—Fiction. 3. Large type books. I. Title.
PS3601.S86M73 2011
813'.6—dc22
                                       2011018065

Published in 2011 by arrangement with Simon & Schuster, Inc.

Printed in the United States of America
1 2 3 4 5 6 7 15 14 13 12 11

For Amanda Patten

CHAPTER ONE

Phoebe Hawkins was twenty years old, handsome, well-born, and with a fortune of fifty thousand pounds. Here she was, at the start of her second London season, the world at her feet, and yet if there were a more miserable young lady in all of London, she would be surprised.

It was mid-morning. Phoebe was standing in the study of her family's London house, a fine building in Aubrey Square, looking across the desk at her father, Sir Giles Hawkins, with a mixture of despair and hatred.

Phoebe had been fast asleep, lost in dreams of present and future bliss, when her maid abruptly awakened her, saying that Sir Giles wanted to speak to her at once. And with the quick sensibility of a young woman in love, she knew exactly why her father had summoned her. Mr. Stanhope must have called, just as he said he would, to ask for her hand in marriage — "As to my heart, you already have it," she had told him. Perhaps he was downstairs now, at this very moment, waiting for her. Phoebe shrugged herself into a morning gown with more speed than care, and stood, wild with impatience, while Miniver did up the hooks and coaxed a brush through her tangled hair.

Phoebe did not for a moment expect her father would raise any objection. To be sure, Arthur Stanhope was some ten years older than she, but that was no kind of an age difference. He was rich, well-bred, and would one day inherit his father's title.

So it was with utter disbelief that she heard her father's cold and definite words.

"There is no possible way that I would give my consent to your marriage to Mr. Stanhope."

Phoebe's heart missed a beat. She had misheard, this couldn't be right. "I don't understand," she cried. "Mr. Stanhope wants to marry me, and I wish to be his wife. How can you refuse your consent?"

Sir Giles shook his head. "You and Mr. Stanhope are not going to marry. I expressly forbid it. It is nearly a year until you are of age, but I will not give you any hope that at the end of that period you will be able to marry him. He knows that I am not prepared to give my consent, now or in the future. You may think that when you are one-and-twenty you will be able to marry whom you please. However, should you go against my wishes in this matter, do not expect to take your fortune with you. I have control of that until you are twenty-five. You may say Mr. Stanhope will take you as you are, without a penny to your name. But he knows that at present he cannot marry you, and I told him that by the time you attain your majority, you will have forgotten him."

"How can this be? When did you speak to him? Has he been to the house this morning? Why did you not call me sooner? Why was I not allowed to see him?" Phoebe put her hand on the corner of her father's desk, feeling quite dizzy. She could not believe that this was happening to her. How could her father, her kind, affectionate father, be speaking to her in this cold and forceful way?

"Mr. Stanhope called upon me to ask formally for your hand in marriage. I told him, as I am now telling you, that there can be no question of my agreeing to him marrying you. I have asked him not to seek an interview with you, and not to approach you, or talk to you, should you meet at any of the parties and functions which lie ahead. I cannot say that he took it in good part, but he is a man with some sense of honour, and when he considers what I had to say, he will see that I am right."

Phoebe pressed her hands to her ears, wanting to shut out her father's cruel words. Why was he behaving like this? Forget Mr. Stanhope, and in the few brief months until her birthday? Impossible! She was in love with him, as he was with her, how could they forget one another? She tried to explain this to her father, but he brushed her words aside. "It is not for you to decide whether you may or may not accept an offer of marriage. While you must have a preference, an engagement is a matter for your family, for their lawyers, and for the family and lawyers of the man to whom you finally become betrothed. That man is not Mr. Stanhope."

Phoebe's dismay began to give way to anger. She was a dutiful daughter, and while she was normally on excellent terms with her father, teasing him and joking with him, knowing that he liked her playful ways, she rarely stood up against his authority, mostly because he so rarely exerted it. This was a stranger sitting in front of her, and she could not fathom what had turned him into a man that she had never seen before: stern, forbidding, and refusing to listen to her.

His face softened. "Believe me, Phoebe, I do understand something of your feelings. However, in this case you must allow me, as your father and as a man with a great deal more experience of the world, to know better than you do what is possible, and what is right. And, forgive me, but your attachment to Mr. Stanhope is of such recent standing that you will accept that any parent would be alarmed by talk of engagement. Am I not right in saying that you were unacquainted with Mr. Stanhope previous to your coming to London this time?"

"You know that to be the case, for Mr. Stanhope has been abroad. He is not a friend of our family, and I could not have met him before this year."

"Exactly. And by saying that he is not a friend of the family, you bring me to one of my principal objections to the match. You are, I suppose, aware of who his parents are?"

Phoebe was irritated by this. Yes, she did know that Mr. Stanhope's parents were Lord and Lady Stanhope. What was remarkable about that? Her father seemed to expect an answer, so she simply nodded.

He continued, "You should also be aware that Lord Stanhope, and indeed Lady Stan-

11

hope, are prominent in Whig circles. Now I am not to be suggesting that simply because a man is a member of the opposition, while I am a staunch Conservative, means that any antagonism existing within the Houses of Parliament should be carried into the outside world. Yet there is a grain of truth in the saying, 'Once a Whig, always a Whig.' And Whiggishness is not simply a matter of how a man votes in the House. It is also a matter of outlook, and going beyond politics, into the realm of morality; public morality and private morality. I do not personally think we will see another Whig government within my lifetime. That does not diminish the power and influence carried by the leading families. They have always worked behind the scenes, and by means of marriages and using family connections have exerted a force beyond what is reasonable."

What had this to do with her and Mr. Stanhope? What was all this talk of Whigs? She knew that Lord Stanhope did not share her father's political views, but was that so important? Certainly, her father had always had a dislike of Whigs, as many Tories did. But this was the nineteenth century, they were not living in the Middle Ages. Was he going to try to pretend that the Hawkins family and the Stanhopes were like the Montagues and Capulets in Shakespeare's *Romeo and Juliet*?

"Fustian!"

"No, it is not fustian. You are very young, Phoebe, and do not yet know what makes the world go round. You have had a protected upbringing, I am glad to say, and know no more than is suitable for a well-bred young lady. You will not have heard the scandals and intrigue that follow every member of these Whig circles. They make light of the marriage bond . . ."

His voice faltered and faded away. He had touched on an unmentionable subject, and his eyes dropped as Phoebe looked straight at him. "I do believe I know something about the loosening of marriage bonds," she said.

They looked at one another for a long minute, the unspoken words clear in both their minds, the knowledge of a time when the marriage bonds of Sir Giles and Lady Hawkins had been stretched to breaking point.

The long-repressed fury finally spilled out of Phoebe as those words rang in her ears, *make light of the marriage bond.* "You say that to me! You who caused Mama so much unhappiness when you set up that woman

13

as your mistress, how dare you criticise other people?"

Sir Giles had risen to his feet, his face thunderous. "That ever I should hear a daughter of mine speak in that way. You sound like a woman brought up in the gutter."

"I sound like a girl who was brought up in a household where her father had a mistress, and her mother —"

"I forbid you to say it," said Sir Giles.

"Feelings are not to be silenced. And you condemn an entire group of people, not quoting any individual circumstances; I find it disgraceful, and uncharitable, and in the circumstances inappropriate."

"It is for me to decide what is and what is not appropriate."

They fell silent. Phoebe's chin was up and she stared at her father with such defiance that he in his turn found it difficult to say anything more. Finally, he banged his fist on to the desk. "Very well, I am sorry it has come to this. You are saying that I have condemned all the Stanhopes, Lord and Lady Stanhope, and therefore by association their son, Mr. Stanhope, merely for being Whigs. This is not so. Your Mr. Stanhope has to my certain knowledge been conducting a lengthy affair with a woman

14

called Mrs. Vereker. You look conscious. You know the lady, an uncommonly beautiful woman, an actress of humble origins who managed to ensnare the late Mr. Vereker, and so insinuate herself into society, where by birth, manners, and behaviour she had no place."

"I do not care if Mr. Stanhope has had a mistress. He is a military man, a man of more than thirty. I do not expect to be his first love."

"No, and if I were fool enough to let you marry him, you would most certainly not be his last love. The man is a rake, Mrs. Vereker is simply the latest in a long line of paramours. I dare say she was at the party last night where you were with Mr. Stanhope. When he came this morning, he swore he had fallen in love with you; I do not consider his words to be worth anything. Were I to give my consent to your marriage, you would, he supposes, go to him as a bride with a substantial fortune. I can only suppose that with high living he finds himself in financial difficulties and so looks for an heiress to wed."

Tears started into Phoebe's eyes, but they were tears of rage, not of weakness. Fighting them back, she looked down at the carpet, where the rich Turkish patterns

15

wavered and blurred before her eyes. "You slander him, you have no justification for what you say."

"I speak nothing but the truth. Ask one of your married cousins about Mr. Stanhope's reputation, about Mrs. Vereker and the others before her, all at the same time, for all I know." He lowered his voice. "Phoebe, believe me, it hurts me immeasurably to distress you in this way, but it is too important a matter for anything less than honesty and clearheadedness." He took a heavy breath, and speaking with apparent difficulty said, "You referred to an episode in my own past life, an episode of which I am ashamed. I will not speak of it, now or ever. It is not a subject to be discussed with my daughter. However, it is because I wish to spare you the unhappiness I caused your mother that I refuse to let you marry a man like Mr. Stanhope. It is my final word. You can weep and wail, although that is not natural to you, or you may rant and rage at me; it will not alter my resolution one jot. You may write to your mother, to ask her to exert her influence with me, but I tell you that it will all be in vain. I know that your mama will be at one with me on this, and you know me well enough to be sure that once my mind is made up I am implacable."

Phoebe left her father's study in a state of greater anger than she had ever known. Her father had risen from his seat and come around the desk to pat her on the shoulder, and had wanted to embrace her, although she drew away from him. Then he said, unforgivably, in her eyes, "One day you will thank me for this. You will meet another man, a better man, who loves you and whom you will love and with whom you will make a very happy marriage. It is not as though you have not had other admirers; indeed, you know I have had more than one young man approach me to ask consent to pay his addresses. You have laughed and scorned them all and asked me to refuse all your suitors, however eligible some of them were. I can understand how a man of fashion and address such as Mr. Stanhope could have caught your fancy, but I assure you fancy is all it is. You could not truly love a man of his character."

The problem was that Phoebe did love Arthur Stanhope, that she had never loved any man before, and that she could see no way that she would ever care for another man as intensely as she did for Mr. Stanhope.

She had come dancing down the stairs, but it was with feet of lead, and a heart as heavy, that she ascended the stairs to return to her room. To her relief, Miniver was not in the room. She did not give way to tears, nor throw herself on the bed, nor take up the pretty vase from beside her bed and dash it to the floor. Instead, she went to the window and looked out over the square, her heart thumping inside her chest like a drum marching men into battle. The weather matched her mood. Lowering grey clouds hung over London, a steady drizzle made the pavements look dark and dirty. The trees in the garden in the centre of the square still had a wintry look to them; spring was late this year. She turned away from the window and went across to her little walnut writing desk. She sat down, took out a sheet of notepaper, dipped a quill into the ink, and began to write.

Dear Mr. Stanhope . . .

She got no further. A letter would not do, how could she say all she had to in a letter? No, she wouldn't write to him, she would go to see him.

Once this plan entered her head, she brushed away all thoughts of how improper such an action would be. If anyone saw her going into his house, then her reputation would lie in shreds.

So much the better, she told herself as she pulled the bell with vigour, calling out at the same time for Miniver, whom she felt sure would be lurking somewhere in the vicinity. She didn't want to take Miniver into her confidence, and so she simply told her to fetch her pelisse, as she was going out.

"Going out where, Miss Phoebe? Shall I ask for the carriage to be brought round? And I'll have to put on my own outdoor clothes, I had no idea of your going out so early, and I've all your jewellery lying soaking —"

"I am going out alone. Go and fetch me a hackney cab, and don't you dare let my father get wind of what I am about."

"A hackney cab? Go alone in a hackney cab? And where to, may I ask?"

"You may not."

"It's more than my place is worth. Sir Giles would scalp me, and then turn me off without a reference. A fine thing that would be!"

"Oh, very well, you may come with me. Go and find a cab, and tell it to wait around the corner."

Miniver pursed her lips. "It isn't right."

Phoebe was not in the mood to put up with Miniver's moral disapproval. "It isn't for you to say what is or isn't right. I will be out in ten minutes, be there with the hackney cab."

Miniver shut the door behind her with a bang discreet enough not to be noticed by other servants, and loud enough to express her disapproval. Phoebe sank down on the chintz-covered sofa. She closed her eyes, as if by doing so she could shut out the images flitting through her mind. She could remember last night with such startling clarity that the scene might be taking place again there before her eyes. She had been at an informal party, given by the rich and amiable Mr. Portal. The season was not yet under way, but Phoebe had come early to town with her father, who had parliamentary business to attend to. Her mother was due to come up to London next week.

It was just such a party as Phoebe liked best. And her pleasure in the evening was capped by the arrival of Arthur Stanhope. She had been standing beside Mr. Portal, and laughing at one of his witty remarks, when she saw Arthur Stanhope standing at the door. Their eyes met, hers brimming with merriment, and his amused and alight with pleasure in seeing her.

They talked, as they had done ever since they first met, a conversation which, Phoebe felt, could go on for the rest of their lives and never grow boring. They went down to supper together, and then afterwards, her cousin Camilla persuaded her sister Alethea to play some dances for the company.

Oh, that exquisite moment when Mr. Stanhope took Phoebe aside and led her into a little alcove, quite deserted, and there took her into his arms, and in a voice quite unlike his usual calm tones, told her he loved her. His kiss, gentle, then growing more passionate, had wrapped Phoebe in a cloud of velvet delight, and when they drew apart to look into one another's eyes, she felt a joy such as she had never experienced.

CHAPTER TWO

As this scene replayed over and over in Phoebe's head, her feelings finally overwhelmed her, and she clenched her fists until the pain of her nails in her palms brought her to her senses.

She must hurry, surely Miniver had been gone ten minutes. She opened the door of her room, looking up and down the corridor to make sure she was unobserved, and then flew down the stairs to let herself out of the front door before the butler or a footman came hurrying to see what she wanted and enquire where she was going. A minute later, she was turning into the street which led out of the square, and there, at the end of the little street, stood a hackney cab, a fat jarvie sitting on the driver's box, and Miniver leaning out and gesturing to her to hurry.

The cabman leaned back to ask where they wanted to go, and Phoebe, panic-stricken, remembered that she did not have Mr. Stanhope's exact address. He lived in Melbury Street, that was all she knew. Well, she would tell the man to go to Melbury Street, and once there, someone, a servant or a deliveryman, would know which was Mr. Stanhope's house.

It wasn't far, and as the hackney carriage rounded the corner, the driver pulled up and asked which number she was wanting. Phoebe was about to ask Miniver to get out and make enquiries, when she saw a door open a few houses down. A tall, familiar figure came down the steps of number 19. Mr. Stanhope. Phoebe rose, and was ready to jump down when she saw the man turn round and speak to someone hidden from sight. She shrank back, all too aware of how improper it was for her to be making a call on a man. Who was he talking to? A servant? In a minute, the door would shut, and he would come down the street. An accidental meeting, that was much better, not the severest critic could find fault with that.

A carriage was coming down the street from the other end, and to Phoebe's dismay, it drew up outside number 19. It was an elegant equipage, a lady's carriage, she would have said. And even as this thought entered her head, a woman came out of Mr.

Stanhope's house. She had an exquisite figure, and walked down the steps with a light gracefulness which Phoebe could not but envy. The woman was wearing a veil, but Phoebe didn't need to see her face to recognise the notorious Mrs. Vereker.

Mr. Stanhope took both Mrs. Vereker's hands, and raised first one and then the other to his lips in a gesture of affection and finesse that caused Phoebe's throat to constrict with anguish. He handed Mrs. Vereker into the open carriage, and as it drew away, she blew him a kiss. He watched the carriage out of sight, and then went back up the steps and into the house. The door closed behind him.

Phoebe sank back into the scruffy seat, and Miniver, alarmed, banged on the roof, calling to the man to take them back directly to Aubrey Square.

"And that'll cost you a second shilling," he muttered as he backed his horse to turn round. "Counts as two journeys, and why bother, that's what I want to know?"

Phoebe's mother reached London two days later, and Sir Giles lost no time in telling her what had happened. "She's taken it badly, won't say a word to me, treats me as though I were an ogre, won't go out. It's to be hoped you can talk some sense into her. She's pining, I dare say, as young ladies will when they fancy themselves in love. It's good for a girl to have an unhappy time in love now and again. It satisfies the romantic side of their nature. You'll be able to deal with her, you'll know just what to say."

Lady Hawkins forbore from telling her husband that he was a fool. She saw that her daughter had been deeply hurt by what had happened, and also, sadly, that the relationship between Phoebe and her father had changed, perhaps for good. Phoebe, in the very short time that she had been apart from her mother, had shed the last of her girlhood and seemed older and more reserved. Certainly the zest had gone out of her life, and it was Lady Hawkins's opinion that she would not get over Mr. Stanhope as quickly and easily as her father predicted.

Phoebe would not discuss it with her mother. No, she didn't care anything for Mr. Stanhope, her father was quite right, she could not be happy married to a rake. No, she didn't want to go out, thank you, not shopping, not to any party, Mama would make her excuses, she could say she had a slight cold and was staying indoors. And when Lady Hawkins tried to make her change her mind, Phoebe turned on her with what was almost savagery, begging to be left alone, and saying that she wasn't at present fit for any human company.

What was to be done? In her own mind there was no question of Phoebe launching into the busy social life of the season, not if she were to be in this state. Sir Giles said that as soon as the balls and parties and picnics and routs started, she would forget about this whole affair, and enjoy herself just as she had done the previous year; Lady Hawkins thought otherwise. Apart from anything else, Phoebe was far from in her best looks, and with that and a listlessness that was not natural to her, she was unlikely to have a successful or enjoyable time. The London season was ruthless, and the mothers of her fellow debutantes would be quick to notice that something was amiss, rumours would spread, and Phoebe would become even more unhappy.

Lady Hawkins, wiser in the ways of the world than her husband, also had a suspicion that the attachment between her daughter and Mr. Stanhope might have been noticed. She held to the old adage that love cannot be hid, and she suspected that Phoebe had made no secret of her liking for Mr. Stanhope. There would be gossip, and to a girl with Phoebe's pride, it would wound. She was coming to the conclusion that it would be better for Phoebe to leave town. If she were not there, new gossip and new scandal would quickly take the place of any stories about her and Mr. Stanhope.

Lady Hawkins did not know the Stanhopes as well as her husband did, but she took his word for it that the match was a wholly unsuitable one, and indeed the last thing she wanted was to see Phoebe married to a rake or a philanderer. And since Phoebe apparently felt the same, they would have to let time do its work and heal her daughter's hurt.

In the end, with some trepidation, she broached the matter with Phoebe, whose response was immediate and adamant. She did not want to do another London season, she would prefer to go home to Hawkins Hall.

That presented a problem. Sir Giles had planned that, while he and Lady Hawkins and Phoebe were in London for the season, the younger girls would be taken to a seaside resort by their governess, to enjoy the sea air and the benefits of sea bathing, while he had some essential works carried out at the house. It was already arranged and the workmen would be moving in within the next week or so. Of course,

Phoebe could accompany her younger sisters and the governess to Ramsgate, but it was a resort which Phoebe much disliked, and when the family physician, Dr. Molloy, was consulted, he said that the seaside would not be beneficial for her.

Phoebe had flatly refused to see Dr. Molloy, saying with truth that there was nothing wrong with her health.

"I would not recommend the waters at Bath or Harrogate, either," he said when Lady Hawkins summoned him for a private talk. "Not for one of her years. From what you tell me, and from my knowledge of Miss Hawkins's constitution and temperament, her complaint lies rather in the mental than physical region. Country air and familiar surroundings would be best for her at this time."

It was Phoebe's cousin Camilla who came up with the obvious solution. Why should not Phoebe go to Pemberley? Camilla Wytton was a Darcy by birth, and had grown up at Pemberley, Mr. Darcy's seat in Derbyshire. Phoebe loved Pemberley, where she had spent many happy times with her numerous cousins all through her childhood. It would be quiet, but there would be some company for her in the form of Lady Mordaunt's governess, as her two boys, together with the young daughters of Camilla's elder sister Letitia, were to spend the summer there. They would be in the charge of this Miss Verney, apparently an excellent young woman, if French, so that Phoebe would not be alone. She could walk and ride, and some of the neighbouring families would be bound to be fixed in the country.

Camilla was concerned about Phoebe, and she had a fair idea of the cause of her cousin's disinclination to stay in London. She had the notion of talking it over with her father, Mr. Darcy, and reported back to Lady Hawkins. "My father is having work put in hand at Pemberley, in the gardens and park; he has a dream of a new landscape there, complete with splendid glasshouses. I dare say he has been reading Mr. Coleridge's poem, and plans a new Xanadu, with a stately pleasure dome to rival that of Kublai Khan, I must say I am wild to see it all when it is all done. However, that need not bother Phoebe. He is very glad for Phoebe to look after all the arrangements for the summer ball he and Mama are holding at Pemberley in June," she went on. "No, do not look so doubtful. I know no one more capable than Phoebe, and it will keep her extremely well-occupied. Any ball at Pemberley will be delightful, Aunt, as you know better than anyone, but I have a feeling that Phoebe will add some special touches that will make it a more than usually splendid affair."

So Lady Hawkins in her turn visited her brother, Mr. Darcy, who was on the point of departing on yet another one of his foreign trips, and he assured her that he would indeed be delighted for Phoebe to stay at Pemberley and manage the ball. His steward and housekeeper would be there to give guidance and advice, and his secretary, the admirable Mr. Tetbury, would not be accompanying him abroad, would be in London, and could be consulted by letter when necessary.

Phoebe was relieved rather than pleased when her mother said she might go to Pemberley. She would even have gone to Ramsgate in order to get away from London, and as soon as the visit to Derbyshire was agreed, her eagerness to leave town increased.

The news brought ecstatic happiness to another member of the family. Her next sister, Sarah, was to have been one of the seaside party; although she was already eighteen. Lady Hawkins had wished Phoebe to have another season to herself before she brought Sarah to London for her come-out. In the circumstances, it made perfect sense for Sarah to do a London season, in Phoebe's place.

Lady Hawkins planned to travel back to Hawkins Hall with her daughter. From there, Phoebe would make the journey to Pemberley, and then Lady Hawkins would return to London with Sarah. Meanwhile, wise in the ways of the world, she made sure that Phoebe, albeit reluctantly, attended one or two small, private parties — although she had taken great care to ascertain beforehand that there was no chance of Mr. Stanhope being among those present. Those who saw Phoebe noticed and commented upon how pale and pulled she looked, and Lady Hawkins was at pains to talk in quiet tones of a tiring, persistent sore throat which afflicted her daughter and the benefits country air would do for this entirely imaginary complaint.

"That should quell some of the gossip," she said to her husband.

Two days later, Lady Hawkins and Phoebe, with Miniver in attendance, left a still-grey and wet London to make the journey to Hawkins Hall, which was situated in Warwickshire. Phoebe's spirits were as dreary as the weather, and as the carriage rattled out of Aubrey Square, she felt as though she were leaving part of herself behind.

CHAPTER THREE

Louisa Bingley was always pleased to receive a letter from her cousin Camilla. The one she held in her hand had arrived from London that morning, and she sat reading it in the old drawing-room of her parents' house in Derbyshire. This was one of the original rooms of the house, not much used by the family now, since a new wing with a large drawing-room had been added to the house some years before. The cosy, panelled room was a favourite place of Louisa's, and had gradually become thought of as her own private sitting room.

Louisa should have been upstairs in her bedchamber, advising Betsy, once her nurse but now her maid, about which of her clothes to pack up to take to London. Louisa was about to embark on her fourth season, a fact which was astonishing to most people who knew her, since Louisa had inherited all her mother's beauty, besides also sharing her good nature and her kind ways. Like Phoebe Hawkins, a connection by marriage, she did not lack for suitors, but she had simply never met a man that she particularly cared for. She resigned herself, quite cheerfully, to a single future. She would be an aunt to her nieces and nephews, for her younger sister had been married these two years, had produced a fine son, and was now expecting a second child.

She read the letter from Camilla through again. So Phoebe would not be in London, but would soon be on her way to Pemberley, to recover from a bout of persistent low spirits, which had led her and her mother to decide that a London season would not be right for her this year. The news surprised Louisa, for she had never known Phoebe to suffer from low spirits; her vitality was one of the most striking things about her.

Louisa was three years older than Phoebe, but despite the difference in age, they had always got on well together, and they shared many happy memories of the summers when various members of the Darcy family and their connections gathered at Pemberley. The Bingleys, who lived some thirty miles from Pemberley, often spent days over there, Mr. Bingley enjoying the company of his close friend Mr. Darcy as much as the excellent fishing, and Mrs. Bingley always pleased to see Mrs. Darcy, her favourite sister.

Phoebe was in trouble. Camilla said nothing explicit about the situation, but reading between the lines it was evident to Louisa that Phoebe had suffered a shock of some kind. And, unless the trouble was a further estrangement between Phoebe's parents — Louisa, with her calm and watchful nature, had been well aware of how difficult things had been for a while in that quarter — then the most likely cause was an affair of the heart. That surprised Louisa, too, since Phoebe had managed her numerous admirers with great skill, a witty tongue, and a refusal ever to take any of them seriously. None of them had ever come close to touching her heart; that was a part of herself that Phoebe kept out of reach of the men she laughed at for being fools or peacocks.

Louisa knew that many in the family hoped that Phoebe and Jack Harlow, the son of a family whose estate was close to Pemberley, might make a match of it. They were almost of an age, had been childhood friends, and had a great deal in common. Although Louisa liked Jack, she didn't feel that he would make a suitable husband for

Phoebe. Amiable as he was, he would be unlikely to stand up to her, and Phoebe could never be happy with a man that she could not look up to and respect.

At that moment Betsy came into the room, summoning Louisa in peremptory tones to come upstairs that instant, or her trunks would never be ready. Louisa followed her maid to her room, deep in thought, and told Betsy in abstracted tones to leave out a dress of pink taffeta that she much disliked, which Betsy, against the express instructions of her mistress, was attempting to pack into one of the large trunks that stood open on the floor.

Betsy upbraided Louisa for not listening to what she was saying, and Louisa, with a start and a guilty smile, apologised and said that she was thinking over the contents of the letter that had come from Mrs. Wytton. "Miss Phoebe is not to do a London season this year but is to go to Pemberley."

"Pemberley? Is she in disgrace? Has she been in some scrape?" From her long service with the Bingleys, Betsy felt herself at liberty to speak her mind, and indeed there was little about the family that she wasn't privy to. And she knew perfectly well that it was a family joke that often, when one of the lively Darcy girls and various other members of the family were in trouble of some kind, she would be packed off to Pemberley to rusticate and keep out of mischief.

"No, no, it is nothing of the kind. Although it does seem — I am not sure, Mrs. Wytton is rather opaque, but I think there may be an affair of the heart, some young man . . . Betsy, I do not want that spencer, I thought last time I wore it that the colour does not become me. Phoebe will be very dull at Pemberley, all by herself. Mrs. Wytton writes to say that Lady Mordaunt's children will be there, of course they are hardly more than babies, but they have a governess, a perfectly respectable, well-bred young woman, Mrs. Wytton says, who will be a companion to Phoebe."

Betsy snorted. "I can't see that a respectable governess, however well-bred, will be the kind of companion to suit Miss Phoebe."

"No, nor can I." Louisa looked at the trunks for a long moment. Then she made up her mind. "Betsy, leave the packing for now. I am going to talk to Mama to tell her that I am not going to go to London this year, instead I shall go to Pemberley to keep Phoebe company."

Not all the questions and objections and arguments of her family could make Louisa change her mind. And in the end, with a sigh, her mother agreed to her plan. As Mrs. Bingley observed to her husband that night in the privacy of their bedchamber, since Louisa had not in three seasons found a husband to suit her in the ballrooms and drawing-rooms of London, why should she be any more likely to this year?

After all, she and Mr. Bingley had met in the country and not in London. "It is not as though every family will be going to town. There will be those who stay in Derbyshire, and I dare say that Louisa and Phoebe, if she is well enough, will be invited to outings and picnics and parties, where Louisa may, who knows, at last meet a man she likes."

Miss Sarah Hawkins was wild with excitement and disbelief when she heard the news that her come-out was to be brought forward to this year. Starry-eyed, she greeted Phoebe, wan and drawn after the journey from London, with a warm embrace and a volley of questions about Almacks, balls, parties, riding expeditions — "Oh, you cannot imagine how glad I shall be to be rid of the schoolroom at last. And not to have to spend the summer at Ramsgate with the children!"

Lady Hawkins, anxious for Phoebe, chased

Sarah away, but Phoebe was amused by her sister's delight, and said that it did her good to see her so happy. Phoebe remembered being just as full of excited anticipation before her own first season. What a difference a season and a broken heart made. She rebuked herself; what she felt in her heart was anger, not sorrow. She would not allow herself the indulgence of dwelling on lost love and a broken heart, like some helpless heroine in a novel.

She went up to her own room, intending to give Miniver instructions about what to take to Pemberley, but she wasn't there for five minutes when she saw Sarah peeping anxiously round the door. "Mama says I'm not to disturb you or pester you with questions, only there are so many things I want to ask you. Are you quite happy again? When Mama wrote to tell me the astonishing news about my going to London, she said we weren't to worry, for there was nothing wrong with you that a few weeks of good country air wouldn't put to rights, but I must say, you aren't in your best looks."

"Thank you," said Phoebe, laughing at her sister's outspoken comments. "No, you do not disturb me, I am only sorting out some of my clothes. I am glad to have someone to talk to."

"This would have been your second season," Sarah said, plumping herself down among the cushions on Phoebe's bed, and heaving a sigh. "And no husband. Oh, Phoebe, there must have been one man you wanted to marry?"

"Perhaps there wasn't one man who wanted to marry me," said Phoebe, her face expressionless.

"I know that isn't true, for I heard Mama telling Aunt Hawkins about the offers you'd had, from the most eligible men, but you turned them all down. I shall be so ashamed if I'm not engaged by the end of the season."

"You will be no such thing. Many a young woman has accepted a man merely for the sake of a ring on her finger, and in order not to be left on the shelf come the summer of her first season, and lived to repent it for years afterwards. You know the words of the marriage service, and it is quite true," she couldn't help sighing, "matrimony is not to be entered into lightly."

"Yes, but then there must be just as many young ladies who meet the right man and fall in love, and then live happily ever after."

"That notion belongs in fairy tales, and you're too old for fairy tales," said Phoebe. "Listen to me, Sarah. Do not let your head be turned by a handsome face or a large fortune or a title, or the prospect of being mistress of a great house. None of those things will make up for not being married to a man whom you truly love, and to whom you are well suited. And above all, find yourself a good man, do not ever allow your head to be turned by a man who — that is, a man whose morals would not pass muster."

"No, Great-aunt Phoebe," said Sarah pertly. "Only I can tell you, I am inclined to fall in love, which you aren't, and therefore I dare say I shall. With an excellent man, perfect in every way. No rakes for me, I assure you, I and my best friend, Lizzy Carlow, are agreed that we both abhor a rake."

"If you expect perfection, you will be marrying the man in the moon, for I assure you, there is no such paragon alive on earth. And," she added, but too quietly for Sarah to hear her words, "when you do fall in love with an excellent, perfect man, you will soon enough find that he is no such thing."

CHAPTER FOUR

As the carriage slowed down to weave its way through the busy main street of Lambton, Phoebe leaned forward to have a better view.

Lambton was a small market town, a mere five miles from Pemberley, and she felt the sense of anticipation and excitement that she always had as she drew near to Pemberley. The great house was an essential part of her childhood and girlhood, a place of her heart, and she still found it strange to think that none of her Darcy cousins would be at Pemberley. They were all married and gone out into the world, with families of their own. There would be no Camilla, always with a scheme and a sparkle of wickedness about her, no Letty with her air of assumed authority, no Belle or Georgina, the ravishing twins. And no Alethea, scowling and filling the rooms with her music.

However, Louisa would be there, and she

was glad of that. This governess might be a charming companion, but Phoebe did not have a high opinion of governesses in general, having seen all hers off in short order.

It was market day in Lambton, adding life and bustle to the normally sleepy little town. A lugubrious shepherd was ushering a small flock of the thick-fleeced local sheep towards a pen at the other end of the street, his dog full of barks and skilful nips, while urchins cheered the beasts on, and one bright spark suggested to the shepherd that he and his friends might have a ride on the broad-backed sheep. "A sheep race, Joe, how about it?"

Here was the inn, the white lion rearing up against a red background on the swinging inn sign, and there a group of towns-women were grouped around a pedlar shouting details of the new ribbons he had in his pack, just what the fine ladies were wearing in London this season.

The carriage drew clear of the crowded street, and the four horses pulled at a steady pace up the incline out of the town. The peaks and woodlands had a clarity to them after a heavy shower of rain, and Phoebe looked out at the landscape with deep contentment at the beauty of it.

The carriage was slowing down to take the fork for the final approach to the house. Oh, such familiar sights! Here they were at the blasted oak, the twisted remains of a giant tree that had been struck by lightning years before, and which her cousin Alethea had once persuaded a timorous young visitor was home to a witch of evil mien and wicked habits.

They were passing a row of neat cottages now, dwellings for some of the workers on the Pemberley estate. A little girl was playing with a kitten in the front garden, and she looked up, thumb in her mouth, as Phoebe waved to her from the carriage.

Now they were passing through the gates at the North Lodge, and driving through more woods. Phoebe let down the glass, despite the chill wind of the early April day, eager to catch the first, enchanting view of Pemberley as the carriage came out of the wood at the crest of the hill. From here she could see the house across the valley, looking just as it always did: a fine Palladian house with its classical façade, perfect in its setting among the parklands. Smooth lawns sloped down to the banks of the river, and the rising, thickly wooded ground behind the house provided a dramatic background.

Phoebe gazed and gazed, feeling the

beauty of the house in its landscape with more intensity than she ever had before. She blinked, caught a gust of chill rain on her cheek, and, with Miniver's tut-tuts ringing in her ears, pulled the glass back up as the carriage began the descent to the bottom of the valley. Once there, it rattled across the bridge and up the sweeping incline to the house.

A footman was waiting to let down the steps of the carriage and she jumped nimbly down, followed by Miniver, who gave a Londoner's sniff as her feet touched the gravel, signifying that she still wasn't reconciled to being dragged to Derbyshire at the time of year when she wanted to be enjoying, albeit at secondhand, all the delights of the London season. Not much opportunity for her to show off her skills here, not at this time of the year. And all the gowns and gloves and wraps and shoes that had been got ready for Miss Phoebe, it was too bad.

Mrs. Makepeace, the housekeeper, had come into the hall to greet Phoebe, a rare mark of favour, and Phoebe's immediate enquiry was whether Miss Louisa had arrived.

"No, Miss Phoebe, that she hasn't," said Mrs. Makepeace. "She's not expected until tomorrow. I'd have thought she'd be here before you, what with your coming all the way from Warwickshire, and Miss Louisa only having a journey of thirty miles or so. But I dare say she had things to attend to, and couldn't get away sooner."

"I haven't come from Warwickshire today, I broke my journey last night at my Aunt Hawkins's house," Phoebe said, stripping off her gloves and rubbing numb fingers back into life. "Am I in my usual room?"

"That you are, and I'll take you up directly." Mrs. Makepeace went up the sweeping flight of stairs with Phoebe, talking all the while, enquiring about her mother and her cousins. Miniver, who thought the servants at Pemberley were inclined to be too familiar with her young lady, brought up the rear, holding Phoebe's jewel case with exaggerated care, as though there might be a highwayman lurking on the landing to snatch it from her.

"There's a nice fire in the upstairs sitting room, and I'll have refreshments sent up directly," said Mrs. Makepeace. "I dare say you started out early enough this morning."

"Yes, and without breakfast," said Phoebe. "I had nothing more than a cup of coffee, and so I am hungry. Goodness, what is that noise?"

They were standing on the landing outside

46

Phoebe's bedchamber, and a loud whooping had broken out on the stairs above them. Phoebe looked up to see four heads peering through the balustrade.

"Why, it is the children," she cried. "Come down, let me look at you."

The children, two little boys who were clearly twins, alike to the last awkward tuft of hair, and two girls of about the same age, tumbled down the stairs. The boys hung back when they reached the landing, their whoops subsiding as shyness overcame them. The older of the girls stepped forward with a bounce and put up her face for a kiss. "Cousin Phoebe," she said, stretching up her arms.

Phoebe picked her up and gave her a hug. Then she said to the boys, "Come Josiah, come William, where are your bows?"

At this, they grinned, and began to caper around her, words spilling out as they recounted some of their doings since they had come to Pemberley.

"So you like it here?" said Phoebe. "I shall come and visit you in the nursery, it is where I used to stay myself, you know, when I was a little girl."

Suddenly, little Elizabeth slipped from Phoebe's arms and Jane clutched at her skirts. The boys fell silent. A figure was gliding down the stairs, and the children watched her with uneasy eyes.

"Good heavens, what is the matter with you?" said Phoebe. This must be the governess she had been told of, the young woman employed by her cousin, Georgina Mordaunt, to look after her children while they were in England for the summer months.

She was an ethereal creature, pale, with huge eyes in an oval face. However, her words were far from pretty or ethereal as she berated the children in a mixture of French and English, scolding them for leaving the nursery without permission and for coming downstairs without her. When the diatribe had finished, she gave Phoebe a cold and unfriendly look, which the thin smile did nothing to hide. "You are Miss Bingley?" she enquired.

"As it happens, no, I am not. I am Miss Hawkins, and I may say that I am very pleased to receive such a joyful welcome from my young cousins."

"They have no manners," was the flat reply. "They are wild, positively little savages. They have been allowed to run free, and it is their father's wish that they learn some decorum, and to do as they are told."

"Decorum! Surely not, at their age, and it

48

is nothing more than high spirits and affection," said Phoebe. And then, not wanting to offend the young woman, she asked her name.

"I am Mademoiselle Hélène Verney."

"Then, Miss Verney, perhaps you would like to join me in the parlour here. I am about to have a late breakfast, and I smell coffee. I am sure there will be something for the children."

The twins and the girls liked the sound of that, but they were quelled in an instant by their governess. "It is out of the question, they must not eat between meals." With that she swept them before her up the stairs, leaving Phoebe unsure whether to feel snubbed or amused. Since it was her nature to laugh rather than to frown, she shrugged her shoulders and went in to have the food which a maid and a footman were carrying into the parlour.

Quick to pass judgement on new acquaintances, she decided that the governess would not be particularly good company for anyone; thank goodness Louisa was coming to Pemberley.

Phoebe helped herself to fresh rolls, spread with the strawberry jam for which the Pemberley kitchens were famous, and then had a second cup of coffee. Refreshed, she went to her bedchamber to change out of her travelling clothes. She didn't linger, for Miniver was at her most disgruntled, complaining about a supposed odour in a clothes press, and full of ill tidings about the household.

"All at sixes and sevens, with the gardeners having to do this and do that, and the service road nothing but a stream of mud, so that the dairymaids bring all the dirt into the kitchens and Mr. Lydgate is troubled with his back, which has put him into a nasty temper. In my opinion, the steward of a house like Pemberley should know better than to go putting his back out. Then there's that French governess, no one likes her. Gives herself airs, and complains all the time. We'd have done better to stay in London, Miss Phoebe, and that's a fact."

Phoebe had expected to dine alone that evening, but as she went upstairs to change out of her dress, which now had a distinctly muddy hem, Mrs. Makepeace waylaid her on the landing and said, with a disapproving sniff, that the governess insisted on dining downstairs and not upstairs in the nurseries. "Being that she's a gentlewoman, it's her right, but with only her in the house, it's not sensible. However, those were our instructions from Miss Georgina — Lady Mordaunt, I should say."

Phoebe found Miss Verney a morose companion. When Phoebe remarked on the pleasantness of the room — the smaller of the two dining rooms at Pemberley, which had recently been redecorated and was now a much lighter and a more airy apartment, with the windows lengthened and giving on to the small, circular conservatory that had been added to the house — Miss Verney raised huge, angry eyes from her bowl of soup.

"My grandfather's house in France had three dining rooms. It had a hundred and twenty-nine rooms all together; in comparison, Pemberley would be no more than a cottage."

The idea of Pemberley as a cottage appealed to Phoebe's sense of humour, and she laughed. Then, seeing that Miss Verney didn't share the joke, she apologised. "Where is your grandfather's house situated?"

"Nowhere," was the reply, accompanied by a regretful sigh. "It was in Normandy, but it was destroyed in 1790, during the revolution. The *sans-culottes*, the peasants, ransacked the house, everything was stolen, and then they burned the house to the ground. With torches. Several servants were killed."

"That is dreadful. I hope none of your family were harmed," said Phoebe.

"Not by the fire," said Miss Verney. "They had been warned by some of the more loyal servants and they escaped in good time. Of course, many of them perished in the Terror, torn apart by the crowds, or despatched by the guillotine. Two uncles, an aunt, many cousins. Since my family are of the nobility, many of the aristocrats who were murdered were relatives or connections of mine."

So Miss Verney came of an émigré family. "It was fortunate for you that your parents escaped."

"Yes, they escaped, with great difficulty and in great danger all the time. And therefore, instead of being the mistress of my own home, I am reduced to being little more than a servant in the house of a rich Englishman. My grandfather, who was a count, would turn in his grave if he could see me now. I am glad that he is not alive to see how his family has been degraded."

Phoebe helped herself to a dish of chicken and peas in silence. It was a far from uncommon story: French aristocrats who had lost everything under the Terror or under Bonaparte, forced to eke out a careful living as exiles in England, finding it hard to exist in a world where the only money they had was that which they earned for themselves.

"I would have had a large dowry, I would have made an excellent marriage," Miss Verney burst out. "Now I am a governess, looking after the children of people who are not noble at all, who do not have —"

She paused, as Phoebe frowned.

"Well, you are lucky in your position, that is some comfort," said Phoebe. "There are many worse households to be employed in, I assure you."

"Yes," said Miss Verney. She stabbed at a piece of meat with her fork. "That is what I am told, but to be shut away in the country, in the cold and the rain, with no one to talk to but servants and children. I would prefer to be in London, particularly now, when the season is on. Although it is hard to see those less well born than oneself going out to dances and parties, when one remains a drudge on the top floor. I am surprised, Miss Hawkins, that you have chosen to come to the country at this time of year. Have you been ill?"

"I? Oh, no, I am seldom ill," said Phoebe. "I chose to come. As has Miss Bingley. I was in London for the season last year, and

Miss Bingley has done three London seasons. The round of parties and balls is always the same, you know."

Miss Verney put down her knife and fork and stared at Phoebe. "*Tiens!* Three seasons? And you, a season and no husband?"

Phoebe felt as though she had suddenly become a creature in a freak show, and Miss Verney evidently considered Louisa, with three seasons behind her, an object of amazement and pity.

"No husband," she said in a repressive voice. She beckoned to the footman, who was standing by the sideboard. He had a faint smile on his lips, but as he approached the table, his face was impassive.

"We shall take tea in the upstairs sitting room, Thomas," she said. She rose, and smiled at Miss Verney. "If you would care to join me?"

Thank goodness Louisa would be arriving soon, because she didn't like to be made to feel so uncomfortable at a meal. Miss Verney might belong to a noble French family, but she had not acquired the manners one would expect from such a background. Soon after they had drunk their tea, Phoebe yawned, patting her mouth with her hand, and said that she was tired, and if Miss Verney would excuse her, would retire to bed.

And I hope she doesn't come down for breakfast, she added silently; that would not be a good start to the day.

CHAPTER FIVE

While Phoebe slept on the next morning, Miniver, an early riser, was sitting at the vast scrubbed wooden table in the servants' hall, exchanging pleasantries with Mr. Darcy's French chef, and bringing the members of the household up to date with all the gossip from London.

The servants' quarters at Pemberley were not, as in so many great houses, below ground, but instead were on the ground floor, in what remained of the oldest part of the house, dating back to Jacobean times. Betsy liked the stone-flagged servants' hall with its oak-beamed ceiling and oak panelling on the walls. The kitchen, adjacent to the servants' hall, still retained a great stone arched fireplace from the times when huge fires were the order of the day. These days, a modern closed stove was installed in the fireplace for M. Joules to create his dishes, and the bread ovens were all of a new and more efficient type.

The Pemberley servants wanted to hear any news about Mr. Darcy's five daughters, who had all grown up in the house.

"We saw Lady Mordaunt when she brought the children," said Mrs. Makepeace. "Looking quite lovely, radiant, you might say."

"Expecting again," said Miniver, and Mrs. Makepeace and the two parlour maids nodded their heads.

"Isn't that what I said, as soon as I set eyes on her?" said Mrs. Makepeace.

"She's hoping for a girl; with twin boys, she wants a child who'll stay at home and not be sent off to school. Now, Miss Letitia" — the household servants all found it hard to give the former Miss Darcys their married names — "she's very happy with all her brood. Mr. Barcombe is spending a lot of time in London, church affairs, he'll end up a bishop at the very least, with his brains and influence."

"He'll make a better bishop than Mr. Collins," put in a pert maid, to be rebuked by the housekeeper.

"It's not your place, Sally, to pass remarks on any members of Mrs. Darcy's family."

"He's not close family," said Sally, arguing her point. "And none of the family likes having him to stay, poking his nose in everywhere and reckoning the value of every piece of furniture and the cost of every strawberry put on his plate."

"Never you mind," said Mrs. Makepeace. "And I hear that Mr. and Mrs. Wytton have been abroad again, in that nasty Egypt. Who would have thought those girls would grow up to do so much rampaging in foreign parts? There's Lady Mordaunt spending most of the year in Paris, and Mr. and Mrs. Manningtree with their house in Italy, and Mrs. Wytton's husband never happy to spend more than a few weeks at Sillingford before he has to be off on his travels again."

"Mr. and Mrs. Manningtree will be back in England next month," said Miniver. "Of course, nearly all the family will be here for the ball."

There was complete silence, and M. Joules, who had gone into the kitchen to give instructions to his under-staff, while keeping an ear open for the conversation from the hall, hurried in, a large spoon in his hand. "Ball? What ball?"

"Oh, did you not know?" said Miniver, pleased at the reception of her startling announcement. "Mr. and Mrs. Darcy plan to hold a big ball here in the summer, for as many as four hundred people, I dare say, and the house full of guests."

Mrs. Makepeace was indignant. "Well, it's not like Mrs. Darcy to leave me to hear such news from the lips of a maid."

"Calm down, Mrs. Makepeace," said Miniver. "There'll be a letter coming, but the post from abroad isn't reliable like it is in England. Ask Miss Phoebe, if you want to know more, for Mr. Darcy's put her in charge of the arrangements. She'll be talking to you and to Mr. Lydgate about what's to be done."

"Did I hear my name?" said a short man with a balding head. He came through the yard door, pink-faced from the wind and rubbing his hands together. "A hot drink, Sally, it's that cold out there this morning. A frost overnight, but at least the wind's dropped."

"Miniver here says there's to be a ball this summer, but we've never had a word about it."

"I have, just this morning," said Mr. Lydgate. He seated himself at the table and helped himself to one of the remaining rolls. M. Joules hovered, calling a swift command through to an underling, too keen to hear about the ball to go back to his pots and pans.

"Four hundred invited, and dozens of

houseguests, is what Miniver's just told us."

"That's right." Mr. Lydgate felt inside his moleskin waistcoat and extracted a letter. "Mr. Darcy's written to Mr. Drummond as well, urging him to press on with the works as quickly as he can. He would like the principal new glasshouse ready by them. Says to bring extra glaziers in from Bakewell and further afield if need be."

"Who's Mr. Drummond?" said Miniver.

"Mr. Drummond, now there's a nice gentleman," said Mrs. Makepeace, pleased to know something that Miniver didn't. "Fancy you not knowing about him. He's living in the South Lodge, and working all the hours God gives, even harder than the gardeners."

"Who're a lazy lot when they can get away with it," said Sally with a sniff; she had recently fallen out with one of the under-gardeners.

"Mr. Drummond is in charge of all Mr. Darcy's estate business," said Mr. Lydgate. "And, yes, Mrs. Makepeace, a most gentle-manlike person. As he should be, with a degree from Cambridge and his father in the church. He's spending some weeks here, getting to know the ins and outs of how the estate is run — he's got a shrewd business head on his shoulders, I can say that for him — and to put in hand all the improvements Mr. Darcy wants. Giving shape to Mr. Darcy's Dream is how he puts it."

"Yes, quite the gentleman," said Sally with a giggle. "And quite handsome too, as that Miss Verney has noticed."

"That's enough of that, Sally," said Mrs. Makepeace. A bell jangled in the little room outside the kitchen, where all the bells connected to the rest of the house hung in rows.

Sally looked up at the line of bells which hung above their heads on the wall. "Upstairs sitting room, that'll be Miss Phoebe. She'll have got up without you, Miniver, what about her chocolate?"

Thomas got to his feet and shrugged his coat back on. "I dare say she's noticed Miniver is sitting gossiping here when she should be attending to her duties."

"I don't need you to teach me my duties," said Miniver. "Sauce," she added to his back as he left the servants' hall.

Phoebe was indeed in the upstairs sitting room, looking out of the window at the rainswept landscape. She wished the weather would improve and was just wondering whether to go to the library and find a more interesting book when she heard the sound of a carriage. Casting her book aside, she ran out of the door and went down the great staircase to be in the hall as Louisa came up the steps into the house.

They greeted one another with great affection, but Louisa was struck by how pale Phoebe looked, Phoebe, who usually had such a glowing complexion. She had inherited the Darcy looks from her mother, but at the moment her features seemed pinched, and her dark eyes were faded and diminished by deep circles beneath them. Her bloom had quite gone, and all the life seemed to have drained out of her face.

Louisa had not expected to see Phoebe quite so lacking in her usual looks and vigour, and she could not help letting out an exclamation of dismay at Phoebe's pallor as she came forward to welcome her.

"Which is only to be expected," said Miniver. "And you don't look altogether the thing yourself, Miss Louisa, if I may say so. Sit down, do, and can I fetch you a glass of water?"

Louisa sat down with a grateful sigh. "Oh, Phoebe, I am so very glad to see you. I am sorry to be such a weak creature, but you know how travelling in a closed coach sometimes affects me, and I came in our old coach, which does sway so!"

"You'll feel better in a trice," Phoebe assured her, and she turned on the footman who was watching the proceedings with interest, hopeful that Miss Louisa might fall down in a swoon. This was more drama than they'd had at Pemberley for many a long month. "Thomas, summon Mrs. Makepeace this instant." She turned to Betsy. "Has she her smelling salts?"

"She did have them when we set out," said Betsy grimly. "Until we reached Bakewell, whereupon she lowered the window and threw them out into a ditch, declaring she never wanted to see them again."

"I can't bear the smell, and they make me even more light-headed than I am already," said Louisa, who looked to be reviving a little.

Mrs. Makepeace arrived and shook her head at the sight of Louisa. "Well, you look as though you've had quite a turn. Your room's all ready for you, Miss Louisa, with a good fire blazing away. That's where you should be, lying down on the sofa there, and I'll have a cup of good hot broth brought up for you directly, just the thing for a stomach made queasy by travel."

Despite Louisa's protests that she had not the slightest desire or need to lie down, this practical plan was immediately put into action, and she was escorted upstairs to her room, a pretty chamber with rose-coloured hangings, and settled on a sofa. "You'll be wanting to have your lunch in here, Miss Louisa, on a tray," Betsy said, but Louisa had had enough of this fussing.

"No, I won't. It is merely the motion of the coach, I shall be completely well again as soon as I've eaten."

Mrs. Makepeace promised an immediate luncheon, and went to give her orders, pausing at the door to say, "And I expect Miss Verney will be joining you — she isn't one to stay upstairs if she can help it."

"Is Miss Verney the governess?" asked Louisa.

"She is. She would have been my sole companion had you not decided to sacrifice the season and join me at Pemberley."

"It was no sacrifice. What is she like? Mama met her in Paris when she was staying with Georgina, and she told me she found her a pleasant enough young woman."

"Your mama finds fault with no one," said Phoebe. "I never knew her to say a harsh word about anyone, and you are nearly as sweet-natured as she is. What can I say about Miss Verney? She is older than both you and me, I should say she must be six- or seven-and-twenty, and is the daughter of

émigrés. And she feels the disadvantages and what she sees as the unfairness of her situation too keenly."

"You do not like her," said Louisa. "I can tell. You make up your mind about people so quickly, Phoebe. My mama may have a propensity to like everyone, but isn't that better than disliking everyone the minute you meet them?"

Phoebe coloured. "I do not dislike everyone. That is, I like some people well enough —"

"Yes, those you have known for ever, and your family. But even there, you have too demanding a standard, you are too rigorous in your judgements. You do not give time for people's virtues to grow on you, you are so quick to dismiss them that you never find out their true worth."

"Oh, as to virtues! Most people have few enough of those, I believe. Very well, I will control my natural instinct, as you describe it, to dislike people, and I will say no more about Miss Verney. But I can't emulate you, you will feel sorry for her, I am sure, and that, for you, is always the first step to liking someone."

Louisa laughed. "That is a rebuke indeed! I hope I feel compassion for those of my fellow beings who are in situations where

65

they are not happy."

"You may feel all the compassion you want, but I still hold that there is something about Miss Verney that puts me on my guard. We are not to quarrel over it, let us talk about something else, the weather, or Miniver's sulks at having to leave town." Miniver, who had stalked into the sitting room, gave a loud sniff at these words, and told them that their luncheon was laid out in the small dining room.

Phoebe tried not to dwell on what Louisa had said. It wasn't true, she didn't dislike everyone, just those people who were boors or fools or laughed too loudly, or danced clumsily or told the same jokes over and over again, or assumed that because they belonged to the male sex, they were naturally and inevitably right in any dispute or argument. And hypocrites and those who were wantonly cruel or malicious. And rakes.

That brought her to her senses, and she forced herself to think clearly about her reaction to Miss Verney. It wasn't a simple dislike, it was just that it was uncomfortable to be in the company of a person such as Miss Verney, who wore her dissatisfaction so clearly on her face and in her words.

A voice whispered in Phoebe's head, a

voice she often heard, but was quick to suppress: "And how dissatisfied would you be, were you to be forced to earn your bread as a governess, when you came from a family of some gentility, who had previously had fortune and position and now had none?"

Phoebe's was a just nature, and she had to give this argument some weight. All the same, there was something untrustworthy about Miss Verney. If she were not mistaken, she was the kind of young woman who brought trouble to those who crossed her path.

CHAPTER SIX

After lunch, although heavy clouds threatened further downpours it was not actually raining, and Phoebe suggested they take advantage of the break in the weather to venture outside. A walk to stretch Louisa's legs after the hours in the carriage would be welcome, she was sure, "And it means that you will be able to escape Betsy for an hour or so."

They went out of the French windows which led from the small downstairs drawing-room into a small, circular conservatory, fragrant with the scent of jasmine. From there, they went down some steps and into the cold, damp air of the gardens.

Phoebe turned left, as Louisa knew she would.

"I thought we might call in at the stables just for a moment," Phoebe said, when taxed with this.

"I know your equine moments, and if you

fall into a discussion with Mr. Jessop as to the points and merits of some horse that Mr. Darcy has bred, then I shall abandon you."

Phoebe laughed, and said she would do no such thing.

The stables were a short way beyond the house, through a handsome arch with a large clock that struck three as they went into the cobbled yard. Mr. Jessop, who was Mr. Darcy's head groom at Pemberley, was there, inspecting the shoe of a handsome grey gelding. Phoebe greeted him as an old friend and ran a hand down the horse's gleaming dappled neck.

"He's new, isn't he?"

"He's one of a matched pair of carriage horses that Mr. Darcy has had sent up from London. They're young and need more work and to learn their manners before he'll trust them to London streets. You looking to take a horse out, Miss Phoebe? Not that you're dressed for riding, but if you're planning to, just let me know and I'll send one of the grooms out with you."

Phoebe laughed. This was an old point of friction between her and Mr. Jessop. She preferred to take a horse out on her own, and dispense with the groom. Jessop, of a previous generation, considered it unsuitable that any young lady should ride out alone, even if she was only riding within the extensive grounds of the Pemberley estate. It wasn't merely a matter of propriety; what if the young lady took a toss, and they had to search the grounds to find her?

"Have you a suitable mount for Miss Louisa?" Phoebe asked.

Jessop released the horse's leg, and signalled to a lesser groom to come and lead the animal away. He scratched his chin and looked at Louisa. "She'd best take out Mrs. Darcy's bay mare," she said.

"Will my aunt mind?" said Louisa.

"It's not often Mrs. Darcy rides, as you know. Your mother, Mrs. Bingley, rode her the last time she was here. She's a keener horsewoman than Mrs. Darcy ever was, and you take after her, if I may say so, Miss Louisa, with nice light hands and a good seat."

"As long as the bay mare isn't too skittish," said Louisa. "I'm not such an intrepid horsewoman as Miss Phoebe, remember."

"The mare's a comfortable ride for any young lady. And what about you, Miss Phoebe? Will you be waiting to take out Viper?"

Phoebe laughed. "I'd love to, Jessop, but I wouldn't dare. It's not that I don't think I could ride Viper, but I do know that if my uncle heard that I had mounted him, I would be in trouble."

"Just give me the word, Miss Phoebe, and I'll have Marchpain saddled up for you. He's in the third stall along, go and have a look. Sir Henry Martindale bred him, and I advised Mr. Darcy to buy him, he's a lovely ride."

Louisa raised her hands in a gesture of defeat. "I knew how it would be. Phoebe, I shall leave you to the horses, and go down to the river. No, you are happy here, and I shall be just as happy on my own."

Louisa walked along the parterre on the southern side of the house and round the west end. From there she walked down the path that took her to the river, walking with care, as it was slippery after the rain. At the bottom, she crossed on to the stone bridge that arched over the river, and stopped to look down into the limpid waters, where green weed was moving lazily in the slow current.

Lost in thought, she didn't hear the sound of an approaching horse until horse and rider were only a few yards away. She looked up to see a complete stranger, a man who looked to be in his early thirties, sitting astride a nervous young chestnut, which he was controlling with some skill. He rode with the straight-backed style of a military man, wore a blue coat, and seemed very much at his ease.

"The house is closed," she said, assuming that he must be a visitor anxious to see round the house, although it was more usual for sightseers to be in a party. "There is no point in going any further."

It was odd that he should be there, for the gates had been closed behind her carriage when she had driven through, and yet this man had somehow entered the park. He looked very much the gentleman, but even so, he had no right to be here, Pemberley was not a public park to be ridden through at any man's whim. "Neither the house nor the grounds are open at present."

"And when they are, it is no doubt only between the hours of ten and one," he replied. He touched his hat with his whip. "Your servant, ma'am. I am not here to see the house, but to pay a visit."

"A visit? Whom are you visiting?" Not her, that was certain, and who else was there? Phoebe? It didn't seem likely.

"Since you ask, I am here to see Mr. Drummond."

"There is some mistake, there is no Mr. Drummond here."

"No? I stand to be corrected, but he was certainly here a week ago, and I have no reason to suppose that he has left."

"This is Pemberley, have you mistaken your destination?"

"No, I believe not. It is Mr. Darcy's seat, is it not?" He ran a knowing eye over her. "Are you one of Mr. Darcy's daughters?"

"I am not."

"No, you don't look like him, although I do see a likeness to Mrs. Darcy."

So he was acquainted with Mr. Darcy; well, that was something, but it still did not justify his appearance here, in pursuit of the mysterious Mr. Drummond.

"Mrs. Darcy is my aunt. But you are mistaken if you think a Mr. Drummond is here. No one of that name is at the house."

"No, he will be about in the gardens at this time of day. And he resides, so I am reliably informed, in the South Lodge."

"The South Lodge?"

"Mr. Drummond is in charge of the works which Mr. Darcy has put in hand. He is also an old friend of mine."

"A gardener, a friend of yours?" Louisa's eyebrows rose in disbelief. Gardeners were excellent people in their way, she herself was on the best of terms with the gardener at home, and had a great admiration for his expertise, but for a gentleman to call such a person his friend was extraordinary.

"An old and close friend," the man said. "You will no doubt make his acquaintance if you are staying here. Good day to you."

And with that, raising his whip to the brim of his hat again, he dropped his hands, and the bay, after a spirited leap sideways, cantered off up the path.

Louisa watched the rider go, a frown furrowing her brow. "Mr. Drummond! 'My friend the gardener'? What was all that about?"

Her mood of peaceful contemplation broken, she gathered up her skirts so that she might walk more briskly. It was beginning to spit with rain, and giving up her plan of a longer walk, she headed back to the house.

Mr. Drummond, seemingly oblivious to the rain which was by now falling quite heavily, put down his measuring rod and greeted the blue-coated horseman with enthusiasm. "Arthur! Good God! What brings you here?"

Arthur Stanhope dismounted and drew the reins over his horse's head. "How are you, Hugh?" He held out his hand, but as Hugh Drummond lifted his own to show the mud on it, clapped him on the shoulder instead. "I'm visiting my sister, she lives not half a dozen miles from here."

"Of course, Lady Martindale. I had forgotten she lived in Derbyshire."

"Yes, and hearing that you were installed at Pemberley, I rode over to see how you do. It is a magnificent house, I have to say."

"It is good to see you, Arthur, it's been two years or more. And so you've finally sold out, no more strutting around in your fine Hussar uniform all day and then dancing the night away in dashing style in every capital city of Europe."

"We cavalry men don't strut," said Stanhope. "Can we go in out of the rain? Or are you obliged to work outside in all weathers?"

"Good lord, no." Drummond called out to a boy who was pushing a barrow almost as big as he was. "Will, leave that. Go to the stable and tell a groom to come and take Mr. Stanhope's horse." And then, turning back to Mr. Stanhope, he said, "We can take shelter in the glasshouse. This is only a shower, it will soon pass."

Hugh Drummond was a lean, wiry man, just the build for a Light Bob, which had been his regiment when he was in the army, while his much grander and richer friend,

Arthur Stanhope, had been destined for a crack cavalry regiment the moment he decided, quite against his irascible father's wishes, to sign up. The two men had first met at Cambridge. Hugh Drummond, a vicar's younger son, and Arthur Stanhope, the eldest son of a noble landowner and statesman, might not have appeared to have much in common, but nonetheless, they became firm friends.

They joined the army at much the same time, and served together in the Peninsula under Wellington. They had both been injured in the assault on Ciudad Rodrigo, and had been invalided back to England for several months. Stanhope had insisted on his friend staying in the Stanhopes' London house, and receiving treatment from the eminent physician who was called in to attend to Arthur himself. "Not that Dr. Molloy will do any better at poisoning you with dreadful potions than any country doctor, but he charges more, and so his medicaments must be more efficacious," Arthur had told Hugh, trying to hide the concern he felt when it seemed likely that his friend would lose an arm.

But Hugh Drummond kept his arm, and stayed in the army until, after Waterloo, when he realised that the chances for advancement would become more and more limited for a man in his position, he returned to England and studied to become a lawyer.

"We can take shelter in the pinery over there," said Drummond, breaking into a run as the rain began to pelt down in earnest.

Stanhope followed his friend through the narrow door that led into a large glasshouse. It was gloomy and a smell of damp, warm earth pervaded the air. "So Mr. Darcy grows pineapples, an expensive and difficult business, I am told," Stanhope said. He walked to the centre of the glasshouse, where a small fountain stood empty, its spout thickened with verdigris.

"Yes, and it's hard to keep an old glasshouse like this at the right temperature and properly ventilated, and Mr. Darcy's head gardener is in a constant state of worry about his plants. You can't do much to improve conditions. Look at all the broken and cracked glass." Drummond pointed to the glass roof above his head, with open spaces where the glass had fallen out all together. "And it's the devil of a job picking up all the glass from the leaves and the plants. Fortunately it's not my responsibility."

"So what is your responsibility, and what

exactly are you doing here?" Stanhope asked. He reached down to investigate a broad, spiky leaf. "By the way, there's a colony of beetles taken up residence here."

"I dare say. I'll tell Grayling, he's the head gardener. Excellent man."

"You were always keen on botany and horticulturalism yourself," said Stanhope. "And your father is extremely knowledgeable, is he not?"

"Yes, and it's that knowledge which explains why I'm here, and not sweating away in a room in London dealing with whatever legal cases I can get my hands on."

"I remember you were going in for the law. Were you called to the bar?"

"No, no, it would have been far too an expensive venture for me to become a barrister, it is so many years before one can hope to make an income, and so private means are essential. No, I qualified as a solicitor, and then, by chance, a most fortunate chance, my name was mentioned to Mr. Darcy. I am now in charge of all his properties and estates, and of course the principal one is Pemberley. Since Mr. Darcy has a wish to improve the park and gardens, and to make some necessary modernization in the way things are run, I have taken it upon myself to spend some weeks here this year, putting the works in hand. One of the plans is to build a modern glasshouse or two, and so, in due course, Mr. Darcy will be able to grow a great many more pineapples for his table."

"Are you intending to pull this one down?" Stanhope asked, looking around him. "I suppose it is quite small, it is the fashion now to construct much larger glasshouses. However, these older ones have their charm."

Drummond frowned, and taking a small knife from his pocket, he crossed to the nearest set of glass panes and dug it into one of the wide wooden struts that held the glass in place. "Soft as butter, it will fall down of its own accord in a year or so, this is all rotting away. And besides, we are much more scientific these days. It is better to have a lighter structure, with narrower glazing bars, so that more light is let in. I will show you the designs for the new glasshouse, if you are interested."

He looked at his friend with a sudden smile. "But I bore you, you are not interested in glasshouses and horticulture. What do you do with yourself now you are no longer in the army? You will be following in your father's footsteps, I dare say; I am sure a glittering political career awaits you. When do you take your seat in Parliament?"

"Never, if I can help it, not until I'm obliged to enter the Lords, and I hope my father lives to be a hundred, to put off that evil day." Stanhope took off his hat and ran a finger along the brim. "I swear this is wilting in the damp, I shall have to change my hat maker." He smoothed his hair with an impatient gesture before placing the hat back on his head. "I am not interested in domestic politics."

"Ah," said Drummond, after a long pause. He didn't need to say more; he knew as well as Stanhope that to be a Stanhope was to be in the forefront of the nation's affairs. Stanhope's father sat in the Lords, and Stanhope, as his eldest son, would in due course inherit the seat with the title. Before then his father would expect him to stand for one of the family's safe parliamentary seats, and take his place among London's active politicians. Clearly, his friend had other ideas for his future.

"It is all talk and air," Stanhope remarked, watching the great drops of rain beat against the glass and then roll down in tiny rivulets. "From my time with Wellington, I know how badly the politicians let us down, how they thwarted him at every turn; I don't ever wish to count myself among their number."

"And then there is your mother," Drummond began.

"I think the rain is slackening off," said Stanhope. "In a minute we can go back outside. Tell me," he went on. "Who is the young lady who accosted me in a rather unwelcoming way, and told me the house was closed to visitors? She said she was Mrs. Darcy's niece, but I am not familiar with all the members of his numerous family."

Hugh Drummond frowned. "That will be Miss Bingley. I have not met her, but I heard she was arriving this morning. We are to be overrun with young ladies, and as the weather improves, they will all be out in the grounds, exclaiming at how inconvenienced they are by the works. I was assured by Mr. Darcy that none of the family would be here until the summer, but I find a governess is installed with some small children in her charge, not that they're a trouble, little imps; in fact, they don't get to run around outside half as much as they'd like, the young woman keeps a tight rein on her charges. Now we have Miss Bingley, and believe it or not, another of them is due in the next day or so."

"Another niece?"

"Yes, a Miss Hawkins, or so I was told." Drummond was tugging at the handle of the door as he spoke, and so didn't notice his friend's change of expression. "Warped, you see," he added as he succeeded in turning the handle.

"Mrs. Darcy has several sisters and a number of nieces, I believe."

"She may have a tribe of them, for all I know, but I just hope they aren't all planning to turn up here."

"I had always regarded you as one who appreciated the fair sex," Stanhope said.

"The governess is well-looking enough, if you like those kind of looks. I don't. Beside, she's half-foreign. And has a very predatory eye, if I'm not mistaken."

Stanhope was laughing now. "My dear Hugh, you always were run after, it is amazing that you are not yet married."

"Married! I should think not. I have my way to make in the world before I can provide for a wife as I would wish. Now you, on the other hand, are in a very different position. You are eligible indeed, I'm sure you have only to show your face in Almacks or at any fashionable party and the mamas flock around you."

"They might do so, but I've been out of London until . . . until earlier this year, and I take care to keep away from all the milk-and-water young ladies."

"Shall we go this way?" said Drummond. "I believe Grayling is in the walled garden, and I need to talk to him. And," with a sly glance, "talking of milk and water, how is the divine Mrs. V?"

"Divine!" said Stanhope with feeling. "There is little divinity about her. No, that is all over. We parted on good terms, and she has landed a bigger fish than me; I have no regrets on that score, none at all."

His liaison with the beautiful and wilful actress, Mrs. Vereker, had been a long-lasting and tempestuous one, so established that it had even ceased to be a subject of gossip in London. "When I marry, it will be to a merry-hearted, well-bred, well-mannered woman, not a termagant."

"Might you not find that dull, after Mrs. Vereker?"

"Not at all, I would not care for a dull woman. It is just that I have had enough of scenes and drama."

"And arguments?"

Stanhope paused for a moment before replying. "I like a woman to have opinions of her own. I do not admire a complaisant woman, who is always agreeing and deferring to a man."

"Have you anyone in mind?" Drummond asked as they left the gravel path and took a short cut across to a stone entrance set in a long brick wall.

"I had, but in the end she turned me down," Stanhope said shortly.

"Did she? And have you given up hope, therefore?"

Stanhope lifted the latch on the door into the walled garden and pushed it open to let his friend through. "Not at all."

CHAPTER SEVEN

Phoebe was up early the next morning, and swiftly fled from her maid's gloomy comments on her sleepless eyes, so that an annoyed Miniver found herself addressing the empty air.

A knock on the door, and Betsy came into the room, a walking dress draped over one arm, and a silk evening gown over the other. She was giving a series of orders to a footman.

"Look at this!" she said to Miniver, holding up a dark grey travelling gown.

Miniver inspected the mark on the skirt. "You always pick up marks and stains when travelling," she said, clicking her tongue. "I've got this mark to get off Miss Phoebe's dress, it's a marvel to me whatever the weather she comes back inside with mud and dust all over her skirts. And look, straw! She's been in the stables, that's what it is."

Betsy sniffed. "That's the country for you."

"Which isn't to say that London isn't as dirty a place as you can imagine. But at least the dirt in the country is nice, healthy dirt. London dirt is the worst kind. And as to weather, it was raining when we left London, and Aubrey Square was no more than a large puddle." Miniver pushed down the lid of a trunk. "Are you taking those gowns downstairs?"

"Yes, and it's to be hoped that this one will need no more than a good brush." She showed Miniver the silk gown. "You may have a little problem with travel stains, but see what I have here. This gown is more than two years old, you'd think Miss Louisa would have had enough of it and passed it on, but no. She insisted on bringing it with her, she says it's her favourite colour, and until she can find another one in the same shade, will continue to wear this one."

"Miss Phoebe has little that's as much as two years old," said Miniver as they passed through the door leading to the servants' side of the house and went down the stairs to the servants' hall. "Everything new, everything of the best, ready for her London season. What a waste. She didn't want to bring any of her clothes with her, saying she

86

wouldn't need them in the country, but I packed them up just the same."

Betsy led the way through the servants' hall, where Sally was scrubbing the big table with vigour. She was singing as she worked, causing Miniver to shake her head and mutter, "Bumpkins!"

Betsy and Miniver went along a stone-flagged passage, and then across a covered yard to the laundry. Besides the main washing and drying rooms there was a small room with a wooden table, several shelves, and a large stone sink. They shook out the gowns and set to work. Betsy hung up Louisa's walking dress on one of the hooks on the wall, and attacked the muddy hems briskly with a brush, talking all the while. "I see no help for it with the silk dress except to wash it."

Miniver mixed up a potion which consisted of fuller's earth and pearl ash. She added some lemon juice, squeezing it out from one of the fresh lemons which an under-gardener had brought into the kitchen from the orangery, and shaped the paste into little balls, which she then rolled to and fro over the stain. "It's risky to wash a silk dress. And it's a nuisance too, all that sponging, and if you don't get it just right you end up with marks on it. Still," she added, "with that dark blue colour, and the moiré pattern, it's not going to show so much."

"It's a shame to see Miss Phoebe looking so poorly," said Betsy. "I wondered when I heard that she wasn't going to do the season at all this year, but as soon as I set eyes on her I thought, Lady Hawkins has her wits about her. Miss Phoebe doesn't look strong enough to go for a walk along the street, let alone dancing the night away at balls and going on all those picnics and outings the young ladies do."

"Miss Louisa missing the season, too, that's a pity, even after she'd done three before."

"She was looking forward to it," said Betsy, keeping her end up. "Not that I was, not with all the work, and all the noise and bustle and disagreeableness of being in London."

Miniver knew not to take what Betsy said at face value. Betsy was never content, wherever she was. When she was in the country she grumbled about the mud, the weather, the cows, and the slow-witted people. In town, it was uneven pavements, dirty streets, traffic, and all the visitors wandering up and down with their mouths open. When she had visited Bath the previous year, she had been very critical of the steep hills, the vulgar people, and the glaring heat of summer days.

Miniver was very sure that Betsy was, in fact, mighty disappointed at Miss Louisa not doing the London season. With such a beautiful young lady, there must be the constant excitement not only of the parties, but of the expectation of an engagement. Someone with Miss Louisa's looks, and her fortune, might hope to make a very good match, maybe even to marry a lord. Even after three seasons — well, those three years hadn't diminished her beauty, quite the contrary. But instead of being in London, and going to balls and parties, Miss Louisa would be here at Pemberley, with Miss Phoebe. It was all very nice for the young ladies when they were growing up, but not the best place to find a husband. She said as much, and got a sharp look in return from Betsy.

"As to that, it's high time that your Miss Phoebe found herself a husband. This was to be her second season, after all, and it's not as though the gentlemen didn't admire her. But from what I hear, she's not yet met the man whose affection she can return. She argues with them and makes fun of them and is very merry about them, and drives them away. It doesn't do for a young lady to be too clever," Betsy went on primly. "Gentlemen aren't looking for clever wives."

"Maybe, maybe not," said Miniver.

Betsy was quick to catch the unspoken message. She went over to the door, which was a little ajar, and shut it firmly.

Miniver lowered her voice to the merest whisper. "Miss Phoebe had an offer, even before this season began. That's what the trouble is with her."

Betsy was agog. "Who was the gentleman? I suppose he was completely unsuitable, and that's what's put Miss Phoebe into such a state."

"Not at all," said Miniver. "Everything fine about him. He is as handsome a man as you could wish to see, and with a fine income and going to become a lord in due course."

"So what was there about that to cause Miss Phoebe to fall into the dismals? And if there was an engagement, why didn't I hear about it? Surely the family would be the first to know."

"Miss Phoebe is very reserved. She keeps her feelings to herself, as you know. What I do know is that she came home from a party in seventh heaven, and the gentleman called on her father the very next morning, to ask for her hand."

"And?" said Betsy, all ears.

"And nothing. One moment she's tripping downstairs to see her father, looking like a young lady ought to when she's met Mr. Right, and the next she's back up sitting down with a face like the crack of doom and writing a letter to the gentleman." Miniver saw no reason to mention the hackney cab. "She was in floods of tears, but all she'd say to me was that she couldn't marry him. Her father refused his consent, that's what it was. The second footman happened to be passing Sir Giles's study, and he heard it all."

"Why ever would Sir Giles say him nay, if the man was as fine as you say, and if he was in love with Miss Phoebe, and she with him?"

"Who's to know? That's what's amiss with her, in any case, it's all on account of her falling in love with a man her family don't approve of."

"Love," said Betsy scornfully. "There's a great deal too much said about love and falling in love by these young ladies if you ask me. In her grandparents' time, marriages were arranged by the family, and I don't see that they were any the less happy for that. I dare say she accepted him before he'd asked her father, and then to be writing to him, and her an unmarried young lady. What behaviour!"

"No worse than three seasons without an offer." Miniver hung the dress up, a rigid back expressive of the disapproval she felt for Betsy's remarks.

"Who said there hadn't been offers? I'm sure I never did. However, no man ever caused Miss Louisa any distress, and I must say I'm sorry to see Miss Phoebe in such a way, merely because of an unfortunate proposal!"

Somewhat mollified, Miniver tucked the skirts of the dress into place, and went over to the door. "There's breakfast being set on the table, by the sound of it," she said. "Drat this stain, I don't believe I'm ever going to get it out. And I'll have to be quick, or the young ladies will have finished their breakfast, and Miss Phoebe and Miss Louisa will be off outside, never thinking of their clothes."

Miniver was quite right. The clouds were still present, but a wind had got up, and was driving them across the sky, and it wasn't, Phoebe said persuasively, precisely raining.

"If this is not precisely rain dripping down the windowpanes, then I wonder what it is," said Louisa.

"We could order a carriage to be brought round."

Louisa was firm. "The last thing I want to do today or tomorrow or the day after is to drive anywhere in any kind of a coach. And it's no good you telling me that the fresh air will do me good. When the weather becomes more spring-like, then it will be a different matter, but at the moment I can think of nothing drearier than to go out in the rain and the wind."

Phoebe laughed, and lifted her hand in acknowledgement of Louisa's point. "Very well, but even if we do not venture out to any of the walks, we can certainly pay a visit to the glasshouses as soon as this shower is over, where you may admire growing pineapples, and be out of the weather you so dislike. And after that, we can sit in front of a good fire, in the little sitting room, and I shall beat you at piquet."

Miniver would have liked Miss Phoebe to take a short rest, but her mistress was implacable. "Do stop fussing, Miniver. I may not look my best, but I am not ill, how many times do I have to tell you? I shall be sitting down, if that satisfies you, for I want to write to my mother."

"And Betsy asked me to say, Miss Louisa,

that when you are free she wants to show you a stain on one of your gowns."

Louisa sighed. "I hope it is a vast mark all across the front of that vile pink taffeta that I know she will have packed, despite my not wanting it. Phoebe, I will be down directly Betsy has finished scolding me."

"You will find me in the library."

The library at Pemberley was one of the glories of the magnificent house, and certainly one of Phoebe's favourite rooms. The present Mr. Darcy's father, Phoebe's grandfather, had employed the famous architect Robert Adam to remodel several of the rooms of the house back in the 1760s. He had chosen to do the library in his classical style, and even the severest critics had to agree that the room was a triumph.

Phoebe paused, as she always did on entering the library, to admire the splendour and elegance of the room. She walked into the room between a fine pair of fluted columns with their Corinthian capitals, picked out with gilt. There was a table in a semicircular recess at the far end and that was where she sat, leaning back in her chair and looking up at the paintings on the ceiling, classical and allegorical scenes set in lozenges and ovals, before she opened the drawer, took out a sheet of notepaper, and, dipping the nib of her pen into the silver inkstand, began to write her letter.

Phoebe usually wrote very much as she talked, and at first her words flowed across the page, describing her journey to Pemberley, the twenty-four hours she had spent with her aunt on the way. She paused at this point; what was there to say? That she was still in low spirits, that she was glad to be at Pemberley, but that try as she might, thoughts of Mr. Stanhope kept intruding on her thoughts? Her mother would certainly not want to read that.

She nibbled at the feathery end of her quill, looking out through the library window. The rain had faded into a thin drizzle, and a figure outside caught her eye. She rose from her chair and went over to the window to have a better look. There was Mr. Grayling, the head gardener, wearing his usual leather jacket and coming round the corner of one of the walled gardens. Coming along behind him was a gardener's boy trundling a barrow full of what looked like manure. Then another man came round the corner, someone that Phoebe had never seen before. Her interest quickened as she studied the new arrival. He was talking to Mr. Grayling now, and she wondered who he was and why he should be engaged in such deep conversation with Mr. Darcy's head gardener.

Upstairs, Louisa was also looking out of the window, while she waited for Betsy to return from a trip to get lavender for the closet.

Who was that man? He was dressed like a gentleman, with gaiters to keep the mud off his legs, a snuff-coloured coat, and, which was surprising, had no hat on his head. His hair was a light brown and thick, and Louisa noticed, for she had a keen eye to such details, that it had been cut and shaped by a good barber. This was certainly no country local, nor yet did he look like a tradesman.

At that moment, Betsy came back into the room. "Come over here," Louisa said. "Since you always know more about what is going on than anyone else, you may look out of the window, and tell me who that man is out there talking to Mr. Grayling. He appears to be a gentleman, but I cannot suppose he is any such thing. Do you know who he is?"

Betsy only needed the briefest of glances out of the window to be able to inform her mistress that that was Mr. Drummond, Mr. Darcy's new man. "He is said to be a gentleman, but I cannot see why it is a gentleman's business to be out and about in the grounds, and dealing with glassmakers and iron men and carpenters and all that kind of thing."

"I rather agree with you," said Louisa. "I always imagined such a person would spend his time in an office, either in London or in one of my uncle's houses." She knew better than to ask Betsy what the servants thought of Mr. Drummond, and although she was curious to know, she didn't care to indulge in too much servants' gossip. She would doubtless find other means of discovering more about Mr. Drummond. He was a personable enough man, although not with the kind of looks she generally admired, yet he had a fine upstanding figure and a direct open look to his face that she liked.

"Miss Phoebe is writing letters in the library," said Betsy, by way of introducing the subject that she was longing to talk about.

"I know," said Louisa.

"It's a shame she's not looking as well as she ought. Downright pale, and not in the best of spirits, although Miniver tells me your arrival has cheered her up. Well, it's a shame about the engagement, but I dare say she'll get over her disappointment."

All curiosity about Mr. Drummond vanished from Louisa's mind as, startled, she withdrew her gaze from the gardens outside and stared at Betsy. "What are you talking about? Miss Phoebe is not engaged, nor has she ever been."

"Not engaged, exactly."

"Why, even if it were not announced in the paper, news of any engagement would have spread at once to the family. I can't think where you came up with such an idea."

"It was what Miniver told me," said Betsy defiantly. "Who should know better than she does what the young lady is up to? And the reason that none of the family heard about it, except her mother and father, was because Sir Giles said no to the man. Miss Phoebe went and picked a wrong 'un, that's clear, she should have known better."

This was going too far. Betsy might have been Louisa's nurse since she was a girl, but it was not her place to pass any kind of judgement on Miss Phoebe. "That is enough, Betsy."

Betsy knew that tone of old. She bobbed a curtsy and left the room, as Louisa, her thoughts in a turmoil of questions and conjectures, turned back to look out of the window. Mr. Grayling and Mr. Drummond had gone, leaving the gardener's boy disconsolately shoveling manure around the base of a plant. Could there be any truth in Betsy's report? She had suspected that an unhappy affair of the heart might lie behind Phoebe's present state of mind; poor Phoebe, if she had indeed fallen in love with an unsuitable man.

She would not let her imagination dwell on it. If Phoebe wanted to confide in her, then she would do so. Until then, intrigued as she was, Louisa would make no attempt to question Phoebe about Betsy's story, or to make any enquiries as to whether any of the events related by Betsy had ever taken place.

CHAPTER EIGHT

Martindale House lay only three miles from Pemberley as the crow flies, but by road it was a journey of nearer five miles. It was a house of a very different style from Palladian Pemberley, with its classical façade. Martindale House was an old manor house that had grown and expanded over the centuries, a stone building, situated at the end of a valley, with a pleasing prospect of a rolling landscape visible from its windows.

Like Pemberley, the house had been modernised and improved over the years, and when its present owner, Sir Henry Martindale, had brought his bride home three years before, he had had several of the main rooms refurbished and newly decorated in her honour.

At forty-three, Sir Henry was many years older than his young wife, but theirs was a love match. They had met at the York races, when Kitty Stanhope had gone to stay in

Yorkshire with her aunt and uncle, who always held a large house party for the races. Sir Henry had been invited, had seen Kitty dancing with some of the young people after dinner one evening, and had been enchanted by her gaiety, gracefulness, and the ready laughter which made her mouth so pretty.

Further acquaintance had convinced him that despite her light and lively manners, she was no mere butterfly, but a young lady of sense and intelligence and warmheartedness. Three weeks later in London, he proposed to her and was accepted, for Kitty had fallen in love with this handsome older man almost as quickly as he had with her.

Kitty's parents, Lord and Lady Stanhope, were far from pleased by the match, but Kitty was of age and it was clear to everyone in the family that she was determined to have Sir Henry. The Stanhopes would have preferred a political marriage for their only daughter, so that Kitty might follow in the steps of her mother and enjoy a success as a glittering hostess among the elite of London society, but Kitty, like her brother, Arthur, had no taste for the political salons and intrigues of London, although their reasons differed. Arthur found that society narrow and self-regarding, while Kitty was at heart a country lover who preferred the tranquillity of rural life to the festivities and bustle of London, and who was very happy to contemplate life as the wife of a rich squire.

That was why, this April, she and her husband were still in the country. Sir Henry Martindale had a seat in Parliament, but went to London as seldom as possible. He enjoyed the life of a country landowner, was on good terms with his neighbours, hunted throughout the winter months, and took his gun out as often as possible when the birds were in season.

Kitty sat in the drawing-room at Martindale House, a slightly pensive look on her face as she regarded her brother. "It is very pleasant to see you, Arthur, but I'm not sure to what we owe the courtesy of your visit. You normally never stay for more than two days at a time before you grow restless and are off somewhere else, and yet you have been here already for two days and are talking of making a stay of several more."

"I have a sudden inclination to rusticate," said Arthur untruthfully. He didn't like the country, was not a sporting man, and found the prospect of a wet English spring positively depressing. Since he had been on Wellington's staff in Paris after the Battle of

Waterloo, he had found himself in his element in the foreign capitals of Europe. After selling out of the army, he had determined on pursuing a diplomatic career, much to his father's fury.

His father, who hated all things French with a deadly passion, had never set foot out of England. When it was pointed out to him that he might make his way to Germany or Italy via the Low Countries, he had simply raised his eyebrows in astonishment at the notion that any Englishman would want to spend a minute abroad that he might spend in his own country. He had no objections to foreigners as such, distinguished men from many parts of Europe were welcomed at his wife's parties and assemblies, but his interests were essentially insular.

Kitty laughed at her brother, her face lightening into the warm smile that Sir Henry had found so attractive. "I don't believe a word of it. You have some ulterior motive, with you there is always an ulterior motive. Have you accrued huge gambling debts and are escaping your creditors perhaps? Or have you killed your man in a duel and are lying low lest you be taken up for the crime?"

Now it was Arthur's turn to raise his

eyebrows, which he did in a very similar way to his father. "I am simply here to enjoy your and Martindale's company, Kitty. What other reason could I have?" He moved across to the fireplace, a wide, deep stone embrasure, and tossed another log on the fire. He kicked it into place with an elegant boot, and dusted his hands. "You seem very dull here at the moment, Kitty," he went on, keen to change the subject. "When I come, I am used to having a house full of guests. Have you given up on your friends?"

"Not at all. You are here at a quiet time, that is all. We are expecting several friends, and will make up a house party on the occasion of the coming-of-age of Henry's nephew, Jack Harlow. You know the Harlows?"

"Of course I do," said Stanhope. "Charles Harlow served in my regiment."

There was a silence as both men remembered Charles, who had fought and fallen with great courage at Waterloo. "And although the family will not be at Pemberley until later in the year, I hear that two of the Darcy family are expected, indeed have probably already arrived, so you see, we are not so thin of company in Derbyshire as you suggest."

Arthur said nothing. Kitty went on,

"Phoebe Hawkins is not very happy, I hear. I am not sure whether you are acquainted with her." She didn't wait for a reply and continued, "She is a girl of character; how I laughed when she argued with Sir Henry at the Portlands' dance in London last year, she quite rolled him up, as you would put it."

"She argues with everyone," said Arthur.

"I know the family are very anxious that she should find a good husband," said Kitty, "but Sir Henry says that he cannot think of any man short of Genghis Khan who would be inclined to take her on. It is unkind, for she is in no way a termagant, and is besides very handsome."

"She is intelligent," said Arthur, striving for a tone of indifference. "Men do not like a clever woman."

While they spoke, Arthur was watching Kitty from under hooded eyelids. There was a slight droop to her mouth, a slight diminution of her usual spirits. Perhaps she was breeding. After all, she and Martindale had been married for three years, it was high time there was a family on the way, and Sir Henry would be glad of an heir.

The door opened and Sir Henry came in. He was still a handsome man, with a good figure. A couple of spaniels gambolled at his heels.

"Not those dogs in here, please," exclaimed Kitty as one of them licked her. "They have such muddy paws."

Sir Henry looked at his wife for a moment, then strode back to the door, opened it, and pushed the dogs through, calling to a servant to come and take care of them. Then he shut the door again and returned to the room.

Last time Arthur had been here, a year ago, Sir Henry would not have come into the sitting room with his dogs, and his first action would have been to go over to his wife and greet her. Now he almost ignored her, instead choosing to tell Arthur about his luck with a rod that morning. "High time you took up fishing, Arthur," he said jovially.

Stanhope could imagine nothing he would like to do less than stand on a riverbank with a rod in his hand on a chilly spring day. He noticed that Kitty had taken up her embroidery frame and was stabbing the needle in and out in a way that boded ill for the neat setting of her stitches. Not breeding, he decided. There were some estrangement there, doubtless a quarrel of some kind. He knew all about women and quarrels and arguments. Although he was surprised that the affection that existed between Kitty and Henry had not got the better of any disagreements they might have.

"I was just saying to Arthur," said Kitty, "that Louisa Bingley and Phoebe Hawkins are to be at Pemberley. I intend to go and call on them tomorrow or the day after, as soon as I hear that they have both arrived. Do you care to accompany me?"

"Perhaps. Or, if not, I am sure that Arthur will go with you." Sir Henry's voice and manner were abrupt.

Definitely something amiss. Well, it was none of his business, although he didn't care to see Kitty looking woebegone. Husbands and wives had their ups and downs, and he himself had never been sure that the disparity in age was such a good thing. Then he saw Kitty give her husband a swift look, an almost pleading look, but with such love in it he knew at once that whatever was the problem with Kitty, there was no lessening of her feelings for her husband.

The drawing-room at Martindale House was a comfortable apartment. The warm red carpet, and the red upholstery of the sofas and chairs, gave it a cheerful aspect on a grey evening, and Sir Henry now rang for servants to draw the curtains and light the candles. "I'm away to my study," he observed, speaking more to Arthur than to his wife. "I have any number of accounts to look over."

After he had gone, Arthur dropped into the chair beside his sister. He hardly knew where to begin, but he felt he must make some effort to find out why Kitty was unhappy. He was some years older than Kitty, and they had never been particularly close, but he was genuinely fond of her. "You're content here at Martindale House, are you?" he began. "Or are you pining for the delights of the London season after all?"

Kitty bent her head, searching in her work basket for a new thread. She didn't look at her brother as she spoke, but said in a calm, even voice, "No, not at all. I am very happy to be here."

Arthur determined on a more direct approach. "Yet all does not seem quite well between you and Sir Henry," he said.

She shook her head. "Sir Henry and I have had a slight difference of opinion, that is all. He has some private worry, which he will not disclose to me, but he will soon be his usual self again, I feel sure." She lay down her embroidery and closed her work basket, and then stood up. "Now I, like Henry, have duties to attend to. Will you come with me tomorrow to Pemberley?" She paused. "And with Sir Henry, of course, if he decides to come."

"Certainly," said Arthur. "In truth, I was there yesterday."

Kitty, who was halfway to the door, stopped and shot an enquiring look at her brother. "Pemberley? Yesterday? You never said. Why?"

"I rode over because there is now in Mr. Darcy's employ an old friend of mine. In fact you may remember him, we were at Cambridge together and also colleagues in the army. Hugh Drummond."

Kitty looked thoughtful. Then she said, "He has sandy-coloured hair, and an open, agreeable countenance."

"That sounds like him."

"What is he doing at Pemberley?"

"He is making a stay of several weeks, I gather. He is in the employ of Mr. Darcy, who has dreamed up some very ambitious plans for the garden, and it is Hugh's job to superintend the whole business. He has invited me to go over to the lodge where he is staying one evening, and I shall certainly do so. But you may renew your acquaintance with him tomorrow, for he is sure to be somewhere around."

"I look forward to seeing him again," said

Kitty politely, although she looked as though she had matters quite other than Hugh Drummond on her mind.

CHAPTER NINE

Phoebe and Louisa were feeling very dull, shut up in the house while the rain lashed against the windows. They had some idea of venturing outside for a visit to the hot-houses, to look at the pineapple plants, but this plan was thwarted by the tumultuous arrival upon the scene of the children from the nurseries. One cousin was exciting enough, but two were better, and the four of them, cunningly managing to escape the clutches of both governess and nursery maid, arrived panting and laughing at the library door, just as Phoebe and Louisa came out. They were welcomed with hugs, but fell silent as their governess appeared, a cross expression on her face.

Louisa greeted Miss Verney with a smile, and the governess, with only a fleeting answering smile, apologised for the noisy behaviour of the children. "They are very naughty, I told them they must not come down and disturb you."

"Oh, no, we are delighted to see them," said Phoebe. "Louisa, it is still so damp and grey outside, let us postpone the trip to see the pineapples and instead see whether some of our old games are still in the sitting room."

So Phoebe and Louisa and the children spent a very happy hour romping in the sitting room. Phoebe played bears with the girls, while Louisa let the two boys beat her at spillikins. Meanwhile, Miss Verney, who did not seem to enjoy seeing her little charges enjoying themselves with such uninhibited shrieks and shouts of laughter, sat at the pianoforte and played some rather mournful tunes. She was an accomplished pianist, Phoebe noticed, in the pauses between growls and pounces, but why could she not play something more cheerful, which the children would enjoy better?

Finally, both Louisa and Phoebe had to admit the justice of Miss Verney's insistence on taking the children away. They were hot and pink-faced and quite probably rather too het up for their own good, as Miss Verney ominously remarked on her way out. "There will be tears before bedtime, I dare say," were her parting words.

Phoebe wasn't in the least contrite. "They

are such fun," she said, plumping herself down in a chair and fanning herself. "I feel quite exhausted."

Louisa agreed that the children were tiring, but she thought to herself that Phoebe looked more relaxed and happier than she had done since arriving at Pemberley. "What do you think of Miss Verney, now that you see her with her charges?" she asked. "Have you changed your mind about her?"

"I think the children may prove to be too much for her. They are so very lively, and she doesn't seem inclined to let them play and romp as they need to. Miniver, I may say, has no opinion of her at all, and says she is not popular in the servants' hall. How that woman does gossip!"

"No more than Betsy does," said Louisa.

"Miniver told me that Miss Verney's parents escaped from France disguised as turnips."

Both of them burst out laughing.

"Of course, it is no laughing matter. A number of aristocrats did escape from France in carts, buried under cabbages and turnips and other such vegetables," said Phoebe. "One has to admire them, and although turnips may seem amusing to us now, I don't suppose they found it amusing at the time at all. After all, only think what the penalty would have been if they were caught."

They were silent for a while, both of them thinking of a cousin of Phoebe's father who had lost her husband to the guillotine during the Terror.

Then Phoebe gave the conversation a more cheerful turn by proposing that they should play a game of backgammon before going upstairs to get ready to dinner. "I suppose Miss Verney will want to dine with us again."

"She could hardly be expected to eat in the servants' hall, nor would it be fair for her to have to eat with the children upstairs. Our governess always had her meals with the family, except when there was company."

Phoebe could not riposte with any stories of her own governess. Lady Hawkins had given up on governesses for her forthright daughter, after the fifth one had given in her notice, exclaiming that she would rather tend the lions in the Tower of London than look after Miss Phoebe. Lady Hawkins had decided instead to take the care of Phoebe under her own command, providing tutors for her in music, languages, and, to the dismay of her friends, she also arranged for

Phoebe to have lessons in Latin and mathematics from the vicar, a scholar and a good teacher, who had coached her brothers.

Not that Phoebe had ever acquired any great proficiency in Latin, but she had enjoyed the history and mythology of the ancient world which the vicar had imparted to her. "Only think if I had had a governess as melancholy as Miss Verney seems to be," Phoebe said thoughtfully. "How dull I should have found her, and how I would have teased her and played tricks on her."

Louisa, who had a more sympathetic nature, wrinkled her brow. "I can imagine nothing worse than having to find employment as a governess, much as I like children. Governesses are in such a difficult situation in so many households, since they are usually gently born, and in many ways the equals of their employers, and yet must always have a subservient status."

"You have nothing to reproach yourself with on that score. Your governess was always one of your family, as you just mentioned, and there she is now, happily married, and the greatest of friends with your mama."

The chef had sent up a most excellent meal, and the three of them dined on spring soup, trout dressed in a Spanish sauce, a very tender cut of lamb served with asparagus, and finished up with an almond pudding and a compote of fruit. Phoebe kept up a constant flow of conversation, amusing Louisa with her droll remarks. Miss Verney seemed less preoccupied, and ventured some remarks of her own.

After dinner, they retired not to the small, upstairs sitting room, but downstairs to the drawing-room. In past centuries this had been a forbidding and formal room, but now, in keeping with the greater informality of the times, it was a delightful room. There was a harp in the corner, and a modern grand pianoforte testified to the musical tastes of the family. Tables and chairs were placed at various points around the room, with a pair of sofas opposite each other in front of the fireplace. The high ceiling was decorated with fine plasterwork, and despite the numerous paintings hanging on the walls, with their heavy gilt frames, the room, which overlooked the gardens to the rear of the house, had enough light coming in through the long windows to prevent any feeling of gloominess.

Phoebe praised Miss Verney's playing, and asked if she would perform again, firmly placing on the instrument some tunes of a more lively kind than the music she had played earlier. Miss Verney played and then accompanied herself in some songs, while Louisa and Phoebe listened and talked together in quiet voices.

"I have a plan for tomorrow," announced Phoebe as Miss Verney launched into another sonata. "I am determined to find out all about these works that Mr. Darcy has planned, and for that purpose I think we need to go to the person who is organising it all."

"You mean Mr. Grayling," said Louisa.

"No, I do not. I am sure that Betsy, while giving you all the latest news about the household, hasn't neglected to tell you about Mr. Drummond. Miniver is full of him. I noticed him from the window when I was in the library this afternoon, and he looks a capable, gentlemanlike man. I wish to discover whether all the beautiful, natural, romantic parkland is going to be destroyed and terrorised into neat parterres and rigid lines."

Louisa laughed at these extravagant notions. "As if Mr. Darcy would plan anything ugly for Pemberley. I dare say it is as much to do with drainage and with improving the productivity of the kitchen gardens as anything else. I have often heard him say that Pemberley lags behind many great houses in what it produces in the horticultural line. I shall be sad, though, if the park is to be altered, for I like the landscape here just as it is."

Louisa took a keen interest in plants and growing things, something she had inherited from her father. "However," she said, "if it turns out that tomorrow is as dreary as today, or we wake to find the countryside shrouded in mist, then I shall not go into the gardens, whatever you may say."

Miss Verney had stopped playing and was listening to them. "I should not be surprised," she remarked, "since it will be all round the neighbourhood that you are now in residence at Pemberley, if you find that people are calling upon you."

"I do hope not," said Phoebe. "I confess that I am not in the mood for company."

"I expect that most of our neighbours will be in London for the season," pointed out Louisa. "So I wouldn't concern yourself with the idea that we are likely to be overwhelmed with callers."

"Sir Henry and Lady Martindale are not in London," said Miss Verney. She closed the lid of the pianoforte and stood up. "Sir Henry was only here last week, he had some query for the steward."

Louisa was staring at Phoebe. Whatever

had Miss Verney said to make her look like that? "You remember Sir Henry, surely, Phoebe?" she said. "And I am sure you are acquainted with his wife. She is the prettiest creature imaginable. She was Kitty Stanhope, of course, before she married."

"Lady Martindale?" said Phoebe. "Oh, yes, of course. I believe I may have met her in London last year."

"Her brother, Arthur Stanhope, is presently staying with her, so Betsy tells me."

"How surprising that they are not gone to town," said Phoebe, who had turned quite pale.

Louisa looked at her with some alarm. "Phoebe, are you quite well? You look as though you had seen a ghost. Ring the bell," she said to Miss Verney, quite sharply. "It will be best if we summon her maid to help her up to her bedchamber. Miss Hawkins has exerted herself too much this evening."

Miss Verney was eyeing Miss Hawkins with a look of intense curiosity. "You would think she had had some bad news."

"I am perfectly well," said Phoebe. "And no," with an effort at a laugh, "there are no ghosts at Pemberley. I am tired, though, and so I will bid you both good night."

Mr. Stanhope in Derbyshire! Within a few miles of Pemberley. Why? Did he know she was here? Her mother had made no secret of Phoebe's departure for Pemberley to spend the spring and summer months in the country, so he could have discovered her whereabouts had he wanted to. She had supposed he would be at present in London, or even abroad; instead, he was here in Derbyshire, and in her own neighbourhood.

What a misfortune! She had promised her parents to have no further contact with him, and she intended to keep her word. Not through obedience, but from her own desire never to see him again. As she turned over in bed for the tenth time, she told herself there was no reason at all why they should meet. He would hardly stay long in the country, and for her part, she would not be calling at Martindale House.

CHAPTER TEN

The clouds began to thin, the rain stopped, and by the next morning there was neither cloud nor wind to mar a perfect day. Phoebe and Louisa were eager to go outside. They walked along the path past the shrubbery and the flower garden, intending to cross the river further down and then walk back through the meadows.

"You may have thought my behaviour rather strange last night," Phoebe began. "Something you said took me unawares."

Phoebe fell silent, and Louisa prompted her. "Is it to do with Kitty Martindale?"

Phoebe shook her head. She wasn't looking at Louisa, but had her head turned away. "No. You mentioned . . . that is, you said that Lady Martindale's brother, Mr. Stanhope, was staying with the Martindales at present."

"Arthur Stanhope. Are you acquainted with him?"

"I shall make a clean breast of it all to you," said Phoebe, taking a deep breath. "But, Louisa, this is to go no further. I have told no one exactly what happened in London, although my parents and Miniver know something of the truth."

"Well," cried Louisa, "if Miniver is in on your secret, then you may be sure that the whole household will know it by now."

Phoebe flushed. "It could not be helped. I wanted to talk to Mr. Stanhope, and the only servant I could trust was Miniver. And then, I had to write to him, and Miniver took the letter for me. No, you don't need to remind me that I should not be writing, or entering into any correspondence with, Mr. Stanhope or any other single man."

"So why were you writing to Mr. Stanhope?"

Phoebe, who had kept her eyes fixed on her feet, now looked up, and directly at Louisa. "Although the season had not yet begun, there were many families already in London, as you must be aware is usually the case at this time of year, and therefore there are small parties of one kind or another. I hadn't met Mr. Stanhope; he spends a good deal of time abroad. However, he was present when I dined with some friends, and then we met again at several other gatherings. I enjoyed his company, and — well, his attentions to me grew more marked. As for me, it is difficult to describe how I felt."

"Was this just dalliance on his part? He has something of a reputation with the ladies, but I would have thought that he was treading a dangerous line with a young lady of your background and situation."

Dalliance! Phoebe had taken it for more than that. He was not flirting with her, there was a look in his eyes when they lighted on her, and that in his voice when he spoke to her, which told Phoebe this went beyond dalliance. She took a deep breath and continued her narrative. "You may judge for yourself whether it was dalliance. I was present, as was Mr. Stanhope, at a very pleasant dinner party given by Mr. Portal. You are acquainted with Mr. Portal, I am sure."

"With Pagoda Portal?" said Louisa. "Indeed I am."

"Later in the evening," Phoebe went on, "there was dancing. Our cousin Alethea was among those present, of course you know what a fine musician she is. She at once volunteered to play, and sitting herself down at the instrument, launched into a waltz. I danced with Mr. Stanhope then, and again a little later. And it so happened that we found ourselves, since I was rather hot after my exertions, in a little antechamber off the big drawing-room where people were dancing."

She paused.

"Go on," said Louisa.

"Mr. Stanhope proposed to me."

Louisa's astonishment showed in her face. She could hardly believe what Phoebe was saying. Lost for words for a moment, she had to pull her wits into order before saying, "Well, he is the most eligible man, in the eyes of the world, that is. But I have heard that he is possessed of a quick temper, and is high-handed in his ways. Oh, Phoebe, is he the right man for you?"

"Louisa, I am — I was, I must say — in love with Mr. Stanhope."

"Phoebe, what were you about? What can you see in him? I have had but a brief encounter with him, when I met him upon the bridge here, not discovering until later who he was — Betsy knew about his visit to see Mr. Drummond — but I am sure he is not the right man for you. I grant you that he is handsome and he has a fine, tall figure and looks that must be generally admired, but he is not at all the sort of man to make you or anyone else a good husband. I knew of his reputation before ever I saw him, and you know the opinion of the world, when it is as well-known as that, is not to be dismissed lightly."

"I knew you wouldn't understand," said Phoebe despairingly. "How can you, when you have never felt any kind of partiality for a man?"

Louisa spoke in a quiet, normal voice, in sharp contrast to Phoebe's agitated voice. "Did he make love to you?"

"Did he kiss me? Yes."

"Whatever was he thinking of to approach you before he had spoken to your father? What if somebody had come in and discovered you in his arms?"

"He kissed me, that is all. And I felt — oh! you would not understand what it is like to be kissed by a man like Mr. Stanhope."

Phoebe hadn't spent a season in London without receiving her share of affection, and although she would not admit it to Louisa, Mr. Stanhope was not the first man to have kissed her. Yet the difference between his embraces and those of other men! Louisa was an innocent in such matters, and no doubt assumed that under the strict chaperonage that existed, no young lady would ever succumb to the temptation to kiss a man before they were engaged. Propriety would forbid it, but as Phoebe had discovered, propriety might well fly out of the window when there had been dancing and wine and a great deal of flirtation.

"When he kissed me," said Phoebe, "I was certain that I loved him, and — oh, I cannot express how I felt, but certainly I had no sense of wrongdoing."

"Well, to be sure, there is a degree of impropriety, but in which case, where was the problem? Don't tell me he jilted you? That would be the most un-gentlemanlike behaviour imaginable."

"I woke the next morning to a degree of happiness beyond anything I had ever known. Only to be summoned downstairs to my father's study, to be told that Mr. Stanhope had called, early that morning, to ask for my hand, and that my father had refused his consent."

"Good heavens, upon what grounds?"

"Because of his reputation. My father would brook no argument. He insists I would not be happy married to a rake, Mr. Stanhope is a rake, and therefore . . ."

They walked on for some way, Phoebe striving to compose herself. Louisa said, "A man may gain a reputation which is unfounded, and not take the trouble to correct the world's view of his character."

126

"I could not marry a man who is likely to be unfaithful. Infidelity destroys trust and honour and has consequences of a far-reaching kind that are unquantifiable."

Phoebe spoke with an intensity that shook Louisa, even though she was aware of some of the difficulties in the Hawkins family that lay behind Phoebe's heartfelt words.

Phoebe had only been thirteen at the time. Her home life until then had been a very happy one: she was something of a wild, noisy child, enjoying running around in the garden, riding her pony, and playing lively games with her sisters and friends of both sexes. At thirteen she had grown a little more restrained, but was still the kind of girl who faced every morning with zest and optimism and who possessed a natural inclination to happiness.

Then a shadow fell across her happiness. Her parents, who had always presented a united front of affection and kindness, seemed to be at odds with one another. Closed doors, whispered conversations, or, much worse, long periods when her parents appeared to have nothing to say to one another brought a dreadful atmosphere into Hawkins Hall.

Now, at twenty, Phoebe could still not forget the deep unhappiness that her father's philandering had caused both him and her mother. She had been too young to fully comprehend what was happening, but intelligent and alert and mature enough to work out for herself what was going on. Servants were careless in their talk, friends made guarded comments, and it wasn't long before she discovered the truth.

Her father, alone in London for several weeks to attend Parliament, while his wife and family remained in the country, had engaged in a dangerous flirtation with the dashing Mrs. Lancey. One thing led to another, and word came back to Lady Hawkins that her husband was making an exhibition of himself in London, and apparently saw no need to keep secret the fact that he was enjoying the full delights of Mrs. Lancey's affections.

Phoebe felt ashamed for him, and angry on her mother's behalf, yet she was old enough and wise enough in the ways of the world to know that many men had mistresses. In fact, her older and more cynical friends said that all men were unfaithful if they could be, and a woman had best make her happiness where she could, busy with domestic duties, children, and the daily round of feminine life.

Her mother had been hurt and upset, but

she was realistic enough to know that this was the way a husband let loose in London on his own might well behave. What was unforgivable was that it turned out to be more than a passing fancy, and when she discovered a passionate love letter penned by her husband to Mrs. Lancey, she found herself unable to forgive him.

Her pride, her dignity, and her reserve did not allow her the natural and immediate outlet of anger or quarrels. She taxed her husband with his infidelity, and he blustered and denied it. And then by one of those sad quirks of fate, an old flame of her own came upon the scene. Colonel Daunton was a military man who had once been her suitor, and whom she had very nearly married. She turned to him, and found consolation with him.

Now it was Sir Giles's turn to be outraged. He had never imagined that this would happen. The old adage that sauce for the goose is sauce for the gander was not, he considered, one that could in any sense be applied to his marriage. For him to take a mistress was normal, for his wife to have a lover was a cause of mortification and rage.

Phoebe, wretched and worried out of her normal lively spirits by all this, could not take sides with either of her parents, both of whom she loved. Then, in 1815, the colonel was killed, gallantly leading his men into action on the field of Waterloo. Her mother found it very difficult to control her grief, but that grief brought Phoebe's father to his senses. He had been suffering from a good deal of guilt, and had come to realise that his affair with Mrs. Lancey was making him a laughingstock. She was not the kind of woman to bestow favours upon one man at a time, and so he felt twice cuckolded.

Slowly, Sir Giles and Lady Hawkins began to rebuild their marriage. There was no question of them ever being on quite the same grounds as they had been; Lady Hawkins could not easily forgive her husband for his infidelity, nor herself for her own, and the shock of being cuckolded and the very physical jealousy Sir Giles had felt when he found out about the colonel and his wife had left him uncertain in his position as husband and father, as the undoubted head of his family and master of his domain.

Even though Louisa knew only part of the story, she knew enough to understand why Sir Giles would reject a suitor on the grounds of his immorality, and why Phoebe herself would shun such a man.

They reached the end of the narrow path

that ran through the rich meadow, thick with poppies now, and clambered over the stile on to the wider path that led across the arched bridge.

"It is possible," said Louisa, "that Mr. Stanhope may not deserve his reputation. You were close to him; did you ever suspect that he was the kind of man to treat women badly?"

"Do rakes treat women badly? Or are the women at fault, for allowing themselves to be made fools of? And I am certain in Mr. Stanhope's case that his reputation is well-earned. I don't want to talk about it; let me just say that I came into possession of information which persuaded me that my father was right to behave as he did."

"Yet —"

"No yets, nor buts. It is over, finished, an incident in my past life on which the door has closed." Phoebe was walking on ahead, wanting to move quickly, as though by so doing she could walk herself out of the melancholy that oppressed her when she thought about Mr. Stanhope. "Let us change the subject entirely," she said briskly, looking back at Louisa. "I need your help."

Louisa lengthened her pace. "I? Help? In what way can I help you?"

"You have heard that Mr. and Mrs. Darcy

131

are to hold a ball here at Pemberley this summer."

"Betsy did mention it."

"Very well, and before he took his leave, Mr. Darcy put the charge for the arrangements into my hands."

Louisa couldn't hide her amazement. "Phoebe, a ball? For how many people? It is a daunting undertaking to plan and arrange everything for a big ball."

"Oh, as to that, Mr. Darcy knows very well that I like to organise things, and in fact I am extremely competent in such matters. He has an excellent housekeeper in Mrs. Makepeace, and Mr. Lydgate will have a very good idea of how things are to be managed. Much can be left to them, but the overall scheme of things needs to be in the hands of a member of the family, and who better than I? I tell you, I shall enjoy it above all things, and you will assist and advise me. Two heads are better than one, as the saying is. I need to be occupied, you know."

"Of course I shall be glad to help in any way that I can. But where to begin? What about invitations? Surely my aunt and uncle do not leave it to you to decide who is to be invited?"

"Of course not. Mr. Darcy's secretary has

all that in hand, and will be sending me the lists shortly. I am also to keep him appraised of all likely expenses, just to make sure that I do not outrun the budget. But much can be done with the resources of Pemberley itself. We have to talk to the gardeners about flowers, because we will need a great many of them and flowers do not grow in a day. And then there is the matter of the works in the garden — we can't have a ball with the garden looking like a fairground. There is much to be thought of and discussed, for I intend the Pemberley ball to be an amazing success, the talk of Derbyshire and London."

Deep in discussion of what they had liked and disliked at the many balls they had been to, and what themes and schemes had been most successful, they walked back to the house, entering up the steps and through the main door. From there they went up the stairs, and were on the first landing when Betsy came running to find them, agog with news. "Mr. Lydgate says that he has seen a carriage turn into the gates. It will either be visitors wishing to view the house, in which case they must be turned away, or, as is more likely, they are some of your neighbours calling upon you. In which case, are you at home?"

Louisa went over to the window and looked out at the carriage that was bowling in great style up towards the house. "It is Sir Henry and Lady Martindale," she exclaimed. "Yes, we must be at home to them."

She turned from the window, hoping that Phoebe would not go to look, but Phoebe brushed her aside and, as she saw who was on the driving seat of the carriage, gave Louisa a speaking look and ran from the room, calling out as she went that she herself was not at home, had the headache, was feeling too unwell to come down and talk to any visitors.

Questions jostled each other in Louisa's head. Did Mr. Stanhope know that Phoebe was staying at Pemberley? It would be foolish to suppose otherwise, since the comings and goings of the family at Pemberley were, she knew, matters of great interest to all the surrounding families. Word of her and Phoebe's arrival would have passed by means of the servants and people in the nearby village of Pemberley, or in Lambton, to everyone in the neighbourhood.

So it was left to Louisa to greet the visitors. Pausing only a moment to tidy her hair, she hurried out of the room and down the staircase, reaching the hall just as the visitors were coming through the front door.

Louisa had a moment to notice that Lady Martindale looked pale and worried when she came forward to take her hands and greet her with great warmth and affection. Sir Henry made his bow and Louisa, holding out her hand to Mr. Stanhope, dropped him a neat curtsy.

Louisa called for refreshments, and soon they were gathered round a table in the small dining room, where cold meats and a delicious array of fruits were laid out.

"Is not Miss Hawkins here?" asked Kitty. "We heard that she was coming to stay, and I thought she had already arrived. I was looking forward to making her acquaintance once more. We were introduced in London, but had no chance to get to know one another."

Louisa, angry at the necessity for the civil lie, said that Phoebe was indeed at Pemberley, but begged to be excused, as she was lain down with the headache. Knowing herself to be a poor liar, she was keen to change the subject, and asked Lady Martindale whether she and Sir Henry were staying in Derbyshire, or were intending to go to London.

Despite Louisa's best efforts, conversation flagged, with neither of the gentlemen appearing to have much to say. So she was extremely relieved when Kitty asked whether it might be possible for Louisa to show them the house. "My brother has not been here before," she explained.

"If I can be forgiven what you took to be my trespass last time I came here," said Stanhope. "Miss Bingley took me for a sightseer, and wanted me turned out of the grounds."

Louisa protested, before she realised that he was teasing her.

"I have heard much of the beauties of Pemberley," Mr. Stanhope went on. "Should Miss Bingley have other matters to attend to, perhaps the housekeeper would be good enough to show me over the principal rooms."

Louisa looked at him suspiciously. It did not seem to her that Mr. Stanhope was at all the kind of man who wanted to look over someone else's house. The people who came to admire the beauties of Pemberley were, for the most part, people of the more middling sort. People who came from large houses and estates of their own only visited similar houses for social purposes, or sport.

It would be impolite, however, not to accede to his request, and so she prepared to lead the little party out of the room. Sir Henry hung back. "I am familiar enough with the delights of Pemberley," he said. "While you are going round the house, I shall, if Miss Bingley will spare me, go and have a word with Mr. Grayling. He has promised my gardeners some seedlings, and I want to make sure that he knows what he is about."

Louisa didn't miss the look that Kitty Martindale gave her husband as he went out of the room with a light step. Seedlings? She supposed that Sir Henry might take a keen interest in his land and be a follower of the modern fashion for horticulturalism, but even so, a desire to talk to the head gardener seemed a weak excuse for not going round the house.

Kitty laid her hand on her brother's arm and together the three of them left the dining room and went through into the state dining room. This was a magnificent room, one of the ones that had been remodelled by Adam, with crimson furnishings and a ceiling painted by the artist Angelica Kauffman for an earlier Darcy.

From there, Louisa led the way upstairs, and into the State Apartments. This was a suite of rooms, used once in Mr. Darcy's great-grandfather's day to entertain visiting Royals, and now seldom occupied except when the house was full of guests. The rooms led into one another without any landings or corridors, in the old style, and Kitty wondered aloud about how differently people had lived in the past century. "From the paintings one sees of the period," she said, "it always seems to me that people were very stiff, in their clothes, in the arrangements of their rooms, and certainly in the formality of their dances."

Louisa had the feeling she was saying these things simply to make conversation; her brother remained strangely silent. She gave him a sharp look. "Are we not to hear your observations on the customs and manners of a past age, Mr. Stanhope?"

Arthur Stanhope did not answer her directly, merely smiling as he strolled over towards a very dull picture of a sea scene, and began to point out some features of the naval battle to his uninterested sister.

"The private family chambers are on the other side of the landing here," said Louisa. "But if we go the other way, there is the library, generally held to be a fine example of Mr. Adam's style, and the picture gallery, which I'm sure Mr. Stanhope would like to see."

The long gallery, with arched beams and tracery from an earlier age, was notable chiefly for the portraits of the Darcy family.

Mr. Stanhope stopped in front of a picture of Mr. Darcy's sister, Phoebe's mother, when she was still Miss Darcy, a girl of about sixteen. He stood for a long while at the painting, and then, at Louisa's prompting, moved on to another portrait, this time of Lady Hawkins with Phoebe, a girl of about ten, dressed all in white, with a scarlet sash, standing at her mother's knee.

"What a charming picture," said Kitty.

Mr. Stanhope did not appear to be listening. He had strolled over to the window, looking out with no great interest over the hills and woods, when something closer at hand seemed to catch his eye. He threw up the sash and leaned out.

Louisa stared at this odd behaviour, but he simply said, in the suavest tones, "Perhaps now Miss Bingley would be kind enough to show us the gardens."

CHAPTER ELEVEN

Phoebe heard the voices recede into the distance. She guessed that Louisa was taking the visitors on a tour of the house; why, she couldn't imagine. Perhaps they had gone upstairs to the picture gallery to look at a particular portrait or painting. Oh, why had they not simply stayed their half hour and then left? During the time they had been in the house she had been pacing up and down in her bedroom, telling herself she should sit down and read a book or take up her embroidery, but finding it impossible to sit still or not to wonder why Mr. Stanhope had chosen to call knowing that she was at Pemberley.

Did he still care for her? In her mind, there could be no doubt that what she had written in her note to him was final. After such a rebuff, what possessed him to apparently seek out her company again, and against the express wishes of her father?

She could stand the inaction no longer. Taking up a cloak, she cautiously opened the door and, seeing that the landing was clear, went swiftly down the stairs and passed through some of the smaller rooms to the rear of the house, judging that even if Louisa were to take the visitors out into the garden, they would not come this way. She smiled at a surprised boot boy whom she encountered in the stone-flagged passage, and escaped into the open air.

The day was still bright, and there was even a touch of warmth in the sunshine. Phoebe hesitated, looking around her, wondering where she should go, where she could be sure of not being disturbed. To one side of the house she could see that some work was going on; that would not be the place to go. Closer at hand were the more formal gardens, including the famous yew garden with its tall yew hedges cut into a wavy pattern. But that was too exposed, and very likely chilly as well. No, she knew what she would do. She would go into the kitchen garden. It was hardly likely that visitors would choose to go into this domestic part of the garden, after all.

She walked quickly along the gravel path and pushed open the door that led into the walled kitchen garden. After looking around to make sure that there was no one else in the garden, she closed the door behind her with a sense of relief.

Spring had come early to the sheltered kitchen garden at Pemberley, despite the bad weather. It covered nearly two acres, and provided the house with vegetables and fruit, and herbs for the table and for the medicinal needs of the household and for all those dependent on the estate. The walls were built of warm red brick and the one which ran along the north side towered above Phoebe, reaching some sixteen feet at its highest point. It was against this wall that the fruit trees were espaliered: peach and fig and apricots.

This was a working garden, and not a place where the family ever sat out, so there were no convenient benches or seats for Phoebe to sit upon. She could have sat on an upturned pot, but she preferred to walk, still feeling restless and wanting to calm herself. She found herself among the herbs, fragrant in the sunshine, with some early bees buzzing at the yellow and purple flowers. The tranquillity of the place began to work its magic upon her, her heart beat more slowly, and her senses began to take in more of her surroundings, the scent of the herbs and flowers, the rich variety of colours with all the greenery of new life, and the mellow colours of the walls, the sound of insects, and birds chirruping in the trees. She bent to pluck a leaf of thyme, and rolled the soft leaf between her fingers, releasing the sharp smell of the herb. A tabby cat was stretched out in a patch of sunshine, and it flicked the tip of its tail as Phoebe bent down to stroke its striped coat.

This garden was full of wonders, a little world of its own, peaceful and fruitful and very soothing to Phoebe's troubled spirits.

That was, at least, until she heard loud male voices approaching. The door at the far end of the garden swung open, and two gardeners came in, one carrying a basket and the other wheeling a barrow. With them was one of the maids, in a print dress and apron, who was obviously enjoying being out in the garden in the company of the young men.

Phoebe panicked. There was absolutely no reason why she shouldn't be in the garden, in fact she could ask them to leave. But she wanted no human contact at the moment, and knew that she would end up trying to explain herself and justify why she was there. Besides, they were so merry, and the minute they caught sight of her they would have to behave in a more subdued way. Why should she be a spoilsport?

So very quickly, and keeping herself behind a long line of potted flowering currants, she reached the door through which she had come without being seen and was out in the main part of the gardens again.

That turned out to be a case of out of the frying pan and into the fire, as now she heard other voices, which she recognised all too well: Louisa and Mr. Stanhope. The sound of his voice made her heart thump; good God, she must get away from here!

She dived through a gap in the hedge, and came out in another part of the garden all together. To her left was one of the glasshouses, a rather ramshackle building, she noticed, even in her present apprehensive state. Surely she could hide in there, surely Louisa wouldn't dream of taking visitors into such a shabby place. She was through the door in a flash, and made her way to the further end, not without difficulty, as the path between the large, palm-like plants was very narrow. There she found a low bench, probably used for potted plants, and after giving it a brushing with her handkerchief, she sat down.

This was ridiculous. All this simply to avoid Mr. Stanhope. Reason told her that if Mr. Stanhope was staying in the neighbourhood, then she would surely have to meet him again sooner or later. Still the questions rattled round in her head. Why had he come? Did he not understand how distressing she would find it to be in his company?

Would Louisa have had the sense to find out how long he planned to be in the neighborhood? Should she simply leave Pemberley and go back to Hawkins Hall — but the workmen would be in, everything would be at sixes and sevens, and no proper staff; it was impossible. And what would her aunt and uncle say if she decamped, how could she explain such an action?

She was so wrapped up in her thoughts and worries and fears and plans that she didn't hear the sound of footsteps approaching. Too late she realised that she wasn't alone in the glasshouse. She jumped up, a defiant look on her face, to find that the man in front of her was not, as she had feared, Mr. Stanhope, but Mr. Drummond.

He bowed, and said in a pleasant voice, "I am so sorry, I fear I have startled you."

Phoebe was for a moment quite tongue-tied. She knew that she was flushing scarlet, and then the humour of the situation overcame her and she began to laugh. The man looked at her enquiringly, and she felt obliged to say, "I am sorry, it is not that I find you funny, or even that I am laughing at a private joke. It is just that wherever I go in all these grounds, there always seems to be someone there."

"I am very sorry," the man said. "Shall I remove myself at once, if you are eager for solitude? However, perhaps I should warn you that there are visitors going round the gardens, and I believe they wish to come in here and look at the pineapples."

The colour had faded from Phoebe's cheeks at these words, and she put her hand to her mouth. Mr. Drummond came to her rescue. "There is another door," he said, "over there in a far corner. I have the key, and if we are quick, we can be out of here before they arrive."

He led the way between a forest of spiky leaves to a small door, produced a key, opened the door, and held it back for her to go through. Then he swiftly shut it behind her and turned the key again. This was a smaller glasshouse, full of ferns with fronds and waving leaves, most of them in pots. He promptly pulled one of those plants across in front of the door.

"There," he said. "Even if they should come into this corner of the glasshouse, they will not suppose there is any way through, nor that there is anything in particular to see here. Now all we need to do is lurk here a few moments, until they have had their fill of the growing pineapple plants, and then you may leave at your leisure, unobserved."

Phoebe felt all the awkwardness of the situation, but was also full of gratitude at his prompt action and his kind and easy manners. She held out her hand. "I am Miss Hawkins," she said. "Mr. Darcy is my uncle, and I am staying here."

"I heard you were expected, Miss Hawkins. I am Mr. Drummond, employed by Mr. Darcy to look after his estates."

"I know, and you are here to superintend the works he is having done." She looked around her. "What is this place?" she asked. "I do not remember ever having been in here; as children, we were most strictly forbidden to go into the glasshouses."

"It is where we bring along the seedlings and the young plants that need extra warmth. It is very full at the moment, because I have already put in hand the demolition of one of the larger old glasshouses, which means that the gardeners have less room than usual."

"Mr. Darcy is planning to build a new glasshouse, I think?"

"Indeed he is, a large and ambitious one, as big, I think, as on any gentleman's estate

147

in the country, and a smaller one as well, for plants from hot countries that Mrs. Darcy in particular is very keen to see grow here. She has made quite a collection while she has been abroad. Some of them are in here. They are very tender, and so need a warm atmosphere all the year round."

Mr. Drummond talked about the plants, pointing out some particularly fine specimens. He was knowledgeable and informative, without being in the least bit dull, and she was amazed at how much he knew. "Are you by profession a horticulturalist?" she asked, puzzled, for that was not an occupation pursued by many gentlemen.

He laughed. "No, my profession is the law, I am a solicitor by training. However, my father, who is a vicar in Norfolk, has always had a great love of plants and brought up all his children to know about gardens and how things grow. That is one of the reasons why Mr. Darcy has employed me, for these days the care and maintenance of grounds and gardens, and applying the newest horticultural techniques, is as important to most landowners as is the management of their houses and estates and farms." He paused and gave a rueful smile. "It's very remiss of me to go on like this, it is rather a hobbyhorse of mine, and I know that others do not find it as interesting as I do."

Phoebe smiled back at him. "Indeed it makes a change to hear a gentleman talking about such things, instead of the usual round of conversation: guns, horses, and dogs in sport."

"Oh," said Mr. Drummond, "I'm afraid I'm also a very keen sportsman, so I'm as guilty as the next man of describing an amazing run across country after a fox, or how a particular stretch of river is teeming with fish."

"We women are just as guilty. We gossip, and talk about clothes and fashions and books, and perhaps, if we are so inclined, about music and paintings. Our world is a smaller one than that of you men," she added.

While they had been talking and walking and looking at plants, Mr. Drummond had kept an ear open as to what was happening in the adjoining glasshouse. He said, "I think you are safe now. I'll let you out of the other door here, and you may make your way further out into the gardens, or back into the house."

Mr. Stanhope had had quite enough of pineapples. Horticulture was not a subject that interested him in the slightest, and he was annoyed at being taken in hand so firmly by Louisa. He was certain that he had seen Phoebe from the upstairs window, which was the only reason he had expressed an eagerness to visit the gardens. He more than once gave his sister an urgent look, but she seemed to be enjoying the plants and flowers, and showed no inclination to leave the pleasant warmth of the glasshouse and go back out into the grounds.

When they did, at last, leave the glasshouse, he looked back and caught sight of Mr. Drummond's figure in another, smaller glasshouse at the other end. He went out with the two ladies, and then with the briefest of apologies set off round the glasshouse to where he judged there must be an entrance to the smaller glasshouse. He was right, and there, standing beside the entrance, was Hugh Drummond. His friend greeted him with a friendly smile and a clap on the shoulder. "Arthur, I thought I heard your voice, but I didn't like to interrupt. What are you doing here? I did not know you were visiting today."

"Paying a formal visit with my sister and Sir Henry, and damned tedious it is too. I have no idea where Sir Henry has gone. He announced that he wanted to talk to Mr. Darcy's head gardener, and I suppose he is still deep in conversation with him."

"I doubt it," said Mr. Drummond wryly. "Mr. Grayling, who is the gardener in question, isn't here today."

Mr. Stanhope was not greatly interested in what might have happened to Sir Henry, but he did want to know where Phoebe might be. He asked his friend if he had happened to see a young lady. "Miss Hawkins, the Darcys' niece, is staying here. Miss Bingley said that she was indisposed, but I'm sure that I just saw her in the garden, and I should not like to leave without paying my respects."

Drummond shot his friend a keen glance. "I have not been introduced to Miss Hawkins," he said, truthfully enough. "Perhaps she is in the yew walk; in my experience young ladies like to walk among the yew hedges."

"Well, if you have not seen her, I shall have to wait for another day to renew our acquaintance," said Stanhope, frowning. "I think we have probably already outstayed our welcome, so it leaves me little to do except find Sir Henry and wait for the carriage to be brought round."

He was somewhat surprised on walking back to the house with Mr. Drummond to see Sir Henry come around the corner, deep in conversation with a strange young woman. He turned to Drummond with a questioning look in his eye, and Mr. Drummond immediately responded, "That is the governess, Miss Verney."

Stanhope said with a laugh, "The one you don't care for. I have to say she seems to be on extremely good terms with Sir Henry."

"Perhaps you had better go and rescue him," said Drummond.

Stanhope strode over to where Sir Henry was standing, and was amused to notice that his brother-in-law seemed slightly disconcerted by his arrival. "I am asking for the carriage to be brought round," said Stanhope. "We must take our leave."

Sir Henry gave a slight cough, and then said, rather to Stanhope's surprise, "I have been talking to Miss Verney. I know her father, the Comte de Verney. He is one of the émigré families and I have known him for many years."

Stanhope and Miss Verney shook hands, Stanhope favouring her with the briefest of glances. His tone was brusque as he said to Sir Henry that they had better find Lady Martindale.

Sir Henry took his leave of Miss Verney, with what Stanhope considered an exaggerated degree of respect to a girl who was no

152

more than a governess, however much she might be the daughter of an old friend. And that, he told himself, was a story which he did not all together believe.

The carriage was brought round, and Stanhope said a civil if chilly good-bye to Louisa. He sprang up into the driving seat, took the reins from the groom, and with a flourish of his long whip set the horses in motion.

CHAPTER TWELVE

The next day was Sunday, and Phoebe and Louisa decided to go to church. There was a chapel at Pemberley, of course, but the family generally attended divine service at the church in the nearby village of Pemberley. They walked to the church, since if they took the path through the grounds of Pemberley, it was no more than twenty minutes to the village besides being a charming walk through the parkland on a bright spring morning.

"How pretty it is," Phoebe exclaimed as they reached the crest of the hill and looked down at the village.

It was a picturesque scene, with the neat houses along the main street, the cottages on the outskirts, the pretty gardens, and the church, many centuries old, with its square tower. Apart from the church and the vicarage, Pemberley boasted several very respectable houses, a butcher, a baker, and a general store, run by the obliging Mrs. Hyslop, where one could buy a dress length, gloves, various items of ironmongery, and anything else ranging from a mousetrap to cheesecloth.

Smoke from various chimneys drifted upwards, as there was not even a hint of a breeze, and Phoebe and Louisa stood and took in the beauty of the scene. This reflective moment was abruptly shattered by the sound of the church bell ringing out, and closer to hand, by Phoebe's suddenly succumbing to a fit of sneezing.

Louisa wondered for a moment if Phoebe had caught a cold, but Phoebe, whose eyes were watering, shook her head. "No, I am not ill, I assure you. It is something that happens at this time of year, I believe it is the grass that irritates one's nose in some way. I will be better directly. We must hurry, however, or we shall be late."

They reached the church as the last strokes of the calling bell were dying away, and hurried inside to take their places. The Darcy family pew was, of course, at the front of the church. The verger, a small man with a round head and frizzy hair on either side of his bald pate, opened the pew door for them, and, with much bowing and scraping, held it open while they went in. In

London, some churches had adopted a more modern seating where everyone was visible to his or her neighbours, but in this county the old ways prevailed and each family was enclosed within the high walls of the panelled pews. Once inside the boxed pew, Louisa and Phoebe were hidden from sight, and Phoebe was thankful for it as she subsided on the velvet upholstered seat and buried her nose in her handkerchief.

Phoebe knew the vicar of Pemberley, but to her surprise, the clergyman who took the service was not Mr. Pontius. This was a man she had never seen before. "Who can he be? He preaches a very dull and prosy sermon," Phoebe whispered to Louisa after he had ascended the pulpit, surveyed the congregation with a suspicious and withering eye, and began to preach.

Phoebe listened to his sermon with rising indignation. "The wretched man has been droning on for more than half an hour, and to no purpose. Hackneyed language and hellfire, it is too bad!"

"Shh, people will hear you. He is the kind of person who likes the sound of his own voice," said Louisa.

"He is an Evangelical, I am sure of it," said Phoebe. "I can't think why he is here, what has become of Mr. Pontius?"

At last the sermon came to an end, the priest uttered the words of dismissal and his blessing, and the little choir of boys fidgeting in their white surplices trooped down the aisle. Phoebe, coming out of the pew, found herself next to Mrs. Hyslop, resplendent in a purple gown, who greeted her with the friendliness of a woman who had known her since she was a child.

"He's Mr. Bagot," the knowledgeable Mrs. Hyslop informed her, "come over from Lambton on account of Mr. Pontius being called away to the bedside of a sick relative. Three quarters of an hour he preached this morning," she added. "T'aint right, it might do for those Lambton folk, who have nothing but cotton wool between their ears, and so don't know the difference, but give me Mr. Pontius any Sunday!"

Mr. Bagot was waiting by the church door. "Ready," said Mrs. Hyslop, "to pounce on the gentry." He introduced himself with obsequious becks and nods to Louisa and Phoebe, who dropped a slight curtsy each and made to move on, but he was as loquacious out of the pulpit as he was in it, and it took them a little while to escape, his compliments to Mr. Darcy ringing in their ears.

"Phoebe, if you dare laugh," began Lou-

157

isa, but Phoebe, in a muffled voice, said it wasn't laughter, but the sneezing come back again, with renewed vigour.

Mrs. Hyslop wagged a finger at Phoebe. "Spring fever," she said. "I remember you always suffered from that when you were here as a girl, Miss Phoebe. Take my advice and ask Mr. Osler to give you some of his new mixture. Mrs. Wellesley gave it to that scullery maid of hers who always had a dripping nose, and it cleared it up wonderfully."

Louisa, who liked Mrs. Hyslop, thanked her for her advice, but Phoebe merely looked annoyed. "Who, pray, is Mr. Osler?"

"He is the new doctor. Mr. Wilson retired a little while ago, and Mr. Osler is his replacement."

"Dripping nose, scullery maid, indeed," said Phoebe, still holding her handkerchief to her streaming nose. "For heaven's sake, Louisa, let us be away from here, before Mr. Bagot offers to drive us back to Pemberley in his gig."

"Perhaps the mention of the scullery maid was unfortunate, but you do have a dripping nose," said Louisa.

"It will stop in a minute," said Phoebe. "It comes and goes without any warning, I dare say that by the time we are back at Pemberley I will have no more sneezes."

Phoebe's predictions proved false. By the time she reached Pemberley, her eyes were red and watering again. Miniver took one look and hurried back down to the servants' hall, muttering as she went: "Consult Mr. Osler? A country doctor? Who suggested that? When I can brew up a remedy myself, which will do her better than any doctor's potions."

CHAPTER THIRTEEN

Whatever was in the rather unpleasant drink forced upon Phoebe by Miniver, it seemed to work, and by the time she retired for the night, Phoebe's sneezes had gone. She woke after a refreshing night's sleep with a clear nose and head, and the rasping voice of Mr. Bagot sounding in her ears.

"I had such a disturbing dream," she told Louisa as they sat in the conservatory after breakfast, enjoying the warmth of the sun as it came through the glass overhead. "That dreadful man, Mr. Bagot, was preaching, and uttering all kinds of nonsense; I wasn't sure whether to laugh or be alarmed when I opened my eyes, but I was extremely glad to find myself in my bed, and not in the Darcy pew!"

A footman appeared with letters. Louisa opened one from her mother and ran her eyes down the closely written words, while

Phoebe stared down at the direction on her letter.

Louisa folded the two pages covered and crossed in her mother's fine hand, and put them away to read later. "Why do you not open your letter?" she asked Phoebe.

"I do not recognise the hand, I wonder who it is from."

"You can find that out in an instant by simply opening it."

Phoebe did so. "Ah, it is from Mr. Darcy's secretary in London, Mr. Tetbury, who is a most estimable man, the model of efficiency and agreeable with it." She ran her eyes down the page of neat copperplate. "He sends me a list of those to be invited to the ball at Pemberley, and a second list of the members of the family and other guests who will stay at the house at the time of the ball." She read on. Mr. Darcy had, Mr. Tetbury believed, asked Miss Hawkins to ascertain if there were others in the neighbourhood not on the list who should be invited. He enquired whether Phoebe would wish to have the invitations engraved in London and sent to Derbyshire, or whether she would have them printed locally.

"This means," said Phoebe, "that we shall need to drive to Lambton. We can have the invitations printed there, and also, Miniver

161

wants me to buy some ribbons to make new rosettes for one of my gowns. Pull the bell, Louisa, and I will order the carriage."

Louisa rose to do as she was asked, and then left the room, saying that if they were going to Lambton, she must change into another gown.

"Oh, do not be too nice, it is of no account what one wears in Lambton," said Phoebe, who had no intention of changing from the dress she was wearing, which was a favourite muslin, so old that the pattern had faded. Miniver had been trying to pass it on to one of the maids for a good while, but Phoebe had always thwarted her attempts to be rid of it.

But Miniver, when Phoebe told her to fetch her a pelisse, was having none of it. "What, go to Lambton in a dress that's hardly fit for going out into the garden, and that only if no one is about?"

"It is only the country. No one pays any attention to what one wears in the country."

Miniver knew that a direct argument with Phoebe would get her nowhere. So she resorted to cunning. "Did you not tell that your godmother, Mrs. Wellesley, is come to live at Lambton? I am sure you wish to call upon her. And besides, if people see you in that dreadful old gown, they will imagine that your father has lost all his money, that you are nothing but a poor Darcy relation."

Grudgingly, Phoebe consented to put on a carriage dress of dark red terry velvet, with a matching bonnet, in which, with her dark colouring, she looked very well indeed. "I thought I had left this dress in London. It is one of my new ones, made to do the season, I do not know how it came to be here."

Miniver did not think this an appropriate time to tell Phoebe that, despite her expressed wishes, she had arranged for nearly all Phoebe's new clothes to be packed up and sent to Pemberley. Most of these clothes were hanging in the press in one of the other bedrooms, where Phoebe would not discover what Miniver had done.

Louisa, charmingly dressed in a dove grey gown, joined Phoebe at the top of the steps just as a groom brought the curricle up to the front door. Thomas was waiting to help them into the carriage, but Phoebe, once she had seen Louisa settled in her place, did not join her inside the open carriage, but instead climbed into the driver's seat and gathered the reins into her hands. Ignoring Louisa's dismayed protests, Phoebe commanded the groom to let go of the horses' heads, and as he jumped up behind, set off down the drive at a spanking pace.

Louisa need not have worried. Phoebe had been taught to drive by her father, and in the last year or so had become a most accomplished whip. And indeed the drive into Lambton was achieved without any mishaps, other than Phoebe having to keep a tight hold on the reins at a crossroads when a goose flapped out from underneath a hedge, startling the horses. However, they were a well-trained pair, and by the time they reached the market town, Louisa's fears had quite subsided.

The groom took the curricle off to the inn, and Phoebe and Louisa walked down the main street of the town. First, Phoebe had business to transact at the printers. The works were situated in a small alley leading off the main street. Mr. Bondwell, the printer, bustled forward to take Phoebe's order, and after some ten minutes' discussion of typefaces and the style of invitations, she thanked him and said that the cards were to be sent up to Pemberley as soon as they were ready.

"And now, of course," said Phoebe as the door closed behind Mr. Bondwell's bows, "everyone in Lambton will know that there is to be a summer ball at Pemberley."

"Do you think they will be very much interested?" said Louisa, stepping to one side to avoid a puddle.

"The family does not visit much in Lambton, and so the inhabitants will not expect invitations," said Phoebe. "However, among the tradespeople and so on, there is always a good deal of interest at what is going on in the great houses within reach of the town. They will hope for some good orders."

They came to the general store, a much bigger shop than Mrs. Hyslop's in Pemberley, and an assistant hurried forward to attend to them. A stock of ribbons was brought out and Phoebe produced the sample of material which Miniver wanted to match. Phoebe would have chosen the first ribbon the assistant suggested, but Louisa would have none of that. "This ribbon will be much prettier with that colour," she said, selecting another one and holding it against the scrap of muslin.

"I liked the original trimming well enough," said Phoebe. "And this first ribbon is much closer to the ones which Miniver is replacing."

"And I dare say the reason Miniver wishes to re-trim the gown is that the original ribbons do not go so very well with this colour; she has excellent taste."

Phoebe allowed herself to be persuaded. "Indeed, I really cannot be very much concerned as to the precise colour of the ribbon or a trim. It is all the same to me."

"You are very lucky to have a maid with an eye and a sense of style, in that case. Otherwise you would go out looking a positive dowd."

"New clothes make me feel uneasy, I admit," said Phoebe. "I am never perfectly happy in them until they are practically worn out. You may laugh at me," she went on, "just as my mother and sisters do, however I think there are more important things in life than dresses."

"When you're a pretty young woman of twenty, clothes are of great importance. Time enough when you are in your dotage to leave off caring how you look."

Phoebe wasn't listening. She was walking now down a narrow street which ran parallel to the main one. "I asked for directions to Mrs. Wellesley's house from Mrs. Makepeace," she said. "There is a lane that runs from behind the vicarage, and we should find the gates to her house further along."

Louisa was curious. "So, if you have not visited her before, she is but recently come into the neighbourhood."

"She moved here this past winter. It is a

coincidence, she has not chosen to reside in Derbyshire because of any family connections. But her friend, Lady Maria Jesper, recently inherited this house and so they have both come to live here."

It was a leafy lane, with the trees arched overhead just coming into their first spring greenery. However, they had to watch where they walked, since the road was muddy in places. "Perhaps we should have driven here," said Phoebe. "I had not realised it was so far from the centre of the town."

As they turned a slight bend in the lane, they saw a pair of gates ahead of them. "This must be the house," said Phoebe as they came up to the gates and looked through. "It is just as it was described to me."

The Red House was a very pretty property, dating from the middle of the last century. They pushed open the gates and walked up the sweep towards the house. To one side was a large kitchen garden, and to the other a very pleasant kind of shrubbery. "They are both garden lovers," Phoebe told Louisa. "I expect they are very pleased to have a house like this with such a good garden."

"You never mentioned Mrs. Wellesley to me before. Is there no Mr. Wellesley? Is she a widow?"

"Yes, she is, which is a great mercy, for her husband was a most disagreeable man. He was a naval officer, and on that account her marriage was not as bad as it might have been, since he was away at sea for many months at a time. However, he was as unpleasant to his men as he was to his wife, and supposedly died in some action or other. Everyone in the family knows the truth of the matter, that the men were on the point of mutiny, there were stories of floggings and inhumane treatment of all kinds. So, as they went into action, one or other of the men put an end to him with a bullet. It often happened, so I have heard, when a severe captain, a hard horse captain, as they call such men, causes his crew to become mutinous."

Louisa stopped and laid a hand on Phoebe's arm. Her eyes were shocked. "Why ever did she marry him, if he was such a monster?"

Phoebe kept walking. "He was rich, well-connected, handsome, and a charming man in his wooing. But wooed and wed are two different states, and the ardent suitor turned into the violent, disagreeable husband. It is an unhappy wife who rejoices at the death of her husband, but it was certainly so in

Mrs. Wellesley's case. I believe she ordered champagne, and ill-wishers claim she danced on her husband's grave."

"What you tell me is incredible, it cannot be true!"

"That she danced on his grave? No, indeed, for he died and was buried at sea."

They had reached the front door, which was set in the centre of the red-brick house, a symmetrical building with matching windows on either side. They were admitted by a maid. Yes, the ladies were at home, would they please follow her?

A small but well-proportioned hall led to a fine staircase. On either side of the front door were two rooms, and the maid opened the door of the one on the right, saying, "Miss Hawkins and Miss Bingley."

Louisa fell back as a tiny figure came hurrying across the room, exclaiming and laughing, and embracing Phoebe with great warmth. She turned an animated face to Louisa. "And this is Jane's daughter? My dear, I am so pleased to meet you. I know your mother, and you are very like her. Maria, come and meet Mrs. Bingley's daughter, Jane Bennet as was. My dear, may I call you Louisa? This is Lady Maria Jesper."

Lady Maria was a complete contrast to Mrs. Wellesley. She was a tall, handsome woman, with a face that seemed severe in repose, but was now softened by a welcoming smile. The two women offered Phoebe and Louisa chairs, tea, refreshments, but Louisa, usually content to remain in the background, asked whether they might see round the gardens. Phoebe silently applauded her friend for picking up her remark as to the ladies' horticultural enthusiasm.

The gardens were enchanting. To the rear of the house was an old walled garden, full of flowers in the first colours of spring: yellow and blue and purple. The espaliered fruit trees still had blossoms on them, and the warmth of the garden, sheltered by its ancient walls, held out the promise of the summer to come. Phoebe walked without speaking, enjoying one of her rare moments of utter calm, listening with only half her mind to Louisa and her godmother discussing tulips, while Lady Maria, who had spotted an unruly weed, was head down in a nearby flowerbed.

She hadn't appreciated before how knowledgeable Louisa was about flowers and gardening. In fact, there was a lot she didn't know about Louisa, whom she had never seen as much of as she had of her Darcy cousins. And she had seldom seen her as animated as she was now, deep in discussion with Mrs. Wellesley on how to train a lilac tree. Lady Maria stood up from the bed, clapping a hand to the small of her back as she straightened herself. "I have a painful back after a fall from a horse many years ago," she explained. "I confess I have never ridden since. You are an uncommonly good horsewoman, I remember. Did you bring your horse with you to Pemberley, or do you ride one of Mr. Darcy's?"

"I shall borrow one of my uncle's horses. And Louisa likes to ride, and will do so once the tracks and roads dry up after all the rain we have had. We both dislike being kept indoors by bad weather, and miss our daily exercise."

They had reached the far end of the walled garden, and now they passed through a small door into an orchard, where Mrs. Wellesley began to expound as to the advantages and disadvantages of the varieties of apples and pears which grew best in Derbyshire. Previously, she told Louisa, she and Lady Maria had lived in Devon, where the weather and conditions were very different.

"As to exercise," Lady Maria was saying to Phoebe, "I am surprised that you are not in London at this time of year, dancing until dawn and spending your days in a round of pleasure."

Phoebe was well aware that Lady Maria had a sharp mind and an ear for gossip, which, combined with a knack of spotting anyone's weakness, meant that one had to take care what one revealed to her; Phoebe felt wary about giving Lady Maria an opportunity to probe further into why she was not in London. By diverting her companion's attention to a small beetle that was climbing energetically up the trunk of a nearby tree, she managed to deflect her interest in a less personal direction.

Another gate led into a small paddock, where a donkey was grazing. It raised its grey head for a moment, and then dropped it to resume its steady grazing of the thick green grass. From there they walked back along the side of the house and into the shrubbery that they had passed as they came in through the gates. Mrs. Wellesley hung back, wishing to talk to Phoebe. She was full of enquiries about her mother, her father, and her sister and her sister's London come-out: "How does she enjoy her first season?"

They had just returned to the house, and had entered the drawing-room again, when there was a loud peal on the doorbell. Two minutes later, the maid appeared, followed by a bowing clergyman, and Phoebe was unhappy to see that it was Mr. Bagot, the vicar of Lambton.

He greeted all the ladies with an unctuous enthusiasm that set Phoebe's teeth on edge. There was a kind of masculine overbearingness to him that Phoebe found particularly irritating. He naturally assumed that, as a single male in a room with women, his voice and his opinions were the ones that most counted. He expounded upon the weather, upon the gardens at the Red House, and upon the undesirability of young women venturing so far from home unaccompanied by a maid.

Phoebe felt that this was none of his business, and was preparing to tell him so when Mrs. Wellesley, no doubt aware of Phoebe's irritation, intervened, saying that there was no possible need for her goddaughter and for Miss Bingley to be accompanied by a maid when they were paying a visit to the Red House, hardly a lonely spot, and but a few minutes' walk from the main part of the town.

"When they leave the grounds of the Red House, however, there is the walk along the lane," he said. "It will be best for me to accompany you."

Phoebe laughed. "I cannot see that we are

in any possible danger walking along the lane the short distance from here to the main street." She turned to Mrs. Wellesley. "Indeed, it is time that Louisa and I took our leave of you. The carriage will be waiting for us."

"And if I know anything about you, Phoebe," said Mrs. Wellesley with a smile, "it will be you and not the groom who drives the carriage back to Pemberley."

Phoebe acknowledged that this was so, and earned herself a wagging finger and a solemn look from the vicar. "I cannot believe that Mr. Darcy would be happy to see his niece driving herself about the countryside. Surely there is a coachman who could have driven you."

"Mr. Darcy is well aware of my habit of driving myself when and wherever I can," said Phoebe. "The only scolding I will get from him is if I drive badly, or do any harm to his horses. And since I stand in awe of him, I shall take very great care to do neither of those things."

Phoebe and Louisa took their leave. Mrs. Wellesley said that she hoped to see them again soon, to hear more of the family news from Phoebe, and to continue her interesting discussion about gardens with Louisa.

They walked quickly down the path, afraid

that despite their protestations, the vicar might put on his black shovel hat and pursue them down the leafy lane. "That was a narrow escape," said Phoebe as they arrived rather breathless at the corner of the main street. "He is as tiresome in the drawing-room as he is in the pulpit. I cannot think how or why Sir Henry chose to bestow the living upon him."

Louisa was less harsh in her judgement. "He was dull, I grant you, and rather too forceful in the way he speaks, given that we are almost strangers, but he may still be an excellent parish priest."

"I very much doubt it," said Phoebe. "If I were one of the poor, I think I would hide in the cellar when he called and only emerge when he had gone. You may be sure he hectors and lectures the poor, when what they need is kind words and hot soup."

Louisa was enthusiastic about her new acquaintances, saying how interesting she had found her conversation with Mrs. Wellesley. "I am sorry I did not have much chance to talk with Lady Maria. Is she also a widow, or is she in some way related to your godmother?"

"No, she's no relation at all. The truth about Lady Maria is dreadful, and I fear you will be even more shocked than you were by the details of Mrs. Wellesley's unhappy marriage." She said this with a sideways glance at Louisa, who tried to look disapproving but didn't succeed in hiding her curiosity.

"In which case you had better not tell me."

"It is good for you, being so inclined to think well of everybody, to learn how much wickedness there is in the world. You will indeed be shocked when I tell you that Lady Maria is divorced."

"Divorced!" Louisa could not keep the surprise out of her voice. It was a rarity for any woman to be divorced. Divorce proceedings were lengthy, expensive, and only ever undertaken by members of the aristocracy. To obtain a divorce, a bill had to be passed in Parliament, and the scandal of it was immense, with the lurid details being published in broadsheets, and passed from one gossiping tongue to another up and down the length of the kingdom.

"It was long ago, when we were children. It was only recently that I learned the facts of the case, for of course when I was a girl, such a matter would never be discussed in front of me. I had it from Miniver in the end, for her sister was in service with the family, and all the servants were outraged at the way that Lady Maria was treated by her husband."

"Don't tell me he was another violent husband, like Mr. Wellesley."

"Captain Wellesley," Phoebe corrected her. "No, Mr. Jesper was a libertine. Now, you will say that many men are philanderers and do not end up in the divorce courts. However, Mr. Jesper had the effrontery to bring his wrongdoing home, in the most literal sense, for he installed not one but two of his mistresses in a wing of his house, and defied Lady Maria to object to their presence. Moreover, he and Lady Maria had no children, but one of his mistresses had three and he wanted Lady Maria to acknowledge them as her own, which would make the elder boy heir to his estate and fortune. Lady Maria's family agreed that she had been badly treated, and urged a separation, but Mr. Jesper issued all kinds of threats against her, hoping by that means to silence her protests and so have his own way, only to find that the affair went further than he had planned, and he lost both Lady Maria and her fortune."

"How very dreadful," cried Louisa.

"You can understand why neither Lady Maria nor Mrs. Wellesley have any inclination to marry again, although as you see for yourself they are both well-looking, good-natured women. I believe they relish their independence, and are certainly much happier living together as they do than they were when they were married."

The groom was on the lookout for them, and in a few minutes they were making their way back down the main street. Louisa, shivering, drew a shawl about her, and called out to Phoebe, "Are you sure you are warm enough? It was a warm spring day when we came this morning, and I declare it now feels positively wintry again."

"I spoke to John Shepherd," the groom put in. "He's the best weatherman in these parts, and he reckons we're in for a storm."

The sky was certainly clouding over, but Phoebe was inclined to dismiss the idea of a storm. "We shall merely have more of this tiresome rain," she said. "April showers, that's all."

CHAPTER FOURTEEN

It seemed that Phoebe had been better in her weather prognostications than the shepherd. The sky lightened as they drove back to Pemberley, and after only a few drops of rain had fallen, a pale sun emerged from behind the clouds.

Louisa had letters to write, and she sat herself down at the desk in the drawing-room. Phoebe sat with her for a while, reading *Ivanhoe,* but then, growing restless, announced that she was going to change into her riding habit and take out a horse. She brushed aside Louisa's objections that driving to Lambton was enough exertion for one day.

She ran upstairs, rang the bell for Miniver, and, ignoring her maid's predictions of the woe that she would be bringing on herself, in less than fifteen minutes was on her way back down the stairs again, this time dressed in a green velvet riding habit. The stable yard was quiet, and Jessop was nowhere to be seen, but her arrival brought one of the grooms out, and she asked him to saddle Marchpain for her. He seemed doubtful, but she assured him that the head groom would not be at all concerned about her taking the horse out.

"He's very lively," warned the groom as he held the horse's head while Phoebe mounted from the block in the yard. "With all this wet weather, none of the horses have had the exercise they should."

"Then he and I will enjoy a good gallop, and shake the fidgets out of ourselves," said Phoebe. The groom hurried to a stall in order to saddle his own mount to accompany Phoebe on a ride, but was dumbstruck when he saw her trotting briskly out of the yard. "Don't worry," she called back to him. "I shall stay within the grounds today, I intend to ride in the park. I don't need a groom to accompany me."

Which left the groom standing in the centre of the stable yard looking after the retreating figure of Phoebe and the horse, and shaking his head. Another groom slid down the ladder from the hayloft and landed beside him. "Miss Phoebe has taken out Marchpain, has she? And I suppose you offered to go with her, and she has ridden off on her own. Well, don't take it to heart. You've only been here for a year, so you aren't yet used to Miss Phoebe's ways. She is as headstrong as they come, and likes to be on her own. Even when she was a girl, she was a rare handful, always taking her pony off by herself if she could get away with it. Don't fret yourself, she's a fine horsewoman, and I dare say she won't be out for long, because if I'm not much mistaken it's going to come on to rain hard within the hour."

Arthur Stanhope had also had some letters to write, but he soon finished them and went off to find his sister, who was picking at some fruit for her luncheon.

"I will ring for some cold meat for you," she said. "I dare say you won't want to eat just pineapple; it was sent over from Pemberley, with Miss Bingley's and Miss Hawkins's compliments."

Sir Henry didn't join them, but then, as Kitty told Arthur, he rarely came indoors in the middle of the day. "Today he rode over to Baxter's farm," she told her brother. "There is some matter he needed to discuss with the bailiff, and he said that he might not be back until the evening."

Arthur Stanhope went over to the window

and looked out. "He'd best not delay for too long, for I think we're in for a storm. I shall take myself off to the stables, and ride over to Pemberley to see Hugh, before it gets too blustery. I shan't be gone above a couple of hours." He turned round and looked at his sister, quiet and pale, and still with that look of unhappiness about her. "Or I could drive if you would care for an outing."

"No, thank you. I went out for a walk this morning, and I need to consult with the housekeeper about the guests who will be coming for the Harlows' party."

"Guests?"

"I'm sure I told you that we expect some friends, people who are coming to Derbyshire for Jack Harlow's coming-of-age."

"Oh, I see. Whom are you inviting?"

"Pagoda Portal, and therefore, of course, Mrs. Rowan. Lady Sackville, and the two Billingham boys. Do you know them?"

"Barely. They were still at school when last I saw them."

"And some others," Kitty added as he walked to the door.

"Well, I shall leave you to your duties."

When Stanhope had left the room, Kitty did not immediately get up and go to talk to the housekeeper. Instead, for several long minutes she sat listlessly gazing into the fire, her hands hanging over the arms of her chair. Her pet spaniel got up from his basket and padded over to her, pushing his wet nose into her hand as though to comfort her. She fondled his silky ears and said, "Daisy, I wish I knew what to do. Or indeed that there were anything that I could do." A tear fell on her hand, and she brushed it off. Then, with sudden resolution, she stood up and, patting the side of her skirt, so that Daisy jumped up in delight, told the spaniel that she would take a brief turn in the garden with her, before she went to find Mrs. Nutley.

Mr. Stanhope's mare was not an easy ride that afternoon. In a fretful mood, with her tail swishing, she snatched at the bit and tossed her head. Along the way, she shied at a stone, at an opening in a hedgerow, and danced on springy legs when a pheasant started from the ditch.

Mr. Stanhope was never impatient with horses, and he kept still in the saddle, exerting a steady pressure with his legs, and uttering soothing sounds. He wondered why the mare was so nervous; possibly it was the gusts of wind which came and went in little puffs, catching her under her tail and making her flick her ears back. It wasn't a comfortable ride, although she behaved better when he jumped a gate into a meadow and let her have her head. She pounded up the rise and then galloped along the ridge at the top, forgetting her fancies, and covering the ground in good style. He reined in as she began the steeper descent through the woods to the boundary of the park at Pemberley. He turned in at the North Lodge, where the gatekeeper ran out to open the gate, observing that the weather was fair blowing up. "Are you visiting at the house? For I saw Miss Phoebe ride out not half an hour since, she won't be back yet."

Phoebe, out in this weather? She must be an intrepid horsewoman. Perhaps he would meet her.

"Thank you, but I am here to call upon Mr. Drummond."

"Now, he is in, for I saw him earlier and he said he was on his way back to the South Lodge, where he's staying, there's no gatekeeper there these days, the family don't use that gate. Got a heap of paper to deal with, so he told me, he fair works hard, does Mr. Drummond."

Arthur Stanhope flipped him a coin, and cantered along the boundary towards the other gate. Rain had begun to fall again, fat drops that spattered the sandy ground beneath his horse's hoofs, and rattled on the new leaves above his head. He kept to one side of the track, where it was more sheltered, ducking to avoid the overhanging branches of the trees which lined the way. He left the solid outline of the house behind him as he turned on to the service road. The mare gave the ice house, a squat brick building, a wide berth, and then he was riding along beside the high walls of the kitchen garden, to the small stone house of the South Lodge. As he swung his horse around the corner of the wall, he had to halt abruptly, to prevent a collision with a rider coming the other way, a rider going at a furious pace, who swerved alarmingly as she saw the horseman sitting there, controlling his horse with difficulty.

He knew her at once, a jolting recognition that drove the breath out of his body. Her face was white, bedewed with rain, a lock of hair falling across her forehead. Her eyes were huge, startled, and for a moment, a flash of delight was there, before they became blank and hostile. She mouthed some words, lost in the rising wind, and then, wrenching at her horse's mouth, swivelled round. Her horse half reared, and he urged his own mount forward to lay a protective hand on her bridle, but she swung away, eyes dark now with anger.

He called out her name, shouting against the wind, "Phoebe! Wait!"

Her horse plunged, then gave a great leap as she clapped a spur into its flank, and in seconds she was gone, leaving nothing but a memory of a face and a swirling habit.

Stanhope reined back, and the mare, ears flattened, gave a buck that nearly unseated him. By the time he had control of the nervous animal, he knew there was no point in setting off after Phoebe. He cursed, fluently and without any awareness of what he was saying, until he was brought back to his senses by Drummond's voice. His friend had come out of the South Lodge, carrying a lamp and calling out into the gloom.

"What is all the commotion? Good God, Arthur, it's you."

Phoebe careered into the stable yard, breathless, and leaning low over her horse's neck. Jessop was there in a trice, putting out a hand to take the bridle, to run a gentle hand down the horse's neck, and to shout to a groom to help Miss Phoebe down.

"Did he bolt?" he asked.

"No, no, it was my fault, driving him."

"You know better than to bring in a horse

in a lather, Miss Phoebe." The tone of reproof was the same one he had used when she was a little girl and had galloped her pony at the end of a ride, instead of trotting back so that the pony would arrive at the stable cool and collected and ready to be put back in its stall. He instructed the groom to take off the sidesaddle, and then told him to take the horse out to cool him down. The groom took the reins and led the horse back out of the yard at a gentle trot, hissing to it as it shook flecks of foam from its bit.

"It was the weather, I dare say," Mr. Jessop said, looking at her closely. "You had a fright."

"I was startled, everything is rustling out there."

"A big storm's blowing up, and the horses are uneasy. Best get yourself inside, Miss Phoebe, as quickly as possible, and change out of that wet riding habit."

Jessop's words flowed over Phoebe, but she hardly took in the sense of any of them. She gathered up the wet skirt of her riding habit, and almost ran along the path and back in through the little conservatory. Once inside she stood leaning against the doorpost, a wave of nausea making her bite her tongue. How could a brief encounter upset her so much? Why had Mr. Stanhope come to Derbyshire, why was he always at Pemberley? That is an exaggeration, she told herself severely. Her father had extracted that promise from her that she would have no further contact with Mr. Stanhope, and she had kept it, apart from the letter she had written. Intense passion, her reading had told her, could fade as quickly as it burst into flame, and so, if she could avoid Mr. Stanhope for weeks — months — a year? Passion might fade, yes, although . . . She clenched her eyes tight, to shut out the image of Mr. Stanhope's face, his hands, the way he carried himself, his voice.

Passion was one thing, love another. When you felt both for a man, what hope was there of the evanescence of affections her father had promised?

London friends had brought her snippets of gossip while she was still at Aubrey Square, every word an unwitting stab in her heart. "Mr. Stanhope, you are acquainted with him, are you not? He is a handsome man, I could fancy him, but he is dancing attendance upon Lady Belinda Cunningham, I can't for myself understand what he sees in her."

Mr. Stanhope was welcome to Lady Belinda; Phoebe knew very well what Belinda was like, as beautiful as the dawn, and with a heart of ice. And another of her informants, a worldly friend, was of the opinion that Mr. Stanhope had no serious intentions with regard to Lady Belinda, or indeed anyone else. Why should he, with so many women sighing for him, and the dazzling Mrs. Vereker to delight him, as she had done for the last five years?

"Of course, Lord and Lady Stanhope will have a bride or two in mind for him, and one of these days he will be obliged to marry. They want him to make a good marriage, parents always do, and especially parents like the Stanhopes. Those Whig families always marry within their own circle, gaining even more influence and power through the intricate web of their connections."

Her father was right, she must shut him out of her life. So said her reason, but the problem was with her heart, which had leapt at the sight of him only to be overwhelmed by a flood of anger, anger with him for being there, angry with herself for falling in love with him, and anger with an imperfect world where the relationships between men and women were so fraught, and marriage nothing but a quagmire of danger.

CHAPTER FIFTEEN

Arthur Stanhope made every attempt to appear perfectly normal as he sat in a comfortable armchair in front of Hugh Drummond's fire. He was angry with himself for being thrown so off balance by his meeting with Phoebe. It was infuriating that she was so close at hand, and so ungettatable. He had come to Derbyshire for the express purpose of seeking her out. Of course, he was concerned with Kitty's well-being, but he was a great deal more concerned with trying to make sense of what had passed between him and Phoebe. She had given a promise to her father not to see him, but although Sir Giles had demanded a similar assurance from him, he had not agreed, he was not to be bound by Sir Giles's authority.

Of course, a sudden and unexpected meeting with both of them on horseback in the pouring rain made an impossible situation for any kind of conversation. And it was clear she was avoiding him. Was that to fall in with her father's orders, or was it her decision? Did she truly want to have nothing more to do with him? Could she have believed the accusations that Sir Giles had levelled in his face — accusations that had made him white with anger, and had sent him away from Aubrey Square with unspoken words of rebuttal on his lips, words which his pride would not allow him to say? He looked moodily into the flames, only listening with half an ear to what Hugh was saying.

His friend soon took him to task, accusing him of not hearing a word of what he had just been saying. "You were commenting upon the likely severity of the weather," Stanhope said.

"Indeed I was, but I also went on to say that although I had hoped you would dine with me and we could spend the evening together, I think that if you are to have any hope of getting back to Martindale House tonight, you had better leave almost at once."

Stanhope protested at this, saying that he was hardly likely to be bothered by a wet evening. "Good God, Hugh, compared to the conditions that we went through in the

Peninsula, let alone at Waterloo, this is nothing."

"We were soldiers then. In time of peace, when social obligations, not military ones, hold sway, one's behaviour has to moderate accordingly. Your sister will worry if you were not to return this evening, although you are perfectly welcome to spend a night here if you wish."

Stanhope got up and went over to the door. As he opened it, a gust of wind and rain blew in, making the fire hiss and emit a burst of smoke. "It does seem to be getting worse," he said. "And my mare doesn't like this weather at all; I think I will have an uneasy ride of it. I shall leave you to your papers, and set off right away. Lend me a cloak, there's a good fellow."

They went into the small kitchen adjacent to the room in which they had been sitting, and from there through a heavy wooden door that led into the small stable. There were two stalls, in one of which was the cob that Mr. Darcy had provided for Hugh's use while he was at Pemberley, and in the other Stanhope's mare, pulling wisps of hay from a net and looking very peaceful. She turned her head as Stanhope came in, and looked at him with knowing eyes. Stanhope slapped her rump. "I'm afraid you've still some work to do," he said, and she flicked her ears back and forth in response.

He saddled and bridled her swiftly and efficiently, while Hugh held a lantern to illuminate the dim stable. Then he led the mare out into the small cobbled yard. She tossed her head, showed the whites of her eyes, and stepped sideways on nervous hooves. Stanhope mounted, raised his whip in salutation to Hugh, and guided the mare out of the yard and on to the track beyond.

Although barely dusk, it was already gloomy outside. It was the night of the full moon, but heavy, scudding clouds obscured most of the moon's light, and Stanhope knew he would have a dark ride of it back to Martindale House. He would normally have ridden cross-country, but instead he struck out on to the main road. It would be a longer ride, but a safer and easier one, given the increasing power of the wind and the rain sweeping down from the hillside.

The wild ferocity of the weather matched his mood. He kept up a steady pace, too experienced a rider to let his attention wander from the road, although all the while a thread of other thoughts were occupying another part of his mind. With this, and his eyes on the road ahead, he rode on for several yards past the still figure lying on the side of the road, before his conscious mind registered what he had seen.

He turned back at once, and flung himself from his horse's back. He threw the reins over the mare's head, and tugged at her bridle to pull her forward with him. She whickered, and he heard an answering whinny come back from the darkness. It was clear what had happened. A rider had been thrown from his horse, which, perhaps lamed, had stayed nearby instead of bolting back to its stable.

Stanhope heard a groan. Which meant that whoever it was certainly wasn't dead. Indeed, even as Stanhope bent over him, the man sat up, clutching a hand to his forehead. His face was smeared with mud; mud mingled with blood, as Stanhope saw quite clearly when the moon for a moment sailed out from behind a cloud, lighting up the whole scene. At the same moment he saw the shadowy outline of a horse, and abandoning the figure to his groans led his mare forward and quickly seized the trailing reins of the other horse.

Stanhope recognised the horse before its rider. The man sitting beside the ditch was Henry Martindale, his brother-in-law. Even as he helped him to his feet, it occurred to Stanhope to wonder exactly why Sir Henry

was a mile or so from the gates of Pemberley, on the road which led in completely the
opposite direction to the one he was supposed to have taken today.

Henry was cursing now, and trying to
wipe the blood and mud from his face with
the back of his sleeve. He uttered a word of
thanks to Stanhope, and reached out a hand
to take his horse's bridle.

"Can you ride?" asked Stanhope.

"I have to," said Henry. "I can hardly
spend a night out here in the ditch."

"No, but if you are badly hurt, or feeling
faint, you are likely to fall off your horse
again. I can leave you here while I go for
help."

Sir Henry felt his ribs and his arm. He
winced. "I landed on that side. But I shall
ride back. If you could just give me a leg
up."

Stanhope helped Sir Henry into the
saddle, and then mounted his own horse
with some difficulty since, disturbed still
further by the strange activities, she was
circling and snatching at her bit. But once
Stanhope was on her back, she calmed
down, and seemed quietened by the presence of the other horse. Sir Henry was
riding an old hunter, a placid enough
animal, luckily for him, for otherwise he

would have had a long walk back to Martindale.

It took them nearly an hour to get back to Martindale House, and as the horses clattered into the stable, a figure came flying through the rain and the wind calling out to them. Kitty flung her arms around her husband, pushing his hair back and exclaiming as she saw the blood on his face.

He pushed her away. "Take care, my dear, I am a very dirty creature. There is no need for you to fly into fancies, I simply had a fall. But Titan here is as solid as a rock and didn't run off, I was in no danger. As it was, Arthur came past, caught the horse, pushed me back into the saddle, and so we rode home. Now I need to wash my face and hands, change my clothes, and I'm sure you will be able to provide us with a good dinner. It is vile weather, and I don't wish to be out in it a moment longer than I have to."

He paused to have a few words with his groom, to make sure that everything necessary had been done in the stables against the forthcoming storm.

"I do not believe we shall have the worst of it here," said Stanhope as they went indoors. "Either the wind is slackening, or the path of the storm lies some way to the

196

west of here. I fancy they will be in for a
rough night of it at Pemberley, though."

CHAPTER SIXTEEN

The groom had been sent indoors by Mr. Jessop to make sure that Miss Phoebe was all right, and, since no one had seen her, a general search was started. Miniver found her sitting on the floor with her back against the conservatory door, grasping her legs with her hands, her head sunk on to her knees. At first, Miniver thought she had suffered a fall, and was in pain. But Phoebe got to her feet, shaking off her maid's attempts to help her up. "I am perfectly all right. Just damp."

A glance at Phoebe's face told Miniver that this was not the time for fuss or comfort or calming words. So instead she became brisk. She drove Phoebe upstairs, told her in sharp tones to remove her habit, and issued instructions for the footmen to bring up hot water so that Phoebe could take a bath in front of the fire in her room.

Louisa, who had been worried about

Phoebe being out in the rising storm, heard she had returned and at once came to her room. She knocked and entered, took a quick look at Phoebe, and then sat quietly down on the sofa to talk about the news that she had had that day from her mother. Phoebe sat in the hot water, sheltered by a screen from any possible draughts, and began to feel the tension and distress drain out of her.

The windowpanes rattled, and Miniver went over to check that the heavy red curtains were properly drawn. With the soft light of the oil lamps and candles, and the glow from the fire, the room was a warm haven of peace and tranquillity. Miniver dried Phoebe in a towel warmed in front of the fire, put her into a dressing gown, and began to lay out an evening dress, for once holding her tongue, and working in silence.

When Phoebe was dressed, and Miniver had brushed and arranged her hair, Louisa invited her to come to her room while she changed. "I do not think that Miss Verney will be joining us this evening," she said. "She has the headache, and has apparently been lying down in her room all afternoon. The nursery maids have been looking after the children, and I had them in the drawing-room for an hour. They are very lively, and

I think you are right in your judgement; I am not at all sure that Miss Verney is the right kind of person to be looking after them."

Phoebe would not allow her thoughts to wander, not for a second. The only way she could cope with her tumultuous emotions was to shut a door on the past and exist entirely in the present moment. She picked up on a word that Louisa had used. "Apparently?"

"I saw a woman in a cloak at the side of the house earlier this afternoon. At first I thought it was you, but she was not dressed for riding. She headed off in the direction of the lake. I am fairly certain it was not one of the servants, and therefore by process of elimination, it must have been Miss Verney."

"Miss Verney may be one of those unfortunates who is much influenced by the weather. With a storm coming, and a bad headache, she may have felt that a walk in the fresh air would do her more good than lying down on her bed."

Louisa, usually inclined to give anyone the benefit of the doubt, was still sceptical. "I think in that case she would have been walking neither so quickly nor so furtively. It is my belief that she had left the house to go to meet someone."

"An assignation," said Phoebe. "In which case she must be carrying on some kind of intrigue with a servant or perhaps a local farmer. It is not very becoming or appropriate behaviour for a governess, I feel. However, if for whatever reason we are to be spared her presence at dinner tonight, I for one will be grateful. I find her a difficult companion."

Phoebe was ready now, and she picked up a spangled shawl and draped it over her elbows. As she did so, there was a knock at the door. A footman was there, asking if he might come in and make sure that her windows were securely fastened. "It seems that this side of the house will bear the brunt of the wind," he explained. "Mr. Lydgate wants all the windows checked."

"Is the storm expected to be so very severe?" asked Phoebe.

Thomas fixed the clasp of the window more firmly into place, and stood back. "As bad as any there's been these last twenty years, they're saying. All the cows have been brought in, and the horses, too, those that were out to grass on the other side of the river. I reckon we're in for a wicked old night."

At first, the footman's gloomy predictions

seemed extreme. Certainly, the wind rattled the windows and sent smoke from the fire in little puffs across the dining-room, but it was no worse than many storms that both she and Louisa had experienced when at Pemberley.

"Weather always seems more violent in the country," Louisa said.

"That is because in town, with so many more buildings, one is protected from the worst of the wind." Phoebe looked down at her plate and wrinkled her nose. "I do hope this is the last of the rhubarb. Mrs. Makepeace persuaded me to order rhubarb tart, for there has been such a glut of the fruit this year. For myself, I find it too sour a fruit, even in a tart."

After dinner, they withdrew to the small upstairs sitting room, as with the wind in the direction it was blowing, the fire in the big drawing-room was smoking too much to make it pleasant to sit in there.

Pemberley was a well-built house, but this evening as they made their way up to their bedchambers, draughts seem to come at them from every side. The candles they were holding flickered, and Louisa's went out when a sudden gust blew in from a nearby window embrasure.

At last, after so many hours, Phoebe was

alone in her bedchamber. She sent Miniver away very quickly, sure that her maid, instead of retiring to her own small room in the servants' wing, would be in the servants' hall with all the rest of the staff, who were, Miniver had told her, in a rare old state on account of the storm.

Phoebe paid no attention to the keening of the wind, the rattling of the windows, or the sound of rain as it began to lash against the windowpanes. The fire in her room burned brightly, and it had not yet begun to smoke, for which Phoebe was grateful. She slid between the linen sheets, carefully warmed by Miniver, but she still found herself shivering. She lay far from sleep, watching the shadows from the fire chase one another over the ceiling and walls of her room.

Why had Mr. Stanhope come to Pemberley? He knew she was there, must have known that she didn't want to see him, when she had refused to come down during his visit, and yet within no more than a few hours he had come back to Pemberley. No doubt calling upon his friend, Hugh Drummond, but did he believe there was no chance of his meeting Phoebe? Was it a matter of such indifference to him? Did he not feel any awkwardness at the situation? Or had he come to find her? The questions ran round and round in her troubled head, and an hour later she felt that she, like Miss Verney, would succumb to a severe headache.

Finally, she drifted into an uneasy, unhappy sleep, only to be woken some few hours later by a tremendous crash of thunder over her head. She leapt out of bed and ran to the window, dragging back the curtains and tugging at the shutters to reveal an extraordinary scene. The sky was pierced by jagged forks of lightning, and every few seconds the whole landscape was brilliantly illuminated by sheet lightning, which made extraordinary silhouettes of the dramatic clouds. She could see trees swaying under the force of the wind and, even as she watched, she heard a wrenching sound, and gazed, appalled, as one of the great elms shook and then toppled, branches hurtling into the ground as it fell across the drive with a thud that shook in her ears.

The door to her chamber flew open, and Louisa was there, in her nightgown, with her hair in curling papers, holding an oil lamp and calling out, "Where are you, Phoebe? Are you all right?"

Phoebe came out from behind the curtain. "Yes, of course I'm all right. It is dreadful out there, a scene from hell. This terrible wind is bringing trees down all over the park."

As she spoke there was another great crash followed by a rumbling sound and voices calling out. Louisa started. "Whatever was that?"

"I think it was one of the chimney pots coming down." Phoebe came back into the room. "There's no point staying in here, Louisa. I would rather be up, I cannot sleep in the middle of all this. I shall dress, and see if there is anything I can do."

Louisa's concern was for the plants. "I hope the walls of the kitchen garden may afford some shelter to what is planted in there," she said. "But as to everything planted in pots, they will be blown to pieces."

She ran back to her room to put on outdoor clothes. Then, meeting Phoebe on the landing, they went downstairs together, finding Miniver coming up the other way. "I was just coming to make sure you were not disturbed, Miss Phoebe. What, are you dressed? You had better get back to your room, I am sure you will be safer there."

"I am sure I will be safe anywhere within the house," said Phoebe. "What's that screaming I can hear?"

"It's Polly, one of the kitchen maids. She's

having a fit of the hysterics, but Mrs. Make-peace is with her and will deal with her. The wind blew the door of the servants' hall open, and leaves and branches and a great deal of rain came in, and everything inside the room was blown to and fro before they could get the door shut again. A saucepan came down and clipped the side of the silly girl's head, not hurting her, but it gave her such a fright that she set up the screeching you can hear."

As Miniver finished speaking, there came the sound of shattering glass. "Oh, Lord save us," cried Miniver, "if that's a window blown in, I can't think of the damage that will be done. Besides, with as many windows as there are at Pemberley, however will we find out which one has shattered?"

Louisa was making to the front door. "That wasn't a window in the house. That was one of the glasshouses going down."

"You can't go out at the front," Phoebe shouted at her. "That's where the wind is driving."

"Miss Louisa must not go out at all," said Miniver, but even as she spoke, Louisa had darted towards the rear of the house, and was gone.

As soon as Louisa was out of the door the

wind struck, quite taking her breath away. She steadied herself, and paused for a moment for her eyes to get accustomed to the contrasting light and darkness, and the cataclysm of the thunder breaking overhead. A pot crashed to the ground from the steps, and another rolled around at her feet. She picked it up; whatever plant had been in it had been blown away, and she found herself clutching a pot that contained nothing but some damp soil. She could hear more glass breaking, and fighting against the rain and wind, so strong it made her stagger, she headed in the direction of the sound.

While Phoebe and Louisa were still asleep, Mr. Grayling, Hugh Drummond, and the indoor and outdoor gardeners had been doing their best to protect the plants, the fruit trees, and the garden buildings, the potting sheds, the glasshouses, and the big pinery.

Most of their efforts had been in vain, and Louisa saw shadowy figures going to and fro, carrying pots and plants and armfuls of greenery. Some were being carried into the stable yard, others were being taken into the house itself. Mr. Drummond saw her and shouted to her to go back in.

"No, indeed, I will not. What are you doing?"

"We are trying to rescue the pineapple

plants," he shouted into the wind. "If we cannot get them under shelter, into a place that is reasonably warm, none of them will survive the night. The big glasshouse is being blown to pieces, and they are exposed to the elements."

So it was that Louisa found herself at five in the morning walking into the hall of the house holding the leaves of yet another of the precious pineapple plants. It wasn't heavy, but very unwieldy, and to carry any plant in that wind and rain was no easy matter. She put it down with a little sigh of triumph, and pushed the hair back from her forehead with a soil-stained hand. Mr. Drummond came over, looking at her with keen attention. "You have done enough, Miss Bingley, you have done more than could possibly be expected of anyone. All the pineapples are now indoors, and I am very grateful for your help, although I feel no plant in the world is worth a young lady putting herself into danger."

She smiled at him and shook her head. "It is all right for a Mr. Drummond to put himself at risk, but not a Miss Bingley?" She was astonished at herself, it was the kind of remark that Phoebe would have made, but that was quite alien to her. At that moment Phoebe appeared on the scene. She had been directing the activities inside the house, issuing orders with an easy command that reminded Mrs. Makepeace forcibly of her uncle Mr. Darcy.

"What a ghastly night!" Phoebe said as she sank on to a stone bench, perched between two large leafy plants that had been balanced on it. "Mr. Drummond, you are a hero. Mr. Grayling is singing your praises, which is a rare compliment, you know. He says that for a city gent you have managed uncommonly well."

Drummond laughed, and coloured up. "Anyone brought up in Norfolk as I have been, Miss Hawkins, is well used to coping with gardens threatened by wild weather."

"And were you not in the army?" Louisa asked. "From what I have heard, the conditions that men fought in during the recent wars would make what has happened here tonight no more than a slight disturbance in the weather."

"I can truthfully say that we rarely saw storms as severe as this during my time in the army. However, here at least I have a roof over my head, and sometimes when I was in Spain my tent blew away and I and my fellow soldiers were forced to spend the night huddled in whatever shelter we could find for ourselves and for our horses."

The last of his words went unheard, as a crash, even louder than those that had preceded it, echoed around the hall. "As to a roof," said Phoebe calmly, "I hope you are right on that matter. But it sounds to me as though Pemberley itself may have lost part of its roof tonight."

Phoebe retired to bed for the second time in a long night as dawn broke, a dawn that was nearly as dark as dusk had been the night before. This time she did not lie sleepless, and no uneasy thoughts troubled her mind as she slipped instantly into a deep and dreamless sleep, waking many hours later when Miniver tiptoed into her room carrying a welcome dish of hot chocolate. She had made it so thick that Phoebe could hardly drink it, and had to resort to a spoon. Miniver drew back the curtains, commenting as she did so that the storm was still raging, although not as strongly as it had been at its height.

Phoebe got out of bed and went to the window to look out on a scene of devastation. The river was rising, and had already overspent its banks. Further up the hillside, the woods looked as though some giant had trodden through, crushing trees and depositing sad relics of branches and even trunks of the smaller trees across the landscape. She was dismayed to see that no fewer than nine of the great elms had been brought down by the storm, although by great good fortune those near the house, which, had they fallen, would have landed on the roof, were still standing. It amazed her how shallow the roots were for such large trees. That was why they had come down, of course.

Louisa had been up for a while, and Phoebe found her downstairs, tending to some of the plants that had been brought indoors. "Such destruction," she exclaimed as she saw Phoebe. "They are all to be moved into the orangery, we did not have time to take them so far last night."

"Well," said Phoebe, surveying the cluttered hall, "I do not know how you will find room for all of these in the orangery."

"Mr. Drummond will find a way," said Louisa with confidence. "The gardeners are full of admiration for how much he was able to save last night. And Mr. Grayling did a most excellent job in protecting the kitchen garden, although he still lost a good many plants. The orchards were ravaged, so Mr. Darcy will not have so many apple pies this autumn as he is used to. However," she went on, "there is one good to come out of all of this. The wind has demolished the big glasshouse, which was going to have to come down in any case, and once the glass is cleared away, Mr. Drummond says that work can begin immediately on the construction of a new, much bigger glasshouse for Mr. Darcy. He has promised to show me the plans he has drawn for it, and indeed it sounds the most remarkable building."

Phoebe was amazed that Louisa, in all the turmoil and work of the night, had managed to have so much conversation with Mr. Drummond. She said as much, and Louisa, with a serious expression, said, "Mr. Drummond is a man with a very calm disposition. He did not allow himself at any time yesterday to become panicked, and it is because of that that so much was achieved, against all the odds."

Phoebe was not particularly interested in Mr. Drummond, although she had liked him well enough, on brief acquaintance with him. For the moment her main concern was to have something to eat and she said to Louisa, "I am amazingly hungry. What is that noise?"

"It is the children. Miss Verney is still indisposed, which I must say is tiresome of her, and so at the moment they're playing in the drawing-room under the eagle eye of Miniver and Sally, the parlour maid, while the nursery maids are attending to their duties upstairs."

After taking some refreshment, and seeing that the rain had died out, Phoebe and Louisa went outside to see what damage had been done to the house. A shocking sight met their eyes. So many trees and shrubs had been blown down, and one whole chimney stack had slid down the slope of the roof, tumbling bricks on to the path below. The house had lost a great number of tiles, and when they went round to the other side of the house, the sad destruction in the flower garden, the shrubbery, and the buildings surrounding the kitchen garden quite upset Phoebe. "It will never be the same again," she said. "This is where the old potting shed stood, where I used to hide from my nurses. I would creep in here with a book, and pretend I was quite on my own. Of course they were perfectly well aware where I was, but even so . . ." Her voice trailed off as she looked around at the pieces of timber from the potting shed which were strewn across the grass.

A weary-looking Mr. Drummond came round the corner. He walked over to them, and greeted them with a warm smile. "Miss Bingley, I cannot say how grateful I am to you for the help you gave me last night. It is incredible to me that a young woman who could have lain snugly in her bed all through the storm chose to come out in the worst of that vicious weather and care for the plants."

Louisa flushed at the compliment. "It is no more than I would have done had I been at home," she said in a quiet voice. "I take great pleasure in gardens and in plants, and it saddens my heart to see how much damage has been done by the wind and the rain."

Mr. Drummond looked towards the woods. "It is true, but at the same time you will see that in a very few years the gash left by the trees that have fallen and been torn out by the wind will have grown over, and indeed the health of the woods as a whole will be improved. It is nature's way of improvement, and carries lessons we can learn from."

"For myself," said Phoebe dryly, "I prefer the improvements done by mankind, as being of a gentler and less savage kind. But I suppose that, given time, everything may be restored just as it was before the storm."

Mr. Drummond shook his head. "That would be a mistake. As you know, Mr. Darcy already had plans to change and bring the garden more in line with modern theories of horticulture, and this will allow him more easily to fulfil some of his bolder plans."

"Bolder plans? What are these?"

"Let me show you." Mr. Drummond led them round to the side of the house. "The grassy slope which runs down to the bend in the river, for example, is very picturesque. But see how it has turned into a veritable mudslide. I have advised Mr. Darcy to stabilise this by terracing the slope, and at the same time, installing a system of drainage. It is much more practical. The way it is now, laid out according to the ideas of the last century, when landowners wanted the park to extend right up to their houses, is today considered old-fashioned and not very functional."

Phoebe shook her head. "The park is the great beauty of Pemberley. I would never wish to see it made into a series of more formal gardens. It has a beauty that can be admired both close at hand and from a distance. What need is there to change a single thing?"

It was Louisa who answered her, not Mr. Drummond. "Surely you appreciate that a house and its gardens and the land around it must change and develop with time. Nothing is constant, nothing can stay the same as it is year in and year out. Only consider the engravings in the picture library here, which show the house as it was in the seventeenth century. You would not wish to have those knot gardens and stiff formal parterres. They gave way to the landscaping you so admire, the landscapes of Humphry Repton and Capability Brown, and now, once again, fashion and taste dictate that such grounds and gardens must take on a new appearance."

"My word, Miss Bingley," said Mr. Drummond. "I have rarely heard a young woman talk so much sense."

Phoebe found this patronising, and replied somewhat tartly, "In that case, Mr. Drummond, I do not think you have spent enough time listening to what young women have to say."

Mr. Drummond took the rebuke in good part, laughing, and saying that he stood corrected.

Something other than the gardens were on Phoebe's mind. She could not help herself. "I know you had a visitor last evening, Mr. Drummond. I trust he left before the storm began to rage."

Mr. Drummond looked rather surprised at this remark, but he replied readily enough, "Arthur Stanhope, who is presently staying at Martindale, called upon me. I sent him back to Martindale pretty quickly, for otherwise he would have had to spend the night here, and I think his sister would have been concerned. I know that he got back safely to Martindale House, for Sir Henry sent a man over this morning to ask whether we needed assistance of any kind. It seems that the storm was not nearly so severe in that part of the county."

CHAPTER SEVENTEEN

Mrs. Makepeace produced long linen aprons for Louisa and Phoebe, who spent the next few hours in the orangery, carefully picking out shards of broken glass from such delicate plants as the African violets. It was peaceful in there, as the wind gradually died down, and for the first time in many hours they could hear what people were saying without anyone having to raise his or her voice. It was not, however, an occasion for intimate conversation, for the indoor gardeners were working there as well.

Phoebe had just added a sprinkling of soil to the top of a plant, and was walking with it towards the back of the house, intending to put it with the others in the hastily cleared out boot room, when she heard the sound of approaching hoof beats. Her heart stood still. Was it possibly Mr. Stanhope, come to enquire how they had weathered the storm?

One of the under-gardeners, bringing in some more fragile seedlings, stepped over to the window to look out on to the drive. "It's a postboy," he said. "It must be an express. He looks in a right state, I reckon he's come off his horse."

The postboy headed round the kitchen quarters, and Phoebe wondered whom the message was for. Most likely Mr. Drummond or Mr. Lydgate; if there were news from her family too urgent to be conveyed by the ordinary mail, she knew her father would send his own servant. He had little faith in postboys. But what was this? More hooves, and the familiar rattle and jingle of a carriage. This time Phoebe put down her pot and went to look. A carriage was indeed coming up the drive. A glance told her this was no fashionable equipage from Martindale, no dashing curricle driven by Mr. Stanhope. This was a workmanlike coach, and indeed it didn't stop at the front of the house, but continued round towards the stables.

At that moment Miniver came hurrying into the room. "I can tell you who is arriving in that coach," she said importantly. "It's none other than Mr. Rutland, Mr. Darcy's butler! I cannot imagine what he is doing here, since he was due to stay in London for the season."

"Perhaps you are mistaken," said Phoebe.

"No, for he was looking out of the window as he went past, and I know Mr. Rutland's countenance as well as I know my own, with that lantern jaw of his."

That was something of a puzzle, since the butler was only at Pemberley when the family were in residence. Could it be that Mr. and Mrs. Darcy were going to pay an unexpected visit to the house? Had they had news of the impending storm, and at once set off? Impossible, they were abroad, and even if they hadn't been, Mr. Darcy was not the man to travel halfway across the country on rumour of a storm.

She put down her pot, confessing to herself that she was curious to know what had brought Mr. Rutland here, whether the postboy had come with an express, and, if so, whether the express were connected to the arrival of the butler.

She went into the hall, and at that very moment another carriage, this one a modern and well-sprung travelling carriage, came up the drive and drew to a halt at the foot of the steps. Phoebe hardly had time to take this in before a frantic footman, tearing off his brown work apron, came running into the hall.

"Miss Phoebe," he blurted out. "Mr. Rutland is here and knows what's in that express he was just going to bring to you, which is that Lady Redburn is to pay a visit to Pemberley. And Mrs. Makepeace says this is her carriage arriving now, bowling up to the house as I speak, and another coach behind, laden with her trunks, and no doubt bringing that dratted French maid to make all our lives a misery."

Phoebe stood and stared at the footman, unable to believe what she heard. "Thomas, you cannot be serious. There must be some mistake."

There wasn't.

Two minutes later, Thomas was holding open the front door as up the steps came the small, straight-backed, elegant figure of Lady Redburn, Mr. Darcy's formidable aunt. His father's much younger sister, she had been born and bred at Pemberley, and since she had all the pride and spirit of the Darcys, with few of their kindlier and warmer ways, her irregular visits always caused consternation in the household.

There she stood, dark eyes snapping as she raked Phoebe from head to foot. "What is this? Why are you wearing that ridiculous garment?"

Phoebe had forgotten the apron. Now she

swiftly untied the ribbons and cast it into Thomas's hands. She went forward and dropped a deep curtsy. "Look at your hands," were her great-aunt's next words. "And why is the hall in such a state? Have all the servants decamped, except for that booby standing there behind you?"

Phoebe gathered her scattered wits. "We were not expecting you."

"Indeed, I can see that is the case. However, I sent an express two days ago from London, so why you should not be prepared for my arrival, I cannot imagine."

"I believe that the postboy has only this minute arrived, ma'am," Phoebe said.

"Nonsense, I do not pay so many shillings to have a letter delivered for it to take two days. And where is Mr. Rutland? Why is he not here, attending to his duties?"

"He, too, only arrived minutes ahead of you," Phoebe said. "Last night we had a most terrible storm; indeed you surely noticed the condition of the woodland and park as you drove along the approach to the house. I expect that several roads will have been blocked, with so many trees blown down. There must have been a great deal of damage done to properties in the county, which will have caused the delay to both the postboy and Mr. Rutland."

It was clear that Lady Redburn was not interested in yesterday's storm. To her what was past was past, and might never be used as an excuse for anything in the present. "Good heavens, look at the dirt on this floor. And these plants, are we living in a hovel? No, I do not want to hear about how and why these plants are brought indoors, I merely wish them to be got rid of."

Mr. Drummond, hearing voices in the hall, emerged from the orangery. He had not had time yet to go back to the South Lodge, therefore he was unshaven, and his shirt, jacket, breeches, and gaiters were all in a most dishevelled and grubby state. He looked with incomprehension at Lady Redburn, who looked back at him with an expression of such disdain that Phoebe had to put her hand to her mouth to quell a laugh.

Lady Redburn did not address Mr. Drummond directly. Instead, she questioned the air. "Who is this person? Why is he indoors? If he is one of the gardeners, which I gather from his costume he must be, then he has no business whatsoever to be in this part of the house."

Mr. Drummond looked thunderstruck at this attack, and Phoebe stepped forward quickly to introduce him to Lady Redburn.

"Great-aunt, this is Mr. Hugh Drummond. He is employed by my uncle to look after all his houses and estates and lands. He is at Pemberley to supervise the new works here, and has been up all night fighting to save plants and buildings from the storm. Mr. Drummond, allow me to present you to Lady Redburn."

Mr. Drummond bowed, but did not receive so much as an inclination of her ladyship's head in return. Phoebe tried again. "Mr. Drummond's family come from East Anglia. His father is vicar of a large parish there."

That brought a glimmer of humanity and interest to Lady Redburn's eyes. "I find it hard to believe that you could be one of the Norfolk Drummonds," she said sharply.

Mr. Drummond, despite his tiredness, saw the humour of the situation, and had to make an effort not to smile. "My name is Drummond, ma'am, and my family does come from Norfolk."

"The family I refer to is an old one, the Drummonds of Moresby Hall."

"Lionel Drummond of Moresby Hall is my uncle," said Mr. Drummond briefly. "If you'll excuse me, I will see about having the rest of these plants removed from here." He didn't wait to hear a reply from her ladyship, but moved swiftly out of the hall, merely pausing to give Louisa a quick wink as he went past.

Louisa's arrival diverted Lady Redburn's attention from the departing Mr. Drummond. Her eyes swept over Louisa, taking in her hastily pinned-back hair, her apron, and the pot she was holding between her hands.

"You will remember Miss Bingley," Phoebe said.

Later, Louisa said to Phoebe that she was sure that Lady Redburn did not recognise her at all. "It was only the name that allowed her to place me."

"You hardly looked the same as when she last saw you in London. Then, if I recall correctly, you were wearing a rather fine pale blue silk evening gown. And you didn't have muddy marks on your face."

Louisa looked horrified, and went over to the mirror on her dressing table to look at her face. "Ring for Betsy this minute! I have to wash and change. And so do you, Phoebe, you look a perfect fright."

Lady Redburn had sailed up the stairs after barely acknowledging Louisa, and without a further word to Phoebe. Phoebe covered her eyes with her hand in a moment of frustration and weariness. Lady

Redburn was already in a bad mood, and when she discovered that the apartments which she customarily occupied when she was at Pemberley would be in no state to receive her, Phoebe knew that everyone in the house would be at the receiving end of her temper.

Her ladyship paid no attention as Phoebe called her name, her mind working desperately to think of a reason to detain her; it was in vain, as Lady Redburn carried on up the stairs. Another familiar figure came into the hall and walked across to the stairs with vigorous little steps, her heels going click-clack on the marble floor. Foujay, Lady Redburn's maid, a woman heartily disliked by all the Pemberley servants. As short as her mistress, she was rather plumper, but her round shape did not go with a sweeter nature, as Phoebe well knew.

There was nothing she could do, except wait for the inevitable explosion when her great-aunt entered her apartment to find the furniture shrouded, the windows shuttered, and the bed not made up.

The minute that Mrs. Makepeace realised that the delay to the postboy and Mr. Rutland meant that Lady Redburn would arrive at any minute, she had flown into action. Rounding up Sally and a young under–parlour maid, she set off towards the back staircase at a pace remarkable for one of her years and dignity.

The servants' stairs were a far cry from those in the main part of the house. No marble floors here, no heating in winter, no great canvases of men on horses or gambolling nymphs hung on the walls above the staircase. The steps were of well-worn oak, the banister a mere rail, and the walls were painted a depressing sludge colour. Small windows at the turn gave some light, but new servants, until they got used to the uneven tread, were always tumbling down the stairs, unable to see the next step. The landing that led off the stairs was carpeted in a serviceable drugget, so that the servants wouldn't make too much noise. Mrs. Makepeace and her entourage hurried along the corridor, only pausing in front of a row of cupboards at the end for her to instruct the youngest girl to take out the linen for her ladyship, and to look sharp about it. "And don't forget we'll need some for that Foujay. She won't sleep in the servants' wing, oh, no, she has to have a bed made up in the dressing room."

They were through the doors and on to the other end of the landing with several

closed doors. These were the main bedrooms, and it was in one of these that Lady
Redburn would expect to stay.

"I can hear her in the hall; lawks, Mrs.
M., she's coming up the stairs already."

The housekeeper and Sally stood and
looked at each other. "We'll never hear the
end of this," said Mrs. Makepeace grimly.

"T'aint our fault, what with everything at
sixes and sevens on account of the storm,
and us only knowing she was on her way
here a few minutes before she tips up at the
front door."

"Much she'll care about that. We'd best
wait till she gets to the top, and then I'll ask
her to wait in the little sitting room while
we make up the room."

"Hark, what's that?" said Sally as a wail
rent the air, followed by a hubbub, running
feet, a child's sobs, voices raised.

"I do believe she's run into the children;
well, thanks be, she never can leave well
alone, she'll take the time to scold the
governess or the nursery maid, and that will
give us our chance."

"Well," said Sally, dashing in through the
door which Mrs. Makepeace held open, "I
hope it's that toffee-nosed Miss Verney, and
not Sukey who's getting it in the neck. I
can't abide that governess, giving herself

airs, and all the time —"

"That will do. Pull back the curtains, and open the shutters so that we can have a light here. Molly," she added as the under–parlour maid came in, staggering under a load of sheets and covers, "put those down on the table, and get that fire lit. Thank goodness I had it laid just last week for when I came to air this room."

Mrs. Makepeace was too good a housekeeper and ran too tight a ship for there to be as much to be done to the room as might have been the case in a less well-run household. The room was dusted, and she knew the floors had been swept. Now she pulled off the dust covers that shrouded the bed, chairs, and sofa, and, bundling them up, told Sally to take them into the room across the way. "Just for now; we can put them away while her ladyship's having dinner."

Sally was inclined to argue. "What if she goes poking her nose in there?"

"Don't be so gormless. When you've done as I say, lock the door and pocket the key. Use your wits, girl."

Sally did as she was told. She had no idea what her ladyship would have to eat for dinner, with the stove gone out, and M. Joules beside himself with the wet soot and twigs and the Lord knew what else all over his kitchen. Miss Phoebe and Miss Bingley weren't a problem, they'd eat a cold meal and think it a joke, but her ladyship would expect a proper dinner. Doubtless M. Joules would be tearing his hair out at this very minute, not that he had so much to tear, him being decidedly bald.

Sally worked while all this went through her head, placing the covers in the room across the landing and locking the door behind her as Mrs. Makepeace had said. Back in the bedroom, a feather duster was thrust into her hand, with instructions to give everything a final quick dust.

"Molly," Mrs. Makepeace said as the little maid sat back on her heels and surveyed the fire, now beginning to crackle nicely, with some satisfaction, "this is no time to sit there gawping. Cut along outside, and see if one of the gardeners can't find some flowers for in here, her ladyship is very fussy about having flowers in her room."

Molly skipped off. Mrs. Makepeace and Sally finished making the bed. Sally smoothed down the heavy brocade cover while Mrs. Makepeace cast a final eye over the room. Then they almost ran through the door and along the landing, reaching the other side of the door just as Lady Redburn turned the corner at the other end.

CHAPTER EIGHTEEN

Phoebe and Louisa retreated to Phoebe's bedchamber, where Miniver was waiting, hands on hips, to take Phoebe out of her disgraceful clothes and put her into something clean and more suitable before she met her aunt again.

Phoebe was laughing too much to protest when Miniver laid out a smart afternoon gown that Phoebe thought had been left in London. She took no notice of it, instead sinking into a chair and waving Louisa, who was almost as helpless with laughter as she was, into the chair opposite.

"Bless those children," said Phoebe. "How well they did! It was the most perfect timing for them to come along just then, and rushing at such speed."

"It is very fortunate that they didn't send Lady Redburn tumbling down the stairs," observed Louisa.

"Little fiends, painting their faces like

that. I hope it was Miss Verney's paintbox that they had out, and not mine or yours."

It was all Miss Verney's fault. She had left the children unattended while she had gone, Sukey said, to answer a letter. Left to their own devices, they had gone exploring. It was only when Sukey, the nursery maid, came back upstairs to the nurseries after taking some washing downstairs that she realised the children were nowhere to be seen. And she was annoyed when Miss Verney turned on her, accusing her of neglecting the children, and not attending to her charges.

But it was Miss Verney who had drawn the full wrath of Lady Redburn upon herself. When the children ran shrieking along the landing, with her and Sukey in hot pursuit, she had certainly not noticed the new arrival, and had spoken to the children in the most unladylike way in front of Lady Redburn. Her ladyship delivered a short and pithy lecture on the manners and behaviour to be expected of a well-bred governess, and then demanded to know exactly who Miss Verney was, what her qualifications were, who had appointed her, and how it was that she seemed to have no idea of how to carry on in a gentleman's house.

"I believe she would have dismissed her on the spot, were she able," said Phoebe. "But of course she can't, for she is in Cousin Georgina's employ, and so nothing to do with the Pemberley staff."

"I should not be at all surprised if a letter were not to be on its way before tomorrow from Lady Redburn to Lady Mordaunt, expressing her displeasure at the governess, and saying that in her opinion she is not fit to be in charge of children. And she is right, Miss Verney does not seem to be very attentive to the children and their needs. The children are too rumbustious for a start, and she is not playful enough with them. It will not do, to be always rebuking them and expecting them to sit still. When we were children at Pemberley, the delight of being here was being able to run about and enjoy the freedom of a country house."

Phoebe felt rather guilty. "I shall talk to Jessop at the stables about letting them go out on the pony. Even though they are so very little, they would enjoy a ride. And I noticed that the swing near the flower garden does not seem to be there any more, perhaps one of the men could put up a new one for the children."

"It is the least they deserve, for taking Lady Redburn's mind off the state of the house, and her fury at all the plants being brought inside. I truly think she would rather that the plants died, than the rooms in Pemberley were sullied with outdoor pots and trays of seedlings."

"Nonetheless, what a fuss she made when she found there were no flowers in her room," said Phoebe. "Poor little Molly, panting up the stairs with an armful of flowers, arriving just too late, and getting the full force of Foujay's tongue. It is too bad of her to speak to her like that, she is not used to their ways, and will now probably give in her notice."

"I dare say Mrs. Makepeace will soothe her ruffled feelings. They must be in despair in the kitchen, for while we would willingly put up with all kinds of inconveniences given the aftermath of the storm, and the extra work it brought upon the whole household, I do not for a moment suppose that your great-aunt will be happy unless everything is just so."

Betsy, coming in to take Louisa away to her room to change, heard this last remark. "And you are quite right in that, miss. Everything is topsy-turvy down in the kitchens, and I would have said there was no chance of preparing even half the dishes for this evening that her ladyship will

expect. But that Mr. Drummond has set all
to rights. He is a most capable man, he
spoke to M. Joules in French, which surprised him and calmed him down so much
that they were able to put their heads
together and talk about what was to be done
to get the big stove working again. And
that's the second shirt that Mr. Drummond
will have ruined today, because by the time
he had finished with his head up the chimney, and clanking around at the back of that
great iron range, he looked like a chimney
sweep."

"Mrs. Makepeace should send the laundry
maid over to collect all his dirty garments,"
said Miniver. "He's got no manservant to
look after him, and a gentleman like that
needs someone to take care of him."

"It's all to be seen to, now that Mr. Rutland is here," said Betsy knowingly. "You
can see he approves of Mr. Drummond.
And even Mr. Grayling has left off his
grumbling, at least for the time being. He
says they wouldn't have saved half the stuff
they did last night without Mr. Drummond's directions and help. Not to mention
that he saved one of the lads from being
crushed by that chimney that came down."

"Did he do so indeed?" cried Louisa. "I
honour him for it, but I would have expected

nothing else."

The door closed behind Louisa and her maid. Miniver and Phoebe looked at one another in silence. Then Miniver, kneeling down to pull the hem of Phoebe's dress into position, said, "That won't do."

"I do not suppose there is anything in it, other than a kind remark," said Phoebe, although she was sure of no such thing. There had been a glow in Louisa's eyes, and a warmth in her voice as she praised Mr. Drummond, that she had never heard or seen before.

Dinner was served late, but it was a remarkable meal in the circumstances. Lady Redburn had, grudgingly, agreed to dine in the smaller dining room, although she said it had been the habit always, when senior members of the household were present, to use the big dining room.

The staff had their pride to consider, and Lady Redburn was not going to be given a chance to complain about the food if they could help it. A clear soup, stuffed fried trout, roast duckling, a salad, and an excellent Charlotte Russe for pudding satisfied even Lady Redburn, who had an uncommonly good appetite for a person of her age. Phoebe and Louisa watched in awe as her ladyship ate her way through the courses, and Louisa whispered to Phoebe, at a moment when Lady Redburn's attention was distracted, that she wondered how she could eat so well and yet retain her slender figure.

"Put it down to her temper. I believe Lady Redburn needs a great deal of sustenance to keep her temper honed and lively."

They were not joined by Miss Verney. Lady Redburn was not of the opinion that any governess should join members of the Darcy family at table. So it was a tray in the nursery for Miss Verney, and Thomas whispered to Phoebe that she was not best pleased by it. "And there wasn't enough trout to go round either, miss," he said with a grin. "So she had to make do with some whitebait." He noted Lady Redburn's eye upon him, and immediately wiped the grin from his face and stood to impassive attention.

After dinner, Lady Redburn led them into the great drawing-room and commanded Louisa to play to them. Louisa, knowing that she had not yet mastered the knack of the pianoforte with its modern double action, sat down with some trepidation. However, Lady Redburn was happy to criticise, and, as Louisa said to Phoebe later when they went upstairs to bed, it would have been a disappointment had she been able to play sufficiently well not to allow Lady Redburn to point out all the inadequacies of her performance.

Phoebe resolutely refused to play, saying with swift ingenuity that she had hurt her finger trying to fasten a catch on the window on the previous night, an excuse that caused Louisa to look at her in a most reproachful way. Lady Redburn merely remarked that it was not Phoebe's place to be fiddling with windows, what were servants for? "Besides, unless you have improved considerably since I last heard you play, which I doubt, your performance upon the instrument gives little pleasure." She then told her great-niece to fetch some cards, and settled down to play a game of solitaire.

Phoebe was much relieved, for she knew that Lady Redburn was a very good whist player, and had been afraid that she would want to have a game. She didn't dare pick up her book, since Lady Redburn did not approve of the novels of Sir Walter Scott, at least not for young ladies, although Phoebe knew perfectly well that Lady Redburn herself liked novels of all kinds and read a great many of them.

The days that followed Lady Redburn's arrival were ones of almost unequalled boredom for Phoebe. Almost, she envied the servants, who were busier than they had been for months, what with the stringent demands of her ladyship, and the work clearing up after the storm. Although it was no longer windy, it was still raining, the roads and lanes were muddy, and in many cases still blocked, and conditions were too bad for Phoebe to take exercise by walking or riding or even going out in the carriage. Neighbours who might have called, knowing that Lady Redburn was at Pemberley, could not visit for the same reason.

Louisa did not seem to be half so bored. Hers was the kind of temperament that took pleasure in small activities, and she was well able to occupy her hours with painting and drawing, practising the piano, doing her embroidery, writing letters, and, with the aid of stout galoshes, which Phoebe refused to wear, venturing out into the damp gardens.

Phoebe did her best to continue with the preparations for the ball, but she was very anxious to keep these hidden from Lady Redburn. She knew her great-aunt's inquisitive and domineering ways well enough to be sure that she would either wish to take over all the arrangements herself, or demand that she be kept informed about everything that Phoebe did, mostly so that she could point out where she was doing it wrong.

It was a mercy that, so far, Lady Redburn was unaware of Mr. Darcy's plan to hold a summer ball at Pemberley. Normally, a maid would have discovered that interesting piece of information from the other servants of the house within ten minutes of arriving, but Foujay kept herself to herself, and wouldn't demean herself by talking or gossiping with the other servants about anything to do with the Darcy family.

Fortunately Lady Redburn was not an early riser, and Phoebe found that she was able in the mornings to shut herself in the library, write the cards of invitation, draw up plans, and dash off notes to Mr. Tetbury about various expenses that she would be incurring, and asking him to undertake certain of the arrangements, such as enquiring about a large marquee to be erected in the garden. It was to be hoped that the weather would be much finer and dryer in June than it was now, but it had been an uncommonly late, cold, and wet spring, and when she questioned the more weather-wise among the gardeners, none of them held up much hope of a very fine or warm early summer.

It came as a welcome relief to the relentless routine of their days, therefore, when Betsy announced to Louisa that the wagons with the ironworks for the new glasshouse were due to arrive later that day. "They've been shipped by canal, so Mr. Drummond tells me," she said, "and then brought on to Pemberley by wagon."

Phoebe had resigned herself to the loss of the old glasshouse, although she was disappointed by Louisa's more robust and practical attitude to its loss. "Mr. Darcy's plans for the gardens and grounds are a marvel," she said enthusiastically. "The new glasshouse, the main one, will be a thing of real beauty. Mr. Drummond has shown me the drawings he has made, he is an excellent draughtsman, you know."

"I do not believe for a moment that it can be at all beautiful. Such types of building, glass or otherwise, are all very well for those newly rich, who wish to have extravagant novelties in the grounds of the houses they have bought, but what place have they in a house like Pemberley, which dates back to the time Queen Elizabeth was upon the throne? No, novel is not always best, and I cannot share your or Mr. Drummond's enthusiasm. It would have been best simply to reconstruct the old house as it was. It worked perfectly well."

"That is what you think, because you know so little about how things grow." Louisa had paid attention to Mr. Drummond's words. "Plants, such as the pineapple, are tender, and susceptible to chill weather and draughts and uneven temperatures. They will not thrive in other than ideal conditions. The old style of glasshouse, with windows being difficult to open, too much sun on bright days, and not enough light when it's cloudy, makes it very difficult for the gardeners to grow the fruit and bring on the early vegetables as they would like. You are lost in a dream of your childhood, Phoebe. I do not know why that should be. Nothing stays the same, we all change, and the landscape around us and the houses in which we live, and the things we use in daily life, all change too. Fifty years ago, there was no closed stove in the kitchen here. I asked M. Joules whether he would be prepared now to cook on the range that old Mr. Darcy's cook had to work with, and he said flatly he would refuse to work in such out-of-date conditions."

Phoebe was stung by Louisa's words. She didn't care to be told that she was clinging to a lost childhood, although with the honesty that was characteristic of her, she

242

had to admit that it was to some extent true. The future frightened her; she was not sure what it held, and because of what had happened in London, she looked forward to the life that lay ahead of her with no particular pleasure. In her present mood, she saw little prospect of fulfilment or happiness.

But then her natural good sense reasserted itself, and she was able to laugh at her melancholy mood, and allow to herself that when the rain stopped, and the days brightened, and she was busy once more not only with the ball, but with riding and walking and perhaps paying visits — she very much wanted to see her godmother again — then her outlook would improve, and she would be more cheerful.

That was what she most missed, the lifting high spirits and the sense of happiness and merriment that she felt she had always experienced when a girl at Pemberley. She had hoped that coming to Pemberley would restore that sense of well-being, but she reflected rather sadly that she now truly appreciated those lines of Horace, where he remarked that a change of climate did not bring about any change of mood.

CHAPTER NINETEEN

Martindale House had only caught the tail end of the storm. There had been some minor damage to roof tiles and chimneys, and the next day Sir Henry had ridden round his estates with his bailiff, making note of fallen trees, broken fences, repairs needed to outbuildings and to tenants' cottages. Sir Henry was a good landlord, taking care of both his land and his tenants. He invited Arthur Stanhope to go with him, but his brother-in-law declined. One day, Stanhope would inherit his father's land and estates, but these represented only a small part of the substantial Stanhope fortune. He knew that when he came into possession of his inheritance, he would employ an able man such as Hugh Drummond to manage his estates; indeed, perhaps Hugh Drummond himself, if he could be weaned away from Mr. Darcy's employment.

Kitty knew how he felt, and rebuked him

for it. "With a population so volatile, and things being so bad for so many people in the country, landowners must shoulder their responsibilities, and look after those who work for them."

"I know my limitations, Kitty. There are others much better qualified than I am to take care of such things. I have served my country in the army, I have played my part in ensuring that her old freedoms have survived. And as far as I can see, I shall spend the rest of my life doing my duty by my country. But my talents do not lie, as Sir Henry's do, in looking after land and property in the country. It is more realistic for me to pay another man to do that, and to do those things which I can do, which others may not do so well."

She shook her head. She was in her own small parlour, where she had just given the directions for the day to her housekeeper, and was now sorting through the letters that had arrived for her that morning. She held one up and stopped. "Here is a letter from Mother, complaining that you are spending so much time out of London. You do not even have the excuse of being called abroad."

Arthur Stanhope had expected nothing else. His mother would have conveniently forgotten that she had urged him to visit Kitty in Derbyshire. He had resigned himself to the fact that he could never please either of his parents. His mother had brought him up with a rigid sense of duty but little affection, and affection was not within his father's range of emotion — other than the casual affection that he might feel for a pretty opera girl, or his latest dashing mistress.

"There is not much news from London," said Kitty. "At least, not the kind of news that would interest you, merely tittle-tattle and gossip. The season has got off to a good start, Mama tells me. Phoebe Hawkins's sister" — she was looking down at her letter, and did not see her brother start at the name — "Miss Sarah Hawkins, is taking the town by storm, apparently, although Mama does not see why when she is not, in her opinion, much of a beauty."

Her brother had turned away, and gone across to the window. "I can't see why my mother takes any interest in the Hawkins family."

Kitty was surprised at the harshness of his tone. "It is only a passing remark, and you know how she resents it when any of the country gentry produce daughters who outshine the progeny of the Whigs. She

246

wishes you to go back to London. I suppose she hopes that you may take your part in the festivities, and doubtless meet and propose to some dashing girl from one of our great families. I wish you would, Arthur. It would do you good to marry and settle down, and my marriage to Sir Henry being such a disappointment —"

He whirled around. "Disappointment? Disappointment to whom?"

There was a long silence. Kitty was looking down at her feet. "A disappointment to our parents, that is all I mean. Henry is rich, which is good, and he is not a Tory, which is also good, despite being a landowner who prefers the country life, but it was not the great match that they would have liked for me. I married for love, which they see as a mistake. I didn't," she finished in a desolate voice, "but who knows, they may be right."

"To the devil with love," said Arthur Stanhope vehemently. "Passion is something that anyone can deal with. But once love's barbed arrows are dug deep in your flesh, there's no escaping."

Kitty laughed, but with no real merriment. "You are very poetic this morning, Arthur. Don't tell me that blind Cupid has been loosing his arrows in your direction, for I shan't believe it. No, you stick to your beautiful actresses, until one day you'll realise you need a heir, and will propose to the nearest available girl, who will proceed to make your life a misery."

Arthur Stanhope took his leave of his sister and Sir Henry that evening, for he was setting off for London early in the morning. He left saddened by Kitty's unhappiness and cynicism about marriage. He was on his way back to London not because of the summons from his mother, but because he had business there that needed attending to. And besides, what point was there in staying any longer at Martindale House? Kitty was miserable, and he wasn't sure why. There might be an obvious reason, but he felt there was more to it than that. It might be possible to help restore good relations between her and her husband, but he felt sure that the deep-seated source of the problem would be less easy to solve. His mother would be triumphant, if he told her half the truth. He wouldn't. He would simply say to her that a long, chilly winter, and sullen spring skies, had pulled Kitty's spirits down.

He travelled fast, wanting to do the journey to London in one day, since he much disliked staying at inns. He changed horses frequently, and keeping up a steady pace was in London by the evening. He was weary from the long drive when he arrived at his house in Melbury Street, and as he went into the house, he told his man, Lismore, to call for something to eat, and a bottle of wine to be ready for him as soon as he had taken a shower. This was a new-fangled contraption, much disapproved of by his valet, which he had recently had installed in a new bathroom next to his bed-chamber. An hour later, with these material comforts satisfied, he sat in his study, flicking through the papers that lay on his desk, making notes in a firm, swift hand, occasionally putting aside some letter or bill to be dealt with or discussed later.

He looked up to see Lismore standing at the door, perfectly quiet and perfectly composed. "What is it?" he said.

"A servant came round from her lady-ship's house," Lismore said with an impassive face. He had no need to say who her ladyship was, it always meant Lady Stanhope. "He brought a message."

"Out with it."

"Her ladyship's compliments, and she hopes that she will see you at the Gowersons' ball this evening."

"The devil she does," Stanhope muttered to himself, carrying on with a letter he was writing. He finished it, signed it, sprinkled some sand on to it and shook it off, then read it through.

"Lady Stanhope's man is waiting for a reply."

"Do you think there is any point in my explaining to her ladyship that I have been driving all day and that my head is full of such places as Leicester and Kettering and Luton, and I have yet to adjust to London life?"

Lismore gave a discreet cough. "I do not believe her ladyship will be much impressed."

No, thought Stanhope. Being a woman of astounding vitality and insensitivity, her ladyship never paid the least attention to anyone else's situation. He knew that if she had been travelling all day, it would be nothing for her to arrive home, change into a ball gown, and sally forth to dine, attend a soirée, and then to spend the rest of the night until the early hours at a ball. He supposed he had his mother to thank for his own superabundance of energy and stamina, but he had often wished, as did other members of her family, that she would occasionally succumb to any kind of weakness.

Reluctantly, he went out to his bedchamber, to find that his valet had already laid out the proper clothes for a ball. He cursed him for his presumption, but allowed himself to be dressed in the breeches, waistcoat, and perfectly fitting black coat. He tied his own stock, shaping the piece of linen into intricate folds with long, deft fingers, and allowed his man to add a final touch of polish to his gleaming pumps. A cloak and a cane, which concealed a slender, lethal sword, and he was ready to go, a perfect example of a well-bred Englishman in perfectly correct evening dress.

As his mother told him, when he finally ran across her some two hours later, "It amazes me how in outward appearance you are simply an English gentleman. Whereas, to anyone who knows you, your head is full of fidgets and maggots that have no place inside any Englishman's skull."

Arthur Stanhope knew better than to respond to this. He enquired courteously as to her well-being, and the health and welfare of his father, "whom I see is not attending the ball this evening."

"He may come later, he is dining with some friends at the club."

Arthur Stanhope waited for his mother to come to the point, which she swiftly did. "I hear that Miss Phoebe Hawkins is at present

251

in Derbyshire. She has been sent to Pemberley, which is what happens to all those Darcy girls when they are in some scrape or other. Have you met her there?"

Stanhope was relieved that he could with almost complete truth say that no, he had not had that pleasure. He was wary. How much did his mother know? It was a mystery how she knew anything about his attachment to Phoebe. God knew, the whole wretched business had been short-lived and conducted in the utmost secrecy. There never was any point, however, in trying to work out how Lady Stanhope came by her information. He had more than once remarked to a friend that had she been in charge of intelligence before the Battle of Waterloo, Napoleon would never have slipped over the border unnoticed.

"I am glad to hear it," his mother said. "I am sure she is a very good kind of girl, if a trifle plain, but as you must know, the Stanhopes and the Hawkins have never been on good terms."

That was all he was going to get out of his mother that evening. What she had to say was full of code and hidden meaning, which he could decipher well enough. With his temper rising, he went into the ballroom, intending to find Phoebe's younger sister and ask her for a dance. That would annoy his mother, and allow him to talk about Phoebe.

This wasn't so easy. Since he had arrived late, most of the more attractive young ladies had filled up their dance cards. But he soon found a friend, a former fellow officer, whom he persuaded to give up his dance with the delectable Sarah Hawkins.

"I wouldn't do it for everyone," his friend said. "And I'll expect a favour in return one of these days. Perhaps an invitation to dine with the divine Mrs. V," and he tipped his friend a knowing wink.

As he waited for his dance with Phoebe's sister, he thought about the divine Mrs. Vereker, the tempestuous, beautiful, wilful actress who had been in his keeping for five unforgettable years. Before he met Phoebe Hawkins, he shunned occasions like this, preferring simply to dine at home or attend small parties with his intimate friends, and then inevitably to go on to spend the rest of the evening and night with Emma Vereker.

The night he met Phoebe, all that had changed. And Mrs. Vereker, nobody's fool and more than wise in the ways of men and lovers, had noticed at once a difference in him.

That evening, she had drawn back from

his embrace and held him at arm's length, searching his face with her voluptuous eyes. "Well, well, what have we here?" she said in her entrancing, husky voice, which always seemed to be on the brim of trembling into either laughter or rage. "I do believe we have the picture of a man in love." He denied it to her, as he denied it to himself. How could he possibly be in love with a girl on first meeting? What was there about Phoebe to arouse such passion? She was well-looking enough, and a young woman who would catch many men's fancy, he would judge, with her sparkling, lively ways and a quick wit, unusual in a debutante. When he'd asked her to dance, she informed him that she wasn't exactly a debutante. This was her second season, and she was enjoying it a great deal more than the first one.

When he asked why, she had laughed, and said that her family had given up on her, and that all the dull men were devoting their time to the new crop of girls making their come-out. "For one's bloom passes very quickly," she said with perfect good humour.

He had seen Phoebe across the room the minute he arrived in Mrs. Rowan's apartments. It wasn't a ball like this one, but a small private dance, the kind of party given before the season proper began by the host-esses who had come to London early. He had almost not gone, but at the last minute the friend with whom he had been going to dine sent round a message saying that he had a foul cold, and proposed to spend the evening not out on the town and eating beefsteaks, but with his head over a pot of steam and imbibing hot toddies.

So he had gone to Mrs. Rowan's party, always glad to see her, and hoping to have a few words with Pagoda Portal, a man he both liked and admired. He had seen Phoebe talking to Pagoda, looking up at him with a wicked expression on her face and flirting outrageously. It was clear that Pagoda liked Phoebe immensely, which was unusual; Pagoda Portal generally found very young women not in the least interesting, preferring more sophisticated and mature acquaintances. It was another point in Phoebe's favour, that she was so at home in Mrs. Rowan's salon. Henrietta Rowan, Pagoda Portal's long-standing companion, and undoubtedly his mistress, was a woman of charm and sensibility, who drew around her the liveliest and cleverest people in London. She had told Stanhope, "I cannot bear a fool. I have nobody to please but myself, and possibly Pagoda, and therefore

I choose only to invite those whose company I enjoy, which means that no one who is a bore, or in any way tedious, may cross my threshold."

So very few young women were to be found at Mrs. Rowan's. Among them, he remembered, were several of the Darcy women. And of course through her mother, Phoebe was a Darcy. She shared something of her cousin Camilla's liveliness, and her more distant cousin Cassandra's intelligence and honesty.

Now he watched Miss Sarah Hawkins dance, with grace and style, and he could see that she was obviously a charming companion. She had more beauty than Phoebe, but his heart would never miss a beat in her company, or as he watched her waltz, while just to think of Phoebe dancing made his heart race.

Phoebe was in Derbyshire, and here he was in London. The music finished, and a few minutes later he was in front of Sarah, bowing and explaining that Justin had yielded a dance to him. She looked up at him with thoughtful brown eyes. "I do not believe that we have been introduced, sir."

"That is easily remedied," he said, holding out his arm. "Allow me to tell you that my name is Arthur Stanhope, and that I am an excellent dancer."

She allowed herself to be led on to the dance floor. "I think you cannot be all together respectable, for I can see that my mama is glaring at me from the other side of the ballroom."

"That is what mothers do," said Stanhope, smiling down at her, catching in her face some likeness to Phoebe that made him warm towards her. "I assure you that I too have a mother, keenly chaperoning me, who is at this moment glaring at us from the other side of the ballroom."

Sarah was delighted at the thought of her handsome partner, no mother's boy, but clearly a man of the world, suggesting that he had a mother who kept an eye on him. "Chaperone?" she said, flashing a dimple.

It was true, he did dance well. But he didn't dance as well with Sarah as he would have done with her sister. To dance with Phoebe was to enter another world, where there were only the two of them, kindred spirits, moving through the music and the dance as one.

"I am acquainted with your sister, Miss Phoebe Hawkins," he said after they had moved apart and then come together again. "I hear that she is no longer in London."

"No, which is very sad for her, but it is to

my advantage, for I was not to be brought out until next year, or maybe not until the year after that, if she did not find herself a husband." She put her hand to her mouth. "Oh dear, that's the kind of thing that I'm not supposed to say. It is not that Phoebe could not have got married, I know for sure that she had several offers, but she does not care for the men who care for her. However, this year she caught a spring cold, and so she has gone to Pemberley."

She threw him a provocative look. She was full of herself, very young, just feeling the power she might have over men, and finding how much she enjoyed the game to be played with the opposite sex. One step forward, and a step aside and round, and she cast him a provocative glance from over her shoulder.

Then, seeing the look in his eyes, the game didn't seem so much fun after all. There was something about Mr. Stanhope that made her afraid. He was too masculine, and she found that the look of hauteur on his face made him seem remote, and somehow dangerous.

She wished with all her heart that she were not going down the dance with Mr. Stanhope, but instead with James Denholm, for example, a fair young man only two or three years older than she was, a man with an engaging smile, and winning manners, with whom she felt completely comfortable.

Mr. Stanhope was talking about Phoebe again, enquiring about her health, asking how she liked being at Pemberley and missing the season. It was better when Mr. Stanhope was talking, and so she prattled on, revealing far more than she was aware of. "Her cold was not so very bad, although it is most unusual for Phoebe to be ill at all." To be sure, she did have a slight cough, but when she came back to Warwickshire, it seemed to her that Phoebe might have after all been well enough to undergo the rigours of a London season, even if she was rather listless and lacking in her usual energy.

"Papa would not have it, however," she confided, her smiles and flirtatiousness quite vanished. "He said she must go to Pemberley, and he would not hear any argument about it."

"Did not your sister protest about being packed off to Derbyshire?"

"Not in the least. She was eager to go. You won't believe it, but she didn't even want her maid to pack any of her smart clothes, all the new gowns that had been made for her to wear in London. It is not so bad, you must not be thinking she is lonely or miserable, for Louisa Bingley is also at Pemberley. She is a far worse case than Phoebe, for she has done three seasons and no sign of an engagement. She's a beauty, although she is twenty-two. I should be ashamed not to be married at twenty-two."

"I am acquainted with Miss Bingley. Is she very close to your sister?"

"I should not have said she was a particular friend, although of course there is the family connection. But she is a quiet person who loves the country, and I have heard my aunt say that she is never very happy when in London. That is, I don't know whether it is London that she doesn't like, or the frivolity of the season. She is rather serious; who knows, she may even be of an evangelical disposition."

Arthur Stanhope had to laugh at the ingenuousness with which Sarah pronounced these words, as though to be an evangelical Christian was to be some kind of freak. "I think you will find Evangelicalism is becoming more and more fashionable, as is rural life."

Sarah wrinkled her pretty nose. "It is all very well to spend some of the summer months in the country, but I hope that when I marry I shall have a house in town, and will be able to spend many weeks here every

260

year, as well as going to the seaside, for the bathing. And I should like to go to Paris. I wanted to go last year, when Phoebe went to stay with Cousin Georgina, Lady Mordaunt. She has the sweetest little boys, and they are at Pemberley too, in the charge of a governess, Miss Verney. Shall I tell you a secret about her?"

Arthur Stanhope wasn't in the slightest bit interested in any governess, except that as she was at Pemberley, she probably saw more of Phoebe than he had been able to do. "Miss Verney?"

"She is French. She was at the school which I attended for a year. She was much older than I am, but I would not have thought at all suited to being a governess. She had to leave in the end, because there was some incident with the father of one of the other girls who was at the school, General Emerson, there was nearly a dreadful scandal, but it was all hushed up."

"In which case, why has Lady Mordaunt entrusted her children to her?"

"It is something to do with France, with her being French. Lady Mordaunt knows her brother or her uncle or some such thing, and I dare say she felt sorry for her, needing to work and to earn a living. And I don't suppose that at Pemberley there are very many men for her to flirt with."

The dance came to its end. Mr. Stanhope enquired whether she wanted to be taken back to her mother, but she said no, she would be dancing again in a minute, and meanwhile was dreadfully thirsty and would like a glass of champagne.

"Lemonade," he said, and at those words Sarah's last vestiges of admiration for his fine figure and air of being a man of the world vanished. He was stuffy, and in fact, probably a very disagreeable man. But she remembered her manners, curtsied when he thanked her for the dance, and then went skipping off to find James Denholm.

Arthur Stanhope decided it was time to leave the ball, but just as he thought he had made good his escape, his mother glided out from behind a pillar in that extremely irritating way she had, and said that she wanted a word with him.

CHAPTER TWENTY

Phoebe awoke with a start, wondering for a moment where she was. There was something different about her room this morning. Then she realised what it was: sunlight, filtering through the shutters. She leapt out of bed and ran to the window to open the shutters. She lifted up the sash to let in the brilliant sunlight of a perfect spring day. It was very early, not long after dawn, and the mist rose from the river and hung gently about the hills beyond. The utter stillness to the air, and the clarity after all the rain, made her catch her breath. Even the scars left by the violent wind seemed, this morning, to be a natural part of the landscape.

Birds were singing, brilliant trills and cascades of notes wafting across to her on the morning air. A pair of doves flew past on their way to the stable dovecote; in the meadow on the other side of the river she could see rabbits grazing on the rich green grass. Certainly the morning was full of sound: the lowing of the cows from the dairy, waiting to be milked, the more distant bleating of sheep, and a very soft whistle emerging from the lips of one of the younger gardeners as he scrunched past on the gravel beneath. Phoebe repressed a ridiculous desire to lean out and wave and call out to him, "What a beautiful morning it is."

If the gardeners were at work, it must be after six o'clock. Phoebe was too impatient to wait for Miniver to bring her morning chocolate. She wanted to be up and out in the fresh, bright air. On impulse, she pulled out her riding habit and tucked her hair under a velvet cap. She picked up her whip and went out of the room, closing the door behind her quietly so as not to disturb Louisa or, much worse, Lady Redburn. Although her great-aunt slept some distance away, Phoebe was well aware of how sharp her hearing was, and how much Lady Redburn disliked the slightest noise disturbing her before she felt it was the right time for her to wake.

Outside the air smelled wonderful, fresh and fragrant with the promise of spring. She felt more lighthearted than she had for a long time, and Mr. Jessop smiled at her as she came almost skipping into the stable yard.

"My word, you're up early this morning, Miss Phoebe. Well, you've saved me a bit of trouble, for you can take Marchpain out for his morning exercise. Mind how you go, though, he is as fresh as a daisy this morning and lively with it."

Mr. Jessop was quite right. Marchpain danced out of the stable yard and pulled at the bit all the way along the road by the flower garden. She took him across the bridge, and he playfully pretended to be frightened of both the bridge and the water, tossing his head and prancing. She turned into the meadow, and there gave him his head and had a glorious gallop, which brought her back — this time at a sedate trot — into the stable yard with glowing cheeks and a very healthy appetite for her breakfast. She dismounted, slid the reins over her horse's head, and handed him over to a waiting groom. Then it was back indoors to be met by a cross Miniver, complaining that her chocolate had gone cold, and what did she think she was doing riding so early and going outdoors while the mist was still on the ground, as if she didn't know how bad the rising damps were for anyone who had the sneezes.

"I don't have the sneezes," said Phoebe. "I haven't sneezed for days. I daren't sneeze when Lady Redburn is about, you know how much it annoys her to hear people's coughing or sneezing. And I don't have a sore throat, and I am not tired, in fact I feel completely well. But I feel extremely hungry, and if I do not have my breakfast at once, I dare say I may fall upon a sofa in a faint."

It was too fine a day, and too delightful to have a world around one that was full of sunshine instead of grey lowering clouds and rain, that she and Louisa agreed, it would not do to sit indoors. Their discussion about how to spend the morning was interrupted by a loud rumbling noise from outside.

"Wagons," said Louisa.

Phoebe jumped up. "The drivers will be able to tell us in what condition the roads are, and whether it is likely that we should be able to get through into Pemberley or Lambton without being mired in the mud."

"If so, let us make another call upon your godmother and Lady Maria," suggested Louisa. "Mr. Grayling told me yesterday that there are several ripe pineapples, more than we can eat, so we could take one with us. Mrs. Wellesley was saying how very partial she is to pineapple, and of course it is not a fruit they can possibly grow at Red House. They will have eaten the one we sent after our visit."

The roads were, the wagoners said, passable with care. Phoebe intended to drive herself, but Louisa dissuaded her. "I know how much you like to drive, and I am sure you are well able to do so, but only think of the scolding you will have to endure from Lady Redburn if she finds you have been driving yourself to pay a social call. On this occasion, let the coachman drive us."

Phoebe wasn't pleased, but she saw the good sense of what Louisa said. She knew that they would be interrogated upon their return as to where exactly they had been, and who had driven them there.

"I pity Mr. Drummond today," observed Phoebe as they drove out to the gates.

"Why?" said Louisa.

"This is the first day that my great-aunt will be able to venture into the gardens. She will want to inspect everything, and hear every last detail of my uncle's plans, so that she may criticise and make all kinds of unwelcome suggestions."

"I can understand how she feels about Pemberley, since she was brought up here, but that is a very long time ago. And surely she has a house and park and gardens of her own to worry about?"

"Indeed she does, Lord Redburn has a fine house and a big estate in Shropshire, apart from a house in London. Lord Redburn is extremely rich, you see. However, she never goes to Shropshire, and that is where her husband spends all his time. It is said that they have not exchanged a single word these last twenty years."

"There was a quarrel?" asked Louisa. "Something quite dreadful must have occurred to cause such a shocking breach."

"I believe not, they simply cannot stand the sight of one another."

"Was it an arranged match? She seems so full of spirit, I can hardly believe that she would have married a man she didn't care for, and I never thought of the Darcys as an oppressive family. Although, of course, in the last century, people took a different view of marriage."

"It was a love match, but after a number of years their love turned sour, and their feelings for one another became dislike and then indifference."

"Was he a rake?"

"A rake?" Phoebe's voice was suddenly sharp. "Oh, if he were a rake, that would be unforgivable in my view. As you know, I could never marry a rake."

"No, but your great-aunt may have done so unawares."

"Is it ever unawares with a rake? Don't they say that a woman marries a rake in order to reform him? And it is unlikely that a man is a rake and his fellow men not know it."

"Perhaps the fault was Lady Redburn's," said Louisa. "I do not wish to cast a slur on the character of any woman, but wives are unfaithful to their husbands, there is no point in denying it. In which case, though, he would surely have divorced her."

"Lady Redburn has often told me and my cousins never to marry a stupid man. So I think that may be at the heart of her disillusion with her husband. If he is a fool, which she is not, then I can see how his presence would irk her, and vice versa."

Louisa shook her head. "She took her vows, and there is nothing in the marriage ceremony about folly or stupidity on the part of either man or woman being an impediment to a marriage."

"Just as well, or the world would be full of unmarried persons."

"Besides, did she not notice he was a fool before she accepted him?"

"Perhaps one can fall in love with a fool,

but not marry him."

"I expect at the time, if she were in love, the only thing she wanted was to marry Lord Redburn, ignoring his true character, or persuading herself that he was something he wasn't. Love is blind, after all."

"Yes," said Phoebe. "And if you're lucky, some kind person tears the blindfold from your eyes before you walk up the aisle."

Louisa was surprised at the bitterness in Phoebe's voice, but didn't press it any further. "That explains Lady Redburn's descent on Pemberley, at any rate, although I am surprised she isn't fixed in London at this time of year."

"She claims she finds the season a bore, that she has endured too many of them, but I think it is rather to take advantage of my uncle being out of the country. Then she may come and rule the roost at Pemberley, which would not be the case if he were in England."

They soon reached the outskirts of Lambton, and in a few more minutes were on their way through the gates of the Red House. The same neat maid answered the door, but she looked a little perplexed. Phoebe could hear voices coming from the drawing-room, masculine voices.

"Mrs. Wellesley already has visitors, perhaps," she said. "Shall we call another day?"

"It is only the vicar with another gentleman, I am sure —"

The drawing-room door opened, and there was Lady Maria. "Ha, I thought I heard voices. Come in, come in, how very good of you to call again." She ushered them in, exclaiming at the pineapple, "See, Cecilia, what a noble gift your goddaughter has brought us. Another pineapple from the pinery at Pemberley."

Phoebe halted at the door, irritated to see Mr. Bagot at Mrs. Wellesley's shoulder, bowing and smirking in what Phoebe felt was an unduly familiar way; after all they barely knew the man. Then the other visitor, a dark, well-dressed man, who was standing by the fireplace, came forward, and Phoebe forgot about the vicar. "Good heavens," she cried. "Mr. Warren! Whatever are you doing here?"

Mrs. Wellesley frowned at Phoebe's outspoken and not very friendly greeting, while Lady Maria watched with grim amusement.

Louisa, startled, stared at George Warren.

"Cousin Louisa, what a pleasure," he said smoothly, advancing and taking her hand.

Phoebe was not well-acquainted with George Warren, but no member of the Darcy family was unaware of his hostility towards them. He was the son of Lord Warren, and that nobleman's first wife. She had died when George was little, and his father had married again. His second wife, and George's stepmother, was the former Miss Caroline Bingley, Louisa's aunt.

Lady Warren had never forgiven her brother for marrying Louisa's mother, Jane Bennet, still less had she forgiven the rich Mr. Darcy for falling in love with Elizabeth Bennet and making her Mrs. Darcy. She doted on her stepson, was privy to most of his intrigues and conspiracies, and resolute in her encouragement of any scheme which might cause embarrassment to the Darcys.

When she was a young woman, Caroline had professed a great friendship for Miss Georgiana Darcy, but Lady Hawkins, Phoebe's mother, had grown to mistrust and dislike Lady Warren, and the two women were on distant terms these days.

How came he to know Mrs. Wellesley? Or was he connected in some way to Lady Maria?

The vicar was eager to explain why George Warren was there, however. He was an old friend, they had been at the same college, he happened to be in this part of the world and had consented to stay for a few days at the vicarage. "Even though mine is a bachelor establishment, and I can hardly hope to offer him any of those comforts which a woman in the house will provide."

Louisa smiled at the vicar, a smile that Phoebe noticed held little real warmth, which was unusual as Louisa was normally the friendliest of creatures. "Surely my cousin's establishment in London is also a bachelor one, Mr. Bagot. And I believe that many men even in households where there are no women manage a high standard of comfort and neatness. Naval men, for example, acquire excellent domestic habits while at sea."

"However, Mr. Warren benefits from the services of a good valet," said Mr. Bagot with what he no doubt thought was an agreeable smile, but which appeared to Phoebe to be an unpleasant smirk.

"My man has been with me for many years," said George Warren smoothly. "You do yourself an injustice, Bagot, I find the vicarage extremely comfortable. Although I agree with you that any home is made more attractive and homelike by the attentions of a woman."

Lady Maria made a sound that was almost a snort, but turned it into a cough. It was clear to Phoebe that she liked neither the vicar nor Mr. Warren. And something else was also clear, which was that Mr. Bagot's slightly patronising way of addressing her and Louisa that had been evident last time they met the vicar had subtly changed. The smiles he was bestowing upon Louisa were wider, he stood a little closer to her than was strictly necessary, and although he still retained his superior expression, he seemed to be making every effort to please.

Mrs. Wellesley was talking about the Martindales. "We met Lady Martindale yesterday, when she drove into Lambton to do some shopping. She does not look all together well, although I think none of us do after this miserable winter and wet spring. She tells me that that brother of hers has been staying with them, but has now returned to London, and I expect she misses his company. He is a clever, lively man and I believe they get on very well together."

George Warren, always agog to catch any item of gossip, pricked up his ears. "Has Arthur Stanhope been in Derbyshire? You astonish me, since I know him to be a fellow who hates the country. I would have thought even his fondness for his sister would not drag him out into the shires in such weather, and at this time of year when London is so lively. Perhaps" — with a sly look at Phoebe — "there was some other attraction to draw him to these parts."

Phoebe bit her lip, and made herself breathe more slowly to try to slow her racing heart, disturbed yet again by the mere mention of Arthur Stanhope's name. So he was back in London. Well, that was a relief, she told herself. At least there was no chance of her meeting him either by accident or socially. She must be glad that he was gone. What had Mr. Warren meant by his last remark? Could he suspect? — but no, that was unlikely.

A sense of desolation swept over her, and it was with difficulty that she managed to smile and speak in a normal voice, and appear to be perfectly at ease. She noticed Lady Maria's eyes upon her, which didn't help; Phoebe suspected that she was the kind of woman who possessed penetrating insight, and it was more than likely that she had noticed Phoebe's hastily stifled reaction to Stanhope's name.

"These scions of the great Whig families are all the same," said Mrs. Wellesley. "It is extraordinary to me that Kitty is so happy in the country. With her breeding you would expect her to be a Whig through and through and to relish life in town in the midst of a great deal of company."

"That marriage was a mistake," said Lady

Maria bluntly. "Sir Henry is himself a Whig, otherwise the match would not have been allowed by Lord and Lady Stanhope, but he is a Tory at heart, combined with the manners and morals of his Whig ancestry. It is not a good combination, and not one that bodes well for Lady Martindale's happiness." She looked at Louisa's face and laughed. "You need not look at me in quite that way, Miss Bingley. When you know me better, you will know this is not gossip, but simply that I speak my mind. I have a great liking for Lady Martindale, and wish her well, but there is no point in disguising the fact that to have a husband who has rakish propensities is not the best ingredient for a good marriage — at least not for a woman like Lady Martindale."

Mrs. Wellesley exclaimed, "What nonsense. Sir Henry a rake? He is no such thing, there has never been a breath of a rumour of any kind of misbehaviour with any of the servants or neighbours. You judge him too harshly."

Lady Maria said, "I do not like men, but I understand them. Perhaps, were he to have a great shock in that area of his life, he might behave better, but as long as he has an adoring wife who will not stand up to him, he will begin to feel that he can get away with infidelity, to put the politest words to it, and you know once a man has acquired a habit like that, it is hard to be rid of it."

She noticed the quick frown on Mrs. Wellesley's face as she glanced at Phoebe and Louisa, and went on in her outspoken way. "You think it is not quite the thing for me to speak about such matters before young unmarried ladies, but you are wrong. Innocence is no excuse for ignorance, and ignorance is the cause of much unnecessary suffering."

"You distress me," said the vicar, his eyes gleaming with curiosity. "I would hope that no parishioner of mine would so far forget his duty to God and his wife as to sin in that particular way."

"If you are saying that you hope that no one in the parish is ever unfaithful, or given to committing fornication, Vicar," said Lady Maria with a hearty laugh, "I think you are in the wrong profession and must go about with closed eyes and also ears. I could name you a dozen in your congregation, pillars of the community, whose private life would not bear close investigation." She gave the vicar a cool look. "And no, I shall name no names. It is part of your duty, not mine, to attend to what your flock is about. As to putting an end to such immoral behaviour, it has been going on since the time of Adam and Eve, and no man of God, however committed or evangelical in his principles, will change human nature."

Phoebe was listening with only half her attention. Lady Maria's remarks about Sir Henry had struck home. Was that not almost word for word what her father had said to her, when he warned her what unhappiness would follow were she to persist in her attachment to Arthur Stanhope? And Lady Maria was right, such behaviour was not restricted to the great Whig families. It was to be found in every village and town in the country, and in the best-regulated of households. As in her own family.

She knew that whole anguished business had alarmed and upset her at a deeper level than she could really appreciate. Was this the common lot of wives? Here was the old story repeating itself with the Martindales, if Lady Maria was speaking the truth. At least with her father it had, she truly believed, been a single incident, bitterly regretted and repented. But with a man who had a natural disposition that way, there could be no long-term hope of happiness.

She came out of her reverie to find that

Mrs. Wellesley was speaking to her, and she had not heard a word of what she was saying. She raised a smile. "I am so sorry, my wits were wandering. I was admiring the blossom out there, and thinking how the trees so heavy with flowers make it look almost as though there had been a snow-storm." She noted that Louisa was looking at her with some intentness, and took the hint. She rose. "I feel we have outstayed our welcome, and we should be returning home. My great-aunt will be wondering what has become of us."

George Warren was suddenly alert. "Great-aunt?" he said. "Would that be Lady Red-burn?"

"I had heard that she was come to Pem-berley," said Mrs. Wellesley. "Lady Maria and I will call upon her, of course. It is some years since I have seen her."

Phoebe and Louisa took their leave, and Warren and Mr. Bagot decided to leave at the same time, escorting Phoebe and Lou-isa to their carriage. Mr. Bagot said his farewells with much bowing, while Warren bestowed a glinting smile upon Louisa, and said that he would do himself the honour of calling upon her and Miss Hawkins and, of course, Lady Redburn at Pemberley in the near future.

"He will not be welcome at Pemberley," said Phoebe fiercely as they drove away. "I know for a fact that my uncle has no time for him at all and heartily despises him, and indeed, given the mischief he has done to several of my cousins and other relations, I'm amazed that he has the effrontery to think that he can set foot in the place. However, I feel sure that Lady Redburn will not greet him with any enthusiasm, and she will send him about his business quickly enough."

CHAPTER TWENTY-ONE

Phoebe and Louisa were greeted upon their return to Pemberley by an irate Lady Redburn, who at once demanded to know where they had been. Upon learning of their visit to Mrs. Wellesley and Lady Maria, she grew still more angry. "I am astonished that you two should have gone out on your own, to pay a visit to neighbours without informing anyone at Pemberley of what you were about. It would have been the least of courtesies to let me know where you were going, and indeed for you to pay a visit by yourselves when it is known that I am at Pemberley will make Mrs. Wellesley and Lady Maria think I am extremely ill-mannered. It is not for you to be presuming to visit in such a way, and on your own."

Phoebe, who had made up her mind not to let herself be riled by Lady Redburn, forgot all her good intentions. "I do not believe we have to ask your permission before we leave the house, most of all when I am merely paying a visit to my god-mother."

"Hoity-toity! While I am at Pemberley, you will remember what is due to your elders and betters, and you must consider yourself to be under my authority. In the mornings before I am up, there are plenty of things for you to do in the house, duties to attend to, letters to write. Then, if any visits are to be made, I will decide when and where they are to take place, and whether it is appropriate for you to accompany me."

This was a red rag to a bull, and Phoebe flared up. "I am not under your authority, I believe, Great-aunt. I am nearly one-and-twenty, and besides —"

"Besides, fiddlesticks. Nearly is not of age. And whatever age you are, as a guest in this house, you must conform to the practices of Pemberley, and not run on in the wild way you are permitted to do at home. I shall at once write a note of apology to Mrs. Wellesley and Lady Maria — a woman whom I must say I cannot bear; it would have been better if she had been born a man, I never met a woman with fewer feminine graces — apologising for your unsolicited visit this morning."

Louisa was making faces at Phoebe from behind Lady Redburn's back, gesturing to her to keep her mouth shut, and to control her temper. Phoebe saw the reason in this, and clamped her teeth together, still glaring at her great-aunt.

"And you need not stare at me in that most unbecoming and resentful way, young lady," Lady Redburn said. "You look exactly as you used to at ten years old when your will had been thwarted. Your father did not whip you, as he should have done, for that would have knocked all this rebellious nonsense out of you at an early age, before you were old enough for it to cause any mischief. It is no wonder to me that you did not succeed in snaring a husband during your first season, and if this is representative of how you behave, I dare say however many seasons you do in the end, you will still not find yourself a good husband."

"Since I am not on the lookout for a husband, ma'am, that is not a prospect that distresses me greatly."

Phoebe was mistaken in her conviction that Lady Redburn would not tolerate having George Warren in the house. When, after intensive questioning, she had extracted all the details of Phoebe and Louisa's visit, she announced that she would be very pleased

283

to see Mr. Warren, a most polished and amiable man, with excellent manners and address.

When she and Louisa finally escaped, Phoebe gave full rein to her wrath. "Polished and amiable, indeed! George Warren is a weasel, he is bad through and through, and I know that Mr. Darcy would not care at all to have him at Pemberley."

Louisa tried to calm her down. "As your great-aunt said, it is very difficult for us to refuse to see him, when he is almost my cousin."

"And I dare say he will bring that dreadful clergyman with him, and no doubt Lady Redburn will greet him, too, with enthusiasm and open arms. I warn you, Louisa, George Warren has told him how big your fortune is, and he thinks he will make a try for you."

Louisa found this very funny, but Phoebe shook her head and said that Louisa had best be on her guard. "For I have to tell you that Lady Redburn does not think highly of the Bingleys, on account of her being such an out-and-out snob. She knows that your grandfather's fortune came from trade, and so despises your father and all of you for having such lowly origins. Just as she despises my aunt, as not being the kind of well-connected bride worthy of Mr. Darcy. She will think there would be nothing amiss in your making a match of it with Mr. Bigot; oh dear, I mean Mr. Bagot. It is a constant source of amazement to me that my uncle's father and mother, who were by all accounts the most delightful people, kind and considerate in every way, should both have had such detestable sisters. My grandmother's sister, Lady Catherine de Bourgh, was a complete tartar, and one of the rudest women imaginable."

Louisa's even spirits weren't ruffled in the least. "It is nothing to me what Lady Redburn thinks of my family, or my origins, or my marriage prospects. I would as soon marry the man in the moon as that vicar. He is a most disagreeable man, and I dare say you are right about his ambition. I am sure he would like to marry a woman of fortune, but although there may be women who would find him good-looking, I find his features and his manners repugnant and therefore I shall not waste another moment thinking about him."

Now began a difficult time for Phoebe at Pemberley. Her great-aunt's displeasure with her over the visit to Lambton was increased when she finally found out about the ball. As Phoebe had predicted, Lady

Redburn at once determined to take all the arrangements and planning into her own hands, saying it was pure folly of Mr. Darcy to entrust so large an undertaking to his inexperienced niece.

In the end, Phoebe wrote a letter to Mr. Darcy, to be forwarded to him by his secretary, saying that she regretted she would be unable to carry out his instructions as to the ball, since Lady Redburn had decided to take the whole matter into her own hands.

More quickly than she would have believed possible, a letter arrived addressed to Lady Redburn, which from the handwriting on the envelope Phoebe at once recognised as being from her uncle. Lady Redburn read it with a heightened colour and pursed lips. "It is very kind of my nephew to be so considerate as to my well-being, saying that I must not trouble myself with the onerous task of the arrangements for his ball. He assures me that you are carrying out his orders, and that with everything in the capable hands of the steward, the butler, and the housekeeper, he is sure everything will be done just as he requested. Well, I wash my hands of it, and should I still be here when the ball is held, which I very much doubt, it will be interesting to see what a sadly managed affair it will turn out to be."

Ha, Phoebe thought to herself. She is afraid of Mr. Darcy! Phoebe had not expected her great-aunt to yield so easily, but in fact Lady Redburn had plenty else to interest her. She inspected the house from top to toe, poking her nose into every nook and cranny, every room and every cupboard, finding fault with the way the maids did everything and driving Mr. Rutland to retreat to his pantry with Mrs. Makepeace, where they took a glass of port together, and expressed their dislike of interfering women.

She sallied forth into the garden, and harangued all the gardeners, informing them that their planting, the situation of their buildings, the arrangement of the kitchen garden, and the state of the flower garden were all wrong. In fact, anything that differed in the slightest from the way things were done when she was a girl at Pemberley was wrong.

Only Mr. Drummond stood up to her. He was extremely polite, and if there was a twinkle in his eye as he listened to her forthright pronouncements of what should and shouldn't be done, he never showed any irritation or contradicted what she had to say. He listened, bowed, and took no notice whatsoever of what she advised or ordered, which, much to Phoebe's surprise, earned him Lady Redburn's grudging respect.

Phoebe herself, given as she was to lamenting over the various changes and modernisations made even in the few brief years she had known Pemberley, was aghast when a laughing Louisa pointed out that in this, and in some other ways, she and her great-aunt were very alike.

Phoebe exclaimed and protested that it was not so, but Louisa insisted it was. "You criticised the bathrooms Mr. Darcy has had installed, and the showers, which I must say I think are a wonderful convenience. The hot-air heating in the halls and stairways is a real comfort, but you insist that the draughts and chills of your childhood days here are superior. You told Mrs. Makepeace you regret the fact that the old stoves in the kitchen have all been replaced with the most modern new ones, and when it comes to the gardens, you don't want to see a blade of grass altered. And there, I can assure you, the changes which Mr. Drummond has in hand are admirable, and will enhance, not diminish, the appearance and style of the grounds."

Phoebe flushed, and said she was in no

way such a stick-in-the-mud as Lady Redburn. "In proof of which, consider how much I like the drawings Mr. Drummond has made for the new glasshouse. It is an amazing structure, with so many panes of glass, and curved as it is, with that dome in the centre. It is quite original, and I wholeheartedly agree that it will be a vast improvement on the old one. Every day as I see more of the iron supports go up, I long to see it finished."

Meanwhile, George Warren paid a visit to Pemberley. He sat quite at his ease in the drawing-room and partook of the substantial refreshments offered, eating most of a pineapple by himself.

Warren set Phoebe's teeth on edge with his barbed comments as to the elegance and opulence of the apartments at Pemberley. He was the kind of man who took it as an offence that anybody should have anything finer or more pleasing than he had. As yet, in fact, he had very little beyond a small property which he had inherited by dubious means, but he stood to inherit his father's title, house, and lands, and considered that as a future peer, he stood higher than any mere Mr. Darcy, and resented the beauty and grandeur of Pemberley.

Phoebe's predictions proved all too true.

Warren brought Mr. Bagot with him, and he nodded and smiled and ogled Louisa at every opportunity. It was clear that he intended to pay court to Louisa, and although she was chillingly indifferent to him, it did little to quell his inclination to sit too close to her, to ask her opinions on every small matter, and praise whatever she had to say, in what Phoebe and Louisa considered a most offensive way.

They were both annoyed to learn that Lady Redburn had organised a dinner party, with George Warren and Mr. Bagot among the guests, together with Mrs. Wellesley and Lady Maria. She had also invited Sir Henry and Lady Martindale, and much to Phoebe's surprise, announced that Mr. Drummond would dine with them.

"Doubtless she considers that otherwise there will be too many women," said Phoebe. "At the least, Mr. Drummond is a gentleman, and behaves like one, unlike the wretched vicar." She was too taken up with resentment at the fact that Warren and Mr. Bagot had been asked to dine at Pemberley to notice the glow in Louisa's eyes, when she remarked that Mr. Drummond would be a worthy guest at anyone's table.

Yet Phoebe's suspicions, first aroused after the storm, had increased and she had a strong feeling that Louisa was becoming more than a little fond of Mr. Drummond. It hadn't escaped her notice how much time Louisa spent in the gardens, and although this was not surprising, given Louisa's love of flowers and keen interest in gardening, Phoebe had more than once found her deep in conversation with Mr. Drummond. In itself that was not a cause for suspicion, as inevitably they were discussing the precise conditions in which some seedling or plant would thrive, or Louisa was telling Mr. Drummond about some variety of azalea which flourished in her family home. But Phoebe was no fool, and she could see that there was a kind of ease between them, and that Louisa, whose beauty had attracted so many men, and who had acquired the habit of holding them all at arm's length, had quite dropped her customary reserve when in the company of Mr. Drummond. It worried Phoebe, who could see no way that Miss Bingley, with a fortune of thirty thousand pounds, would ever be allowed to marry a man in Mr. Drummond's station of life.

CHAPTER TWENTY-TWO

Miniver was on her mettle as she dressed Phoebe for the dinner party. This was the first chance she'd had since coming to Pemberley to turn her mistress out in prime style, and she intended to make the most of it. Phoebe objected strenuously, she would wear her old lilac evening gown, thank you; she saw no reason to dress particularly fine, not for the company that would be there that evening, and had she not told Miniver in the clearest terms not to bring those dresses to Pemberley? She could not imagine what they were doing here, and had no intention of wearing one of them.

Miniver won, as was inevitable. Phoebe came downstairs looking, Louisa thought, quite lovely, in a gown of palest yellow, caught up in rosettes along the hem, and with a pretty detailing of more matching tiny rosettes around the neckline. She wore an elegant diamond necklace, and another diamond ornament sparkled in her dark hair. Even Lady Redburn, casting a swift eye over her, approved. "I am pleased to see you looking like a young lady of quality at last, Phoebe. That colour becomes you. Although I think a less fussy style of gown would be better for you."

She had no compliments for Louisa, who simply looked the beauty she was. Betsy had taken a great deal of trouble with her, although, as she complacently remarked to Miniver as she watched Louisa go down the stairs, with those looks, there was very little that needed to be done.

The company gathered in the drawing-room. Phoebe kept herself well in the background, while Lady Redburn greeted the guests as they arrived. She gave George Warren a warm welcome, which annoyed Phoebe, and was gracious to Mr. Bagot, which annoyed her even more. Then her godmother arrived with Lady Maria, and Phoebe was soon swept up in conversation, and was able to forget for the time being her irritation at the make-up of this gathering. Sir Henry and Lady Martindale were the last to arrive, and Phoebe looked closely at Kitty Martindale. She had to agree with Mrs. Wellesley's judgement: Lady Martindale looked neither well nor happy. And there seemed to be a degree of constraint between her and her husband, who quickly left her side and wandered over to engage in conversation with George Warren.

Phoebe was pleased to see that it was Mr. Drummond who took Louisa into dinner, and not Mr. Bagot, who had been angling for the privilege. Mr. Drummond cut him out very neatly, holding his arm for Louisa, so that the vicar was obliged to fall back on Mrs. Wellesley, who, with what Phoebe considered commendable goodwill, went into dinner beside him. She herself hung back; she would rather sit next to the outspoken Lady Maria than be obliged to make conversation with either George Warren or Mr. Bagot.

The dinner was excellent, with M. Joules in his element. Asparagus, purée of wood pigeon, red mullet, a *chaud-froid* of chicken, lamb cutlets, and duckling with green peas were rounded off with a vanilla soufflé of exquisite lightness and a delicious lemon cream. Phoebe relaxed under the influence of the good food and plentiful wine, until she heard Lady Redburn, in a loud and commanding voice, inform George Warren that she would make sure that he was sent a ticket for the Pemberley ball in June, were he still to be in the neighbourhood at that time.

Phoebe dug her nails into the palm of her hand with fury. How dare her great-aunt? She knew with certainty that Mr. Darcy would not welcome George Warren in his house while he was there, not to mention the other members of the family that George Warren had wronged in some way. Now that Lady Redburn had given an invitation, it would be impossible for her to rescind it, even if Phoebe explained to her great-aunt just why George Warren would not be an acceptable guest.

She knew Lady Redburn would not listen to her; she would pooh-pooh the whole idea of there being any unpleasantness between Warren and the Darcys, saying that the Darcy girls were always up to some scheme or other, and that their remoter cousins in particular were always involved in intrigue and scandal. That was where the blame lay, not at the feet of George Warren, whom she had known since he was a little boy, and could find no fault with. She liked men to have some backbone, she couldn't be doing with all these milk-and-water young fellows that you met these days.

Phoebe took a gloomy mouthful of her pudding. Lady Maria was eyeing her with some amusement, and said to her in a low voice that she should take care not to show in her face what she was feeling. "Mr. Warren is an unpleasant rogue, I warrant you, but it does not do to show in public one's distaste for such a man. He will notice it, be amused by it, and attempt to set you up to be one of his victims. You would do better to ignore him, and to take your great-aunt's fancy for him in your stride. She herself is one who likes to make mischief, and the more she knows that you find George Warren's company objectionable, and that your uncle also would prefer not to see him, the more she will see to it that he spends time at Pemberley. It is her way, she has always been like that."

The conversation at the other end of the table turned to the subject of a forthcoming celebration for Jack Harlow's twenty-first birthday. Phoebe pricked up her ears; she and Jack were old friends, and she had every intention of attending the fête that had been arranged for his coming-of-age. The Harlows' house was some seventeen or eighteen miles distant, and at first Lady Redburn had instructed Phoebe to decline the invitation, telling her the Pemberley carriage was not there to encourage girls to gallivant about the country, and piling up the reasons for her objection: "It is too far, there will be no man available to escort you, and you would not be back, most likely, until the early hours of the morning. It is not fitting for you to jaunt about the countryside in that manner."

Phoebe exclaimed at this. "I have known Jack forever. He taught me to play cricket when I was a girl, and we used to race one another on our ponies."

That didn't go down well with Lady Redburn, and so the matter rested, until Mrs. Wellesley unthinkingly mentioned to Lady Redburn that there had always been a hope that Phoebe and Jack might make a match of it. Lady Redburn didn't listen to Mrs. Wellesley's opinion that it would not be a successful marriage; in her opinion, Phoebe, who should certainly be married, could do much worse than to marry a Derbyshire man.

Lady Martindale said something which made Sir Henry, sitting across from her, laugh, and Phoebe saw for the first time how attractive he was, and could understand why Kitty Martindale had married him, although he was so much older than she was. She also noticed the grateful but uneasy glance Kitty gave her husband, and a chill went down her spine as she thought of what Lady Maria had said about his unfaithfulness. Phoebe wondered if he, like her father, had a mistress in town, or whether he was carrying on an intrigue with some local woman. She gave her head a little shake; it wasn't a subject which she cared to dwell upon.

Lady Redburn rose, and took the ladies back into the drawing-room. She instructed Louisa to entertain them upon the pianoforte, took the best seat by the fire, and told Mrs. Wellesley and Kitty Martindale to come sit with her. Lady Maria proposed a game of backgammon to Phoebe, which she accepted with relief, not wishing to join in the conversation at the fireside, nor to be commanded to sing by her great-aunt.

Tea had been brought in, Phoebe was beating Lady Maria at backgammon, the gentlemen were still in the dining room, and Louisa had embarked on a second sonata, when Phoebe heard voices in the hall. A moment later the door opened.

There, in immaculate evening dress, stood Arthur Stanhope.

CHAPTER TWENTY-THREE

Lady Martindale looked up, saw her brother, and sprang to her feet, holding out both hands to him, a look of delight on her face. "Arthur! What an unexpected pleasure. I had no idea you were coming back to Derbyshire from town. When did you arrive? And now you've come all this way to Pemberley, you are too late for dinner, you know."

Arthur Stanhope greeted his sister with affection, but he could not stop his eyes flickering around the room until they rested on Phoebe, who had her head down and was concentrating on her pieces. Lady Maria chided her. "What are you about, Phoebe, are you not acquainted with Mr. Stanhope? It is your duty as much as Lady Redburn's to welcome him to Pemberley."

Lady Maria was quite wrong. Phoebe had no wish to welcome him to Pemberley, she did not wish to see him at Pemberley, she did not wish to see him at all. And now, having paid his respects to the other ladies, he was coming across to their table. Lady Maria waved a hand at him. "Pray, do join us. Pull up a chair. Miss Hawkins and I have almost finished our game, and besides, she was set to backgammon me, so I think we may call an end to it. What brings you here? I thought you were in London."

"I was," said Mr. Stanhope. He addressed Phoebe. "I was dancing with your sister yesterday night. She sends you her love."

For the first time, Phoebe lifted her eyes and looked directly at him. She immediately lowered them, hating herself for the blush that rose to her cheeks. "You were at a party, I suppose," was all she managed to say. Then she took a deep breath and composed herself. "I hope my sister was well."

"Well, and in the most lively spirits. She is enjoying considerable success, from what I hear."

Phoebe did not know where to look nor what to do with herself. Her heart had leapt at the sight of him, and yet she wished he were not here, she ardently wished that he would simply go away. His presence caused feelings that she could not control, and indeed did not fully understand, to overwhelm her. She must get away, she could not bear to stay in this room so close to him. Why had he come? He must have known she would be at Pemberley. She made as if to get up from the table, but Lady Maria restrained her, putting a hand on hers, and saying, "Let Mr. Stanhope take my place at the backgammon table, Miss Hawkins. I have something I wish to ask Lady Martindale."

Phoebe sank back into her chair, trapped. She fiddled with one of the pieces, wishing she could simply get up and run from the room, like a child in a tantrum. Mr. Stanhope was rearranging the pieces, his long, firm fingers moving them into position swiftly and surely. She couldn't take her eyes from his hands, she felt she would have known them anywhere, they seemed to represent the quintessence of his being. She averted her eyes and looked across the room to the large painting which hung above the fireplace. It was of a classical subject, showing Europa being abducted by Zeus disguised as a bull. The painting disturbed her, and so instead she looked at a painting of a nautical scene that hung beside the door, with a man-of-war under full sail surging through stormy seas, firing a broadside. She made herself count the little woolly puffs emerging from the muzzles of the cannon;

anything to divert her attention from the man sitting opposite her.

"You are very quiet, Miss Hawkins," said Mr. Stanhope. "Have you nothing to say to me?"

"Nothing," said Phoebe. "Nothing at all." She rolled the dice unthinkingly, and moved a piece into a different position, hardly aware of what she was doing. He watched her with an ironic smile. "It is a good thing you are not a gambler, or you would lose a great deal of money. It is important to pay attention to the game one is playing."

"It is not a game, sir." She blurted the words out before she knew what she was saying, and she spoke with a ferocity that startled her. It seemed to startle Mr. Stanhope as well, but he quickly recovered his infuriating calm.

"Then I shall roll my dice, and move a piece, and although this game is nonsense, it will appear to the others in the room that we are playing."

Phoebe cast a desperate glance at Louisa, hoping that she might come to her rescue, but Louisa, who was a true musician, was absorbed in her music and did not notice her friend's look of appeal.

"Do you plan to stay long in Derbyshire?" asked Phoebe, striving for a light, indifferent tone, falling back on the polite nothings of conversation.

"Do you care?"

"Not at all, your movements can be of no concern to me. One must say, thus and thus, when at such a gathering as this. It would not be polite to sit in silence, and when one does not have very much to say, one must fall back on banalities."

"Oh, Miss Hawkins, I have a great deal to say to you."

"Oh, Mr. Stanhope, I have no wish to hear anything you have to say to me."

Phoebe had never spoken a greater untruth.

And he knew it, by God he knew it. Her heart was in her eyes, she couldn't deceive him. Damn this room, damn this company, would she never give him a chance to talk to her alone? When he had got back to Martindale House, and heard that Sir Henry and Lady Martindale were dining at Pemberley, he hoped that it might be a large party, one where he could draw Phoebe to one side, and finally have the conversation with her that he so wanted to have. But this was too small, too intimate a gathering for him to be able to take her aside unnoticed, and there was his sister already turning curious eyes to their side of the room.

"I think we should make at least a pretence of playing," he said, shaking the dice. He spilled the dice out on to the board, and made his move. "You may have a turn now, and take one of my pieces."

She did as she was told, mechanically, unaware of what her fingers were doing.

"You lie when you say you do not want to hear what I have to say. Yet you have a reputation for honesty. Perhaps, by being less than honest with yourself, you are learning to be less than honest with others. A pity; honesty is a quality I admire in anyone, and especially in a woman."

"Since I neither seek nor want your admiration, it is of no consequence to me what you think of my or anyone else's honesty," she flashed back.

Phoebe turned her head away, not wishing to look at him, and saw George Warren, who had come unnoticed into the room, standing and regarding them with a supercilious and unpleasant smile. Arthur Stanhope noticed him and the sneering look, and frowned. What the devil was Warren doing here? He had no time for the man; he distrusted him, disliked him. And from what he'd heard, there was no love lost between Warren and any of the Darcys. Yet here he was, lounging into the room, looking as though he belonged at Pemberley. Ah, that was it, he had charmed Lady Redburn, that was why he was here. She cared nothing for a man's morals as long as he wore a well-fitting coat and had a virile air to him. Well, she was welcome to him, but he still didn't like the way the fellow was looking at Phoebe.

A suspicion leapt into his mind. No, surely not. Yet someone had sent those abominable rumours floating around town, rumours that had reached his mother's ears, but not, he felt sure, Phoebe's, but which he felt equally sure would be passed on to her before long. Some so-called friend would say she felt it was her duty to tell Phoebe what people were saying about her; it was odd how a sense of duty always impelled its possessor to impart unpleasant news, never to pass on a compliment or overheard words of praise.

And who was that fellow standing behind Warren? He didn't like the look of him at all. Good heavens, it was a clergyman. Come to that, where was Henry? He could see his sister's eyes fixed on the door, an anxious look in them. Who else was here? It looked to him a very dull party: Warren, the cleric, Lady Maria with her coarse tongue and abrupt ways, Miss Bingley, seated at the handsome grand pianoforte, and the insufferable Lady Redburn. Poor Phoebe. Not a set of people he would choose to spend any time with, with the exception of his sister and Mrs. Wellesley, who was a woman he liked and admired. Wasn't she some connection of Phoebe's?

He winked at Kitty, hoping to see her smile, but it was a wan smile that she gave him in return. Drat Sir Henry. He would have to do something about the man, he couldn't stand by and see Kitty dwindle into a shadow of her former self. He had seen too many women go that way, and Kitty wasn't going to be one of them, not if he could help it.

Warren came sauntering over to where he and Phoebe were sitting. He looked down at the backgammon board, a knowing smile on his face. "It is a very interesting game you appear to be having, I never saw such poor play. Lost your touch, have you, Stanhope? Do you have things on your mind other than this game?"

Arthur Stanhope closed the backgammon board with a snap. "Well, Warren, what brings you to Derbyshire? Rusticating? Settling-up day too much for you?"

An angry flash spread over Warren's dark countenance. "It's none of your business why I should be in Derbyshire. I might ask the same question of you."

"You might, and I would reply, with perfect civility, that I am visiting my sister and her husband."

"Thus displaying an unusual amount of family feeling," said Warren. "Are you often in Derbyshire?"

"As often as I want to be," came the cool reply.

While the men were talking, Phoebe slid out of her chair and went over to the piano. She nudged at Louisa to move along, and sat down on the long piano stool beside her, reaching out to turn the page for her. Lady Redburn, noticing this, called out to Phoebe to sing for them. "You have had a good master these last two years, so your mother informed me, and your singing was always better than your playing; pray, let us see what progress you have made."

Phoebe shot her great-aunt a look of pure hatred, which made Arthur Stanhope smile. It was impossible for her to refuse such a request, however, and after shuffling through some of the music on top of the instrument, she placed a score in front of Louisa, and looked through the pages until she came to the song she wanted. It was a lyrical ballad, a haunting melody, a song penned in Elizabethan days of love won and lost. Her voice, and the feeling she put into the words, made Stanhope's heart stand still.

There was a moment's silence when she finished the song, and then Mrs. Wellesley clapped her hands in appreciative applause. "My dear, I had no idea you had such a good voice. It is not unlike that of your cousin Alethea."

Phoebe laughed. "Oh, Mrs. Wellesley, you cannot compare me to Alethea, who has such a remarkable voice. But I thank you for the compliment."

At the general request of the company, she sang two or three more songs, and Stanhope noticed that as she became absorbed in the music, the tension which had been evident in her posture and face left her.

He hadn't noticed Hugh Drummond come into the room, and he looked up to find his friend standing beside him. He got to his feet, and shook Drummond warmly by the hand, and clapped him on the shoulder. "What a pleasant surprise. I did not know you were among the guests this evening."

"It came as rather a surprise to me," Hugh Drummond said dryly, with a quick look at Lady Redburn.

"Aha, you are having trouble in that direction, I can imagine how irksome you must find it."

Hugh Drummond smiled and shook his head.

"You prefer not to discuss your hostess's ways while she is in the room. You are quite right, of course," said Stanhope. He noticed that his friend's eyes were drifting over to where the two girls were sitting at the piano. He stiffened. Which of the two was he looking at like that? Not Phoebe, surely, although how could anyone look at Miss Bingley, when next to her was a Phoebe? He watched Hugh; there was both warmth and a kind of despair in his eyes. Louisa Bingley; yes, it was Miss Bingley.

"We were saying, Mr. Stanhope, that Derbyshire appears to have a sudden influx of visitors. Here is Pemberley opened up, and Mr. Warren visiting at Lambton, and now you are back in the county. How do you account for it?"

Lady Maria's voice was gently mocking, and Arthur Stanhope had the uneasy feeling that she was well aware of why he might be back in Derbyshire. He adopted a light tone of easy amusement. "Surely, the delights of Derbyshire are too well-known for it to be a surprise that you should have so many visitors." He knew Lady Maria to be a formidable correspondent, and had no doubt that some of the rumours flying around London, imparted to him by his mother, would have come to her notice. He would dearly love to know what or who was the origin of the rumours. Phoebe's father? It seemed unlikely, Sir Giles had considered it imperative that Phoebe's name not be linked in any way with his.

Lady Redburn was setting up a four to play whist, a game she loved. The vicar, Lady Maria, and Mrs. Wellesley were soon seated at the table while the cards were laid out. Warren, still with a mocking expression on his damned face, sat himself beside Kitty, and was clearly setting out to make himself agreeable. Arthur Stanhope wished he could get Phoebe to himself, but knew it would look too particular, and in any case, he suspected that she would resist any such attempt on his part to get her alone. So, with a last glance at the piano, he rose and strolled towards the door. Hugh Drummond looked up questioningly. "Just slipping out for a smoke," Stanhope said in a low voice. In fact, his intention was to find out where the devil Sir Henry had got to. An intention which cost him very little effort, since as he entered the hall, Sir Henry was coming in from outside. He had a relieved look on his face, which annoyed Arthur Stanhope.

Sir Henry's gaze dropped under Stanhope's grim expression. "Just going in to join the ladies," he said.

"You have been missed."

Sir Henry gave one of his blustering laughs. "I do not expect so." He went into the drawing-room, closing the door behind him. While Arthur Stanhope hesitated, reluctant to return to the drawing-room himself, another figure came sliding into the front door and, seeing him, gave a considerable start. A hand flew to her mouth.

"Forgive me, sir. I did not think — that is, I supposed that everyone was in the drawing-room."

She was not wearing an evening gown, and so was not a guest, but he had seen her before. Of course, she was the governess, looking after some of Mr. Darcy's grandchildren. "What are you doing here?" he asked abruptly.

She looked up at him from beneath long lashes, a shrewd and knowing look, which startled him considerably. No governess he had ever met would have looked at a man like that, a complete stranger. Not a governess in a respectable household, anyhow.

She flitted past him, and in a flash was on her way up the stairs, before he could ask any more questions. Not that he needed to, he had a very good idea why she had been outside, and her presence and that look answered several of the questions that he had recently been asking himself. Definitely, he would have to do something about it, he couldn't have this going on at Kitty's very doorstep. Kitty was no fool, and he felt sure that she, too, had a good idea of what her errant husband was up to, although he also felt quite sure that she didn't know with whom Sir Henry was entangled.

He might consult his mother about it, but she would merely shrug her shoulders, and say in an indifferent voice that it was the lot of wives. He would prefer to teach Sir Henry a lesson; that way he might learn to curb his roving eye. Of course, another solution was simply for his sister to find her own consolation elsewhere, but he knew his sister too well not to be aware that for that to happen, she would have to have become completely estranged from her husband.

Nodding at the hovering footman to open the door, he went outside and down the steps. He walked along the side of the house, which this evening was outlined against a still-brilliant waning moon. The sound of the piano came faintly through the drawing-room windows. He was excluded from the scene within, and the poignancy of the music and the intensity of his emotions at that moment caused his spirits to feel an unaccustomed anguish.

In the distance an owl hooted, and there was a dull plop from the surface of the river as a fish rose for a second to the surface. His senses were super-alert; it was as though he could hear creatures from halfway across the county. From nearby came the sharp bark of a fox, and the soft sounds of the cattle on the other side of the river mingling in the stillness of the night, as the beasts grazed and moved in the darkness.

He walked slowly back towards the front door, hesitated for a moment, and then went back inside.

CHAPTER TWENTY-FOUR

At last, the evening came to an end. As they stood in the hall, waiting for the carriages to be brought round, Phoebe strove to keep her distance from Stanhope. She refused to meet his eyes, turning her head to one side to talk to Louisa. When Stanhope's carriage was finally at the door, she presented him with the tips of her fingers placed in his hand, and dropped him the briefest of curtsies, still not looking at him.

Lady Redburn was in a snappy mood, on account of not winning at whist, and both Phoebe and Louisa were glad to escape from her and go upstairs to their bed-chambers. Alone in the darkness of her bed with the curtains drawn around it, Phoebe did not sleep. She was trying to make sense of the emotions which had been raging through her all evening. She had not imagined that it would be so painful to see Mr. Stanhope again, nor that her feelings for him would not have altered one jot, despite her father's very just comments, and her own determination not to think about him.

Then there was the problem of the Harlows' fête. What if Mr. Stanhope were still in the county? It was the forthcoming weekend, he had only just returned to Derbyshire from London, and so there was every prospect that he would make up one of the party from Martindale House.

Why had he come to Derbyshire? Her heart told her that it was to see her, and indeed she could hardly mistake the glow of ardour in his eyes when he looked at her. Reason told her that a man rejected as he had been would have too much pride to seek her out again, and remembering why she had rejected him, remembering the agony of seeing him with Mrs. Vereker, she told herself yet again how right she had been to reject him.

She could not go to the Harlows'. She could not spend an entire day avoiding a tête-à-tête with him, not if he were determined to speak to her alone. Nor could she trust herself to tell the lie that must be told, that she did not care for him, that her feelings as expressed in her letter to him were unchanged, and that she hoped he would be gentlemanly enough not to approach her again on this matter. How could she form those words on her lips? And yet she would have to. She had given her word to her father, and besides, her father was right. She could never expect any happiness married to a man like Stanhope.

Her thoughts turned from herself to Louisa. Were her suspicions correct, was Louisa falling in love with Hugh Drummond? Was he in love with her? If so, Phoebe could see nothing but difficulties ahead for them. Louisa's parents, she knew, cared a great deal about the happiness of their children, but they would believe, as would many parents, that it would be impossible for their daughter to be happily married to a man in Mr. Drummond's position. And she shuddered to think what would happen when Lady Redburn noticed their growing affection for one another.

It was not until the first pale light of dawn was creeping through the shutters that Phoebe finally drifted into an uneasy slumber. Miniver, when she had helped Phoebe to bed the night before, had noticed that all was not well with her, and she didn't come into the room until long after the sun was up. She opened the curtains and unshuttered the windows before drawing back the curtains around Phoebe's bed with enough vigour to make the brass curtain rings rattle. The noise awoke Phoebe with a start, and she sat up abruptly, pushing her hair out of her eyes, and blinking at the sunlight streaming in through the window. For a moment her heart rejoiced at the brightness of the day, and then the memory of her problems flooded into her mind, and she sank back on to the pillows, her eyes shutting out the glad day.

Phoebe took Louisa into her confidence. "I cannot go to Harlow Park this weekend."

Louisa, who was looking rather pensive, shook her head. "You have to go, you know that; once an invitation is accepted, it is impossible for you not to go. And there can be no reason for your not going. They know you are here at Pemberley; short of your being carried away by some family emergency, which heaven forbid, you must fulfil your obligation and go."

Phoebe sneezed. It was a perfectly natural sneeze, and not the forerunner of watering eyes and streaming nose. Perhaps the condition which had afflicted her when she went to church was returning. She could hardly go to Harlow Park like that.

"No," said Louisa. "It is not the same, that is just a sneeze, nothing more. It is a bad habit to get into, to fall back upon a chill or a fit of sneezing or some other illness to excuse you from what you don't want to do."

Phoebe was indignant. "It is something I have never done in my life. But you are quite right, I can't see there is any way that I can escape from going to Harlow Park."

"You will just have to ensure that you are never alone with Mr. Stanhope. There will be a large number of persons present, and I'm sure it will be possible for you so to arrange your day that you need not see much of him at all."

"I can and shall avoid him," said Phoebe. "However, if he is intent on not avoiding me, what am I to do?"

Louisa shook her head. "It's a difficult situation." She paused, and said, with some diffidence, "Is Lady Redburn aware of what happened between you and Mr. Stanhope? Were you to explain to her —"

"Impossible!" cried Phoebe. "If she were to get wind of it, I should never hear the end of it, and she would be bound to try and interfere in some way. She might pack me off back to London, or try to send me home to Hawkins Hall, which would inconvenience and annoy my parents."

Louisa had another suggestion, but it was

one she made after a definite hesitation. "Mr. Drummond is a very close friend of Mr. Stanhope's. Might it be possible for you to speak to him, and he could explain to Mr. Stanhope —"

Phoebe didn't let her finish her sentence. "I hardly know Mr. Drummond, and I would not wish to put him in such an extremely awkward position, as to be advising his friend about my desire not to be in company with him."

"I suppose not, but I believe Mr. Drummond to be a man with a very good heart, and I am sure if he knew of your distress, he would be more than willing to help."

"No. I have got myself into this scrape, if you can call it a scrape, for I feel it is worse than that, and it is for me to deal with. I had hoped that by leaving London I would not have to see Mr. Stanhope again, at least not for some considerable time. As things have turned out, I am to be thrown into his company, and I shall have to manage as best I can."

"You are far from indifferent to Mr. Stanhope, I believe," said Louisa. "Why is an attachment between you and him not possible? You have convinced yourself that he is a rake, but you have never given me any sound reason why you are so sure of his nature. You will soon be of age, and although I would never recommend any daughter to go against her parents' wishes, I cannot believe that your parents would want you to break your heart."

"I shall not break my heart. I don't hold with that kind of sentimentalism, I do not believe that hearts are so feeble and weak as to be easily broken. Yes, I liked Mr. Stanhope more than any man I have ever met, and I did think at one time that I could imagine no greater happiness than to be his wife. However, circumstances are such that I know I would not be happy with him, and that is not something that can be altered."

The click-clack of heels on polished floors alerted them to the imminent arrival of Lady Redburn. "Not another word, not in front of Lady Redburn," whispered Phoebe as the door opened, and her ladyship sailed in.

Phoebe made Miniver cross, by refusing to take any interest in what she was to wear to the Harlows'. "It is of not the least importance how I look."

"What, you don't wish to look your best, with so many people there? And Mr. Jack —"

"What, Jack? Who knew me as a little girl,

with my dress all torn and muddy, and bits of grass in my hair, from rolling down the bank? I hardly think I need to dress up to impress Jack."

"Even if Mr. Jack was not to notice that you were poorly dressed, his mother certainly would."

"Lady Harlow will have far too much to do to care how I may look."

Louisa made no such objection as to what Betsy wanted her to wear, although she was as disinclined to go to the forthcoming party as Phoebe, and would have much preferred to remain at Pemberley. She laughed a little at this, how absurd it was that she and Phoebe, isolated as they were at Pemberley, would both much rather stay at home. She listened with half an ear to Betsy's prattle and, as soon as she could, left the room and went downstairs to go out into the gardens.

Where she received a most delightful surprise. She would not, when she went outside, make any efforts to seek out Mr. Drummond, but it was pleasant how often it seemed that their paths crossed. It was so today, as she made her way to the flower garden, with a book in her hand, intending to sit beneath a tree for an hour or so. She knew that Phoebe would find her there, but it was Mr. Drummond whose pleasant voice interrupted her steps. He held a letter in his hand.

"Good morning, Miss Bingley," he said. "Here is a charming thing. Lady Harlow, hearing I am presently at Pemberley, has written to invite me to Harlow Park. I was acquainted with her eldest son, you know, who was in the army. I am not sure that I should accept, not with so much work in hand at Pemberley at the moment. The iron structure will be finished today, you know, and then by next week the glaziers will be hard at work."

Louisa smiled. "You have a very strong sense of duty, Mr. Drummond, but surely you are entitled to a few hours to yourself."

"I am employed by Mr. Darcy, I am not a gentleman of leisure and private means. The gardeners here at Pemberley work twelve hours a day, six days a week, and even on Sunday they are expected to work for ten hours. It is hardly right for me to take time off purely for private pleasure, however much I should like to do so."

"I should much prefer not to go to Harlow Park," said Louisa. "I am not so well acquainted with the Harlows as Phoebe is, and I am sure I shall be very dull, and obliged to make conversation with people I hardly know. I had far rather be here at Pemberley, enjoying the gardens, with no strangers to have to exert myself to please." She flushed, feeling that she had spoken too freely.

Mr. Drummond took it in very good part, laughing at her, and saying that he never yet heard of a young lady who did not care for putting on a fine dress and going to a party. "And I wish I might come, then I might beg your hand for a dance or two, for Lady Harlow says there will be dancing in the evening. I should much enjoy that."

The words were barely out of his mouth, when the conversation was interrupted by the arrival of Lady Redburn. She held her parasol above her head, and once she moved into the shade, she snapped it shut and used the point to tap the ground in front of Mr. Drummond.

"Good morning to you, Mr. Drummond, have you no work to be about this fine morning? I am sure that Mr. Darcy does not pay your salary for you to stand gossiping in the flower garden."

Louisa exclaimed at this; she could not help herself. "It is I who detain Mr. Drummond, ma'am. He was passing by, and I wished to ask him about one of these flowers that has just come into bloom here. It is not a species with which I am familiar."

Lady Redburn was having none of this. "There is no need for you to know what a species of plant may or may not be, Miss Bingley. You have no garden of your own, and when you do so, when you are a married woman, then you may take an interest in the names of plants, and enquire of your own staff on such matters. Your ignorance is no excuse for causing Mr. Drummond to be idle."

Mr. Drummond raised his eyebrows at Louisa, and bowed to Lady Redburn. "I assure you, Lady Redburn, that my work will not have suffered by my taking a few minutes to answer Miss Bingley's questions." And with that he walked briskly out of the flower garden, and away down the path in the direction of the shrubbery. It was as well that Lady Redburn could not see his face; while good manners, and good breeding, had enabled him to keep the serene countenance while she was upbraiding him, now that she was out of his sight, he let fly with a few hearty curses and observations on her ladyship's character which would have surprised Lady Redburn had she heard them.

Meanwhile Louisa, trapped in the flower garden with Lady Redburn, was obliged to walk slowly around the beds, while her lady-ship pointed out how badly it was planted, how this shrub was covered in insects, how that plant looked in a poor way, and how all together the whole scheme had been carried out with no real taste. "The flower garden was very pretty in my day," she said. "It is a pity that my nephew has allowed the gardens and grounds here at Pemberley to be so badly managed. They are nothing like as fine as they used to be."

Louisa was too wise to argue, although her naturally placid temperament was ruffled by Lady Redburn's bad manners, and by her attack upon Mr. Drummond. She had nothing but admiration for him, putting up with Lady Redburn's arrogance with such calmness. And then she had to suppress a smile, as she saw Phoebe come round the corner of the path, catch sight of Lady Redburn, and turn on her heel to whisk herself out of sight.

Lady Redburn noticed the smile, and demanded to know what she was smirking at.

"Nothing, ma'am. I assure you, I was not smirking, I was smiling with pleasure at the beauty of the flowers and the findings of the day."

"Stuff and nonsense. You were smiling at

some private joke, and that is something that young ladies should never do. If you have something amusing on your mind, or that you wish to say, then it is only polite to come out with it, so that others may hear it and share the joke."

"I assure you, Lady Redburn, there is no joke," said Louisa.

CHAPTER TWENTY-FIVE

Never had Phoebe set out to any kind of a party with so little enthusiasm. She and Louisa were travelling in the barouche, and the children were coming in a separate carriage, accompanied by Miss Verney, looking far too elegant for a governess in a gown of pale green, and Sukey, the nursery maid. It was Phoebe who had insisted that Sukey should come as well, for, as she said to Louisa, she did not trust Miss Verney an inch, and what if she were to wander off on her own pursuits and leave the children to their own devices?

May had brought almost perfect weather, neither too hot nor too cold. The countryside was burgeoning into the lush greenery of late spring, and the hawthorn blossom was heavy against the myriad colours of greening trees and meadows. The hay was ripening well now, and the air was full of the scents and sounds of busy insects and singing birds. Such beauty in the landscape did much to cheer Phoebe and Louisa up, and for at least the first part of the journey, they both forgot their troubles and simply enjoyed the drive.

However, as they drew near to Harlow Park, Phoebe no longer noticed her immediate surroundings, as all her thoughts were focused on what she considered the ordeal ahead.

Harlow Park was an old house, which had been much enlarged and improved by the present owner, Mr. James Harlow. He had a taste for the Gothic and the old house, which had been quite plain, had been embellished with pointed windows, crenellations, and a tower at the east end.

James Harlow also had a passion for fountains and waterworks of all kinds, and his grounds were famous for their pools, fountains, cascades, and basins. There was a lake in front of the house, and as their carriage drove up the long drive, Phoebe and Louisa saw that boats had been put into the water for the amusement of the guests.

Phoebe's spirits rose. She had known it was to be a large party, but she had not quite appreciated just how many people would be there; among such a throng, it must surely be possible to avoid Mr. Stan-hope.

The Harlows, like many landowners, were acutely sensitive to the messages that the French Revolution had sent out, and took great pains to look after their tenants and those who worked for them. Today, their son Jack's twenty-first birthday, was a day of celebration not only for family and friends, but also for all the people connected with the estate. Huge trestle tables had been set out beneath the trees on the other side of the lake, and here, Mrs. Harlow informed Phoebe as she greeted her with warm affection, the tenants and their families would sit down to lunch.

"And afterwards there are to be the usual country festivities. Although May Day is past, there is the maypole, and morris danc-ing, and various games and entertainments. I am so pleased you have brought the children with you, for several of our grand-children are here, and the offspring of our guests as well, and we have taken pains to make sure that the children will also enjoy the day. Now, here is Jack, waiting to see you."

She went away to attend to some of the numerous duties that fell upon her shoul-ders on such a day, while Jack greeted

Phoebe with unrestrained delight. He was a tall, fair young man with very blue eyes and a naturally smiling face. He had frank, open manners and Phoebe was extremely fond of him.

"Let me congratulate you on your birthday and upon your coming-of-age, Jack. It is only a sadness that Charles isn't here."

A cloud passed over Jack's face. "It still seems wrong to me that I shall be the one to inherit the house and the land. I was always very much the younger brother, and you know how much I admired and looked up to Charles. I'm glad to say that some of his fellow officers are to be here today; are you acquainted with Mr. Stanhope? And Hugh Drummond, a capital fellow, we only recently learned that he was in Derbyshire. Phoebe, I shall later claim a dance with you, and you too, Louisa, if you will allow me."

Phoebe was wearing a white muslin dress with a pattern of tiny cherries on it. She wore it with a dashing red sash, and her bonnet was trimmed with little bunches of cherries. Despite her protestations that she did not care how she looked, Miniver had turned her out looking her best, and she and Louisa, who was as beautiful as ever in pale blue, turned heads as they walked along a shaded path towards an area of the garden which Phoebe particularly liked. At the end of the walk was a large circular fountain with two smaller ones at either side. The theme was oceanic, with Poseidon holding a trident and his horses rising from the waves in the big fountain, and frolicking dolphins and mermaids in the two smaller ones.

Phoebe perched herself on the broad marble surround of the larger fountain, and dabbled her fingers in the ruffled water. "This fountain is a great joke with the family," she said to Louisa. "I don't think you knew Mr. Harlow's father, but this Poseidon is modelled on him, and it has his features to perfection. It is an especially good joke, because you must be aware that Poseidon was not the sweetest-natured of the gods, and old Mr. Harlow was notorious for his bad temper and high-handed way with servants and tenants. It is remarkable how unlike him the present Mr. Harlow is, and Jack will be just the same as his father, a good landlord and kind and considerate to his dependants."

It was calm and peaceful there by the fountains. Phoebe thought that if only she could enjoy such solitude for the rest of the day, it would not be so bad. The gentle splash of the water soothed her spirits, and the cool breeze made it extremely pleasant to be there.

She was just about to remark upon this to Louisa, when they heard the sound of voices and approaching footsteps; seconds later the peace was shattered by the arrival upon the scene of Lady Martindale and her brother, Mr. Stanhope.

Phoebe shut her eyes in disbelief. With all the extensive grounds of Harlow Park, why, within minutes of their own arrival, had Lady Martindale and Mr. Stanhope ventured into exactly this part of the park? It was as though fate were determined to throw her into Mr. Stanhope's path. For a moment she contemplated turning on her heels and fleeing, but Louisa, as though sensing what she might be going to do, put a restraining hand on her arm and whispered, "I shall not leave you, let us just greet them, and then I am sure we may get away."

Although Lady Martindale had said nothing about it to her brother, her suspicions had been aroused at Lady Redburn's dinner party at Pemberley. She knew her brother well, and was aware of his longtime relationship with Mrs. Vereker, and some of the other women who had preceded her. She had never seen Arthur look at any woman in the way that he was now looking at Phoebe Hawkins. It was evident to her that he was overflowing with admiration; he was in love with the girl, there could be no doubt about it.

And that explained his presence in Derbyshire. She smiled wryly; she should have guessed that her brother would not have paid so long a visit, nor returned from his trip to London, simply to be in her company. Yet it did not look to her as though her brother's feelings were reciprocated. It was evident that Phoebe was extremely uncomfortable in his company, she appeared tongue-tied and took great pains not to look at him. That could be embarrassment, or an unwillingness to show her own affection before others, or simply, it was possible that she did not care at all for Arthur.

Her next thought was that her mother and her father would not approve of a match between Arthur and Phoebe at all. Not, of course, that it would matter a jot to Arthur, who was not of an age or temperament to allow his parents to rule his life.

Phoebe had turned on her heel, clearly eager to get away. Arthur stepped forward, but now it was Kitty's turn to put out a restraining hand. "Let her go," she said quietly. "I am sure you will find an opportunity to talk to her later."

Phoebe and Louisa were gone, with more speed than was polite. Stanhope watched them go, and when they were out of sight, he turned back to Kitty with such a look of hurt and perplexity in his eyes that it wrung her heart. "Arthur, how long has this been going on? For how long have you been in love with Phoebe Hawkins? You have never mentioned her."

"Is it so obvious?"

"To me, yes indeed it is. I think it would be plain to anyone who saw you looking at Miss Hawkins just now."

"I met Phoebe the first time but a few weeks ago. Kitty, I was overwhelmed. Dazzled, enchanted, what can I say? I don't have the words to describe my feelings for her. Dammit, here I am, a man of thirty years old, and I can truthfully say that I have never felt for a woman what I feel for Phoebe Hawkins."

Kitty looked at her brother with a puzzled expression in her eyes. "She runs away from you. Why is that?"

"You're asking whether her feelings for me are as intense as mine for her. I believed that they were. Kitty, I wanted her to marry me, and I had every reason to suppose that

334

she was willing to accept me."

She stared at him, astonished. "Are you telling me that you are engaged? Why has the engagement not been announced, to the family, to the world?"

"Ask Sir Giles that."

"Young women today reserve the right to make their own choice as to their husbands. Although, from what I have heard, he is a Tory of the old school, and no doubt sets store by some of the old ways."

"Phoebe is only twenty, she is not yet of age, and therefore, yes, I should have asked for Sir Giles's permission to marry her before I told her that I wished her to become my wife. Such niceties did not at that time seem important to me and all I wanted was to make sure that Phoebe could love me. She swore she did, and I tell you, Kitty, there was no happier man in the whole of England than I was that evening."

"So what went wrong? What reasons did Sir Giles give for refusing his consent?"

Arthur Stanhope could not stand still. He set off to walk around the fountain, and speaking to his sister across the water, said, "The Hawkins family are Tories. The Stanhopes are, of course, Whigs."

Kitty had to raise her voice to make herself heard over the sound of the water.

"That might be an inconvenience, but not a reason for refusing his consent. I never heard of anything so Gothic."

Arthur Stanhope went over to one of the smaller fountains, and gazed morosely at the shapely form of a mermaid clutching a large shell. "That was just the beginning. Sir Giles does not approve of my morals."

"Morals! As to morals, I should have thought yours were a great deal better than most men's. Oh! Does he mean Emma Vereker? Arthur, I do hope that that affair had come to an end before you offered to Phoebe. To take a mistress after a marriage is bad enough, but to have one on the go even while you claim to be with another young woman would be despicable."

"What do you take me for?" said Arthur Stanhope, torn between laughter and rage. "Should I have the great good fortune to make Phoebe Hawkins my wife, I can promise you, Kitty, that there will be no question of a mistress."

"All men say that when they marry, they say that when it is May and the sun is shining and their hearts are full of love. But what happens in the dog days of August, or when autumn winds begin to blow through the matrimonial home?"

Arthur Stanhope had returned to his

sister's side. He took both her hands in his. "I do not pretend not to understand that what you say has a strong personal element to it. I can see your own unhappiness, and I can have a very good guess as to the cause of it."

Kitty drew her hands away and shook her head. "That is my affair, Arthur, and it is something that I will discuss with no one, not even you. But this conversation is about you, not about me. Can you really believe that you will be faithful to Phoebe, if she becomes your wife?"

"It is not so extraordinary. I agree with you that many of the Stanhopes haven't set a good example as to fidelity, but there are others in the family who have made happy and lasting marriages. I do not resemble our father in appearance, nor in attitude, nor in the way I conduct my life, and certainly not as to morals. And remember, the marriage between him and Mother was made in another century, it was a marriage of convenience, an arranged match, with no very great pretence of any affection from either of them."

"It is better to marry with love than without it, certainly," said Kitty with feeling. "But no degree of love and affection can be sure of lasting forever."

CHAPTER TWENTY-SIX

Phoebe felt a mixture of relief and despair. Relief that the encounter with Mr. Stanhope that she had both expected and feared had come so early in the day, and despair at the intensity of her feelings for him, and the misery which it caused her to see the chasm that had to exist between them.

She walked alongside Louisa, mingling now with others as more and more guests arrived, not taking in a word that Louisa said and quite oblivious to her surroundings. She smiled when she saw people she knew, made her curtsies, extended her hand and said everything that was proper. It was as though she were a mere simulacrum of the real Phoebe, as though this person walking around the grounds was a stranger, another person all together. She had never felt so remote from herself and from her surroundings, and the detachment frightened her.

"You are in a state of shock," observed Louisa. She looked around, and led Phoebe towards a lilac tree. "Sit on this bench, here in the shade. I am going to fetch you a glass of wine. No," she went on in a firm voice. "You will do as I say for once, Phoebe. If you are not here when I return, I myself will go and find Mr. Stanhope and together we will come and find you." With these daunting words, she set off at a good pace in the direction of the house.

And what if Mr. Stanhope appears again, Phoebe said to herself, while I'm sitting here? He seems to have a knack of finding me. This thought caused her so much alarm that instead of sinking back and allowing herself to relax, she sat bolt upright, her eyes darting to and fro in case that tall figure in a blue coat should appear again.

To her consternation, she was discovered by a man wearing not a blue but a green coat, someone she was even more reluctant to meet. George Warren drew level with her, bowed, a supercilious smile on his face, and without asking her permission flicked up the tails of his coat and sat on the bench beside her.

Phoebe fiddled with the catch on her parasol, looking down, and choosing to say nothing to this unwanted companion.

"That is not a very friendly greeting," Mr. Warren observed. "You had better come down off your high horse, Miss Hawkins, and treat me with a little more civility than you have shown to date. The Darcys are well-known for their pride and haughtiness, but I assure you, it is unwise for you to look down your nose at me in that way. Tell me, how is Mr. Stanhope? Have you been in his company today? I know how warm your feelings towards him, and surely you would wish to take advantage of the opportunities offered by these lovely gardens to sneak into the shrubbery, or perhaps that little Roman temple at the other end of the garden, where you and he may indulge in yet another passionate embrace."

Phoebe stared at him, aghast. What was he saying? Why was he saying it? What could have caused him to make such a deeply offensive remark, unless he had a very good idea of how things had been between her and Mr. Stanhope? How was that possible? She did not trust herself to speak to him, and instead, without a word, she rose and ran away from him, down the path, taking a left turn, a right turn, heedless of her direction, only anxious to get away from him.

It was not long after her disappearance that Louisa returned. She was accompanied by Mr. Drummond, whom she had met while on her way back to Phoebe, carefully carrying a glass of champagne. He had taken the glass from her, and asked where she was going with it. She explained that Phoebe was not feeling quite the thing, and she thought a glass of champagne would refresh her.

"An excellent notion," said Mr. Drummond, falling into step beside her. "May I accompany you? I know hardly anyone here today, and so I am glad to see a familiar face." He held out his arm for Louisa, and after a moment's hesitation, she smiled, and laid her hand on it.

Louisa stopped short as the two of them turned the corner and came into the broader path where she had left Phoebe. There was a figure sitting on the bench, but it was certainly not Phoebe. "George!" she said with displeasure. "What are you doing here? Have you seen Miss Hawkins?"

Warren got lazily to his feet, and extended a hand to Louisa, while giving a brief nod in Mr. Drummond's direction. "I think the sun has affected Miss Hawkins's wits," he said. "She bounded away from here as though the hounds of hell were after her. I suspect a guilty conscience."

"Knowing you, George," said Louisa with

asperity, "you said something deeply unpleasant to her, as is your way. No, do not raise your eyebrows and look at me in that way, I have no time for a politeness which you do not deserve. Phoebe was not feeling quite the thing, I left her sitting here while I fetched her something to drink, and now I find you have driven her away. Which direction did she take?"

Warren sat back on the bench and stretched his legs out in front of him, crossing them at the ankles, quite at his ease. "As to that, I couldn't say. She flitted off like a madwoman. If you find her, tell her that I take no offence, and merely put it down to the effects of the sun."

Mr. Drummond cleared his throat, but Louisa gave him a speaking look, and saying to Warren that she considered it a great pity that he had ever come to Derbyshire, she set off down the path without taking any further leave of her cousin.

Mr. Drummond gave Warren a hard look and then followed Louisa. She was walking extremely fast, and it took him a few minutes before he caught up with her. When he did so, she stopped and turned to him, an apologetic look on her face. "I'm sorry about that, Mr. Drummond."

"I am sorry that you were having to put

up with that insufferable man's bad manners. What is he thinking of, to speak of Miss Hawkins in that extremely unpleasant way?"

"There is no love lost between any of the Darcys and Mr. Warren, I'm afraid. His stepmother is my aunt, you know, which is why he calls me cousin although we are not in fact related by blood. I cannot speak ill of my aunt, but I will say that she dotes upon George Warren, and he has perhaps been too much indulged all his life. He delights in schemes and intrigues and is always pleased if he can catch any member of the Darcy family at a disadvantage; he has a long-standing grudge against all the Darcys."

They walked on together in silence, Louisa marvelling at how very comfortable she found his company. She would not admit to herself that this was more than the comfort of friendship, or that the feelings she had for him were growing beyond the companionable. At the moment she had no time for her own feelings, she was far too worried about Phoebe. She stopped again and looked directly at Mr. Drummond.

"Mr. Drummond, I believe you have been acquainted a long while with Mr. Stanhope."

"Arthur?" said Mr. Drummond, somewhat surprised. "Yes indeed, I have known him since we were at college together. He is the best of good fellows, and an excellent friend. Why do you ask?"

Louisa began to speak, then hesitated, and shook her head.

Mr. Drummond was watching her closely, and he spoke in a gentle voice. "It seems to me, Miss Bingley, that you are troubled about something. If there is anything that I can do to help, you have only to ask."

Louisa made up her mind. "Since you are such a good friend of Mr. Stanhope, I am sure you will have his best interests at heart. I betray a confidence in telling you this, but I do it for the best of reasons, and because I judge that it may in the long run be of great benefit to both Mr. Stanhope and to Phoebe Hawkins. They formed an attachment —"

Mr. Drummond interrupted her. "I knew it," he exclaimed. "I could not mistake the signs."

"Oh dear, I do hope that does not mean that falling in love is a regular habit of Mr. Stanhope's."

They walked on, and had gone some way before he spoke again. "I can't deny that Mr. Stanhope is far from averse to the female sex. And it is the same the other way, that is to say, that women find him a man easy to admire. Yet I would not call him a libertine, nor a philanderer. He has had a long-standing relationship with an actress, you may have heard of her, a Mrs. Vereker. No, do not look like that, it is not an adulterous affair, for Mr. Vereker died several years ago. From some words that Arthur let drop recently, I have reason to believe that his feelings for Mrs. Vereker are no longer what they were. So he has fallen in love with Phoebe Hawkins, has he? She will make him an admirable wife, she is the very woman to suit Arthur. But I take it that there is a problem. Perhaps Miss Hawkins does not return his feelings?"

"A match between Phoebe and Mr. Stanhope has been forbidden by Sir Giles Hawkins, Phoebe's father. I gather that the reasons he gave were partly to do with the Stanhopes' politics, and partly his mistrust of Mr. Stanhope's morals. He forbade her to have any contact with Mr. Stanhope, and so you see what a quandary she is in. I am sure that she is as much in love with him as ever she was, but she is a dutiful daughter, and her father did give reasons for the attitude he was taking, which she felt were just. He does not approve of Mr. Stanhope as a husband for Phoebe, now or at any time."

"I do not see what possible objection there can be. Arthur is an excellent fellow, a clever man, who is sure to make a name for himself. And besides that he is rich, and will one day inherit the title. I cannot see why any father in his right mind would turn down such a match for his daughter."

"The two families come from opposite sides of the political spectrum, but I think it is rather that Phoebe's father objects to Mr. Stanhope as a man, not because of his political background. You say that Mr. Stanhope is neither a libertine nor philanderer, but he has a reputation as a rake. However undeserved this reputation may be, there is a particular, personal reason, which I am not at liberty to divulge, for Sir Giles Hawkins's reluctance — no, refusal — to sanction a match between him and his daughter."

"A rake!" said Mr. Drummond in surprised tones. "I assure you, Arthur is no such thing. Lord Stanhope, now, that is a different matter. That man deserves the bad reputation he has acquired, and although you will not find Arthur ready to criticise his father, he knows this as well as the next man."

They had come to a sloping lawn, which led down to the lake, and Louisa, who had excellent sight, exclaimed as she saw Phoebe on the other side of the lake. "There she is, but she will be gone long before we can come up with her."

Mr. Drummond gestured to the row of boats which were pulled up alongside the jetty, under the care of an aged man who lacked most of his teeth. "I suggest we take one of these skiffs which Mr. Harlow has so obligingly placed here for the use of his guests. That will be much quicker than taking the path round the lake; I can row you across in a trice."

Mr. Drummond handed her into the boat, and settled her down on the cushions that had been provided for the comfort of the ladies. Then he took his seat at the other end, and seizing the oars in his capable hands, told the man holding the rope to let it go, and began to row with steady, sure strokes towards the centre of the lake.

Louisa sat in silence, enjoying the cool breeze on the surface of the lake, and admiring the easy strength of Mr. Drummond's movements. She was considering what Mr. Drummond had said, which reinforced her own idea that, while she felt it was very wrong for children to go against their parents' wishes, in this case it might be Sir Giles who was in the wrong. "So you would say that Sir Giles has misjudged Mr. Stanhope?"

Drummond lifted his oars, to let the boat drift past some large water lilies. "I think that possibly Sir Giles has been listening to too much gossip and hearsay and rumour. Since he does not move in the same circles as the Stanhopes, it would be difficult for him to form a just opinion of the kind of man that Mr. Stanhope is. Perhaps there is something in his own life that has caused him to make a rather sudden and unfair judgement."

Louisa gave him a quick look, but she was not going to say anything more upon that topic. "In which case, I am going to ask your help. I am convinced that Phoebe is unhappy at the forced estrangement between her and Mr. Stanhope. Her feelings for him are intense, I am sure of it. It is not made any easier by the fact that Phoebe has a great deal of reserve. To the best of my knowledge, no other man has ever come close to winning her heart. Most of all, I fear there is a danger that if she were permanently separated from Mr. Stanhope, she might never find another man that she could care for in the same way, which would mean her ending her days as a spinster. There is of course nothing wrong with spinsterhood, but I think that for Phoebe —"

"The single state may be a cause of blessedness for some people," remarked Mr. Drummond drily, "but I cannot see that it would be the right kind of life for Miss Hawkins."

The smiles they exchanged were smiles of complicity. Their shared concern for their two friends, and their unspoken decision to do what they could to reconcile Phoebe and Mr. Stanhope, bound them together, completing a pattern that had begun on the night of the storm, and that had been shaped by Louisa's real interest in the work that Mr. Drummond did. For his part, what had begun as admiration had grown into liking and then deepened into love. The realisation that this had happened to him, and the implications of it, made him pull on his oars with unnecessary strength, with the result that he caught a crab and fell backwards over the bench he was sitting on.

Louisa laughed, and extended a hand to help him up. Then she began to speak again of Phoebe's troubles, her resolution strengthened by the support and interest of Mr. Drummond.

"If she were to discover that the grounds upon which her father refused to let her marry Mr. Stanhope were false, or of no real significance, then I suspect that she would go against all her upbringing and her natural feeling for her father, and would defy him in this matter. And," she added defiantly, "I think she would be perfectly right to do so."

CHAPTER TWENTY-SEVEN

Louisa might be happy, but for Phoebe, the day was turning into a nightmare. She moved restlessly among the crowds of people, greeting friends in an abstracted way, cutting others as, lost in thought, she failed to notice or recognise them. Everywhere she seemed to see Mr. Stanhope; glimpsing him across a lawn or through trees or across one of the rooms of the house, she would turn in another direction only to catch sight of him in front of her: at the end of a corridor, walking past a statue, talking and laughing in a group of men.

She told herself that it was ridiculous to think that he was pursuing her, that it was her own thoughts and fancies that were coming after her, but her nerves were in such a state of excitation that this reasoning did her no good at all. Exhausted, she sank down on a Roman marble bench in a secluded knot garden, a relic of the much earlier main garden of the house which Lady Harlow had chosen to preserve. There, crouching down to peer at a clump of minute, pink flowers, was Lady Maria.

Satisfied with what she had found, Lady Maria rose from her knees, dusting down her dress in a careless way. She saw Phoebe and came over to her.

"Why the hunted look? Is some arrogant male of the species in hot pursuit of you? My dear," she added in a worried voice, seeing Phoebe's expression, "I was joking. But if indeed there is some man who is harassing you, tell me and I shall speak to him. Men are such tiresome creatures, the whole race of them."

Phoebe looked round the old-fashioned garden, still expecting to see Mr. Stanhope's tall figure appear from behind one of the rectangular hedges. But there was no one there apart from herself and Lady Maria.

"I suppose you do not care to share with me what is bothering you?" said Lady Maria. "I have a name as a gossip, and it is justly earned, but I am also the soul of discretion when it is necessary."

"It is kind of you, but there is nothing wrong. I'm perfectly all right."

"Perhaps you are affected by the heat."

Phoebe shook her head.

"I suppose it is Mr. Stanhope who is causing all this trouble. I knew him when he was a boy, always wanting to go his own way. His tutors and parents called him a difficult child, one that chose to have things as he liked them, yet I think even then he had a strong sense of what was and wasn't important to him. I should have said he was the very man to suit you, if you are interested in my opinion."

"You are mistaken. Mr. Stanhope and I are not at all suited — and indeed, I don't know why we are talking about that man."

"Then I shall change the subject," said Lady Maria cheerfully. "Do you think Miss Bingley and that pleasant man employed by Mr. Darcy will make a match of it?"

Phoebe, her attention at once diverted from her own troubled thoughts, stared at Maria. "Louisa and Mr. Drummond? Why do you ask me that?"

"I saw them just a little while ago, together in a boat on the lake. I may be a cynic, but I'm no fool and I can tell when a young couple have eyes for no one except one another. Will Mr. and Mrs. Bingley approve of him as a husband for their daughter, that is the question. I suppose she has a tolerably good fortune, and I'm sure that Mr. Drummond has not a penny except what he can earn by his wits. His father is a clergyman with a large family, I believe; he can have few expectations there."

"I am sure that Mr. and Mrs. Bingley care far too much about Louisa's happiness to be concerned about money," Phoebe said, although she was sure of no such thing.

"Such a remark reminds me how young you are. Everyone cares about money. Louisa is a beauty, and could be expected to make a very good marriage. No one could call Mr. Drummond a good catch."

"I do not know how it is between Louisa and Mr. Drummond, Louisa has not spoken about any attachment to me, and if she had, I should not tell you. But I will say that Louisa has had her chances to make what you call a good marriage, and has not taken them. Mr. Drummond is an excellent man and one whom I feel sure will make a success of his profession."

Lady Maria laughed. "Tell that to your Great-aunt Lady Redburn, and see what she has to say about it."

Phoebe gave Lady Maria a direct look. "It is nothing to do with Lady Redburn whom Louisa marries."

"That is irrelevant. She wants anyone within her sphere to be as well-connected as possible, and I can tell you that she will not approve of a match with Mr. Drummond."

"As it happens, Lady Redburn likes Mr. Drummond."

"Lady Redburn likes people in their places. And she won't believe that Mr. Drummond's place could ever be at Miss Bingley's side. Take my advice, warn Miss Bingley to be on her guard, for Lady Redburn is obstinate and overbearing when she feels things are not going just as she wants them to."

Phoebe was finding Lady Maria's bracing personality too much for her at the moment. She rose, gave the slightest of curtsies, and said that she was going to go into the house where it might be cooler. Before Lady Maria could say another word, Phoebe was on her way out of the knot garden and hurrying across an open stretch of lawn, charmingly ornamented with a little Greek temple, to the shelter of the sunken garden.

Where, to her disbelief, she saw Mr. Stanhope, walking alone, bound at any moment to look up and see her. She spun round and, as he called out her name, turned left and hurried into the Harlow Park yew maze, famous for the height and thickness of its hedges and the complexity of its paths.

■ ■ ■ ■

Lady Redburn furled her green parasol, and tapped George Warren smartly on the shoulder with it. He turned round, a scowl on his face, which changed to a smooth smile as he saw who it was.

Lady Redburn ignored his companion, a stocky man with a round head, who looked rather surprised at this interruption, and demanded that Mr. Warren walk with her. He raised his eyebrows at his companion, took his leave of him, and obligingly announced that he was at Lady Redburn's disposal.

They turned into a quiet path, a shady walk which ran between linden trees. Lady Redburn lost not a moment in coming to the point. "Mr. Warren, tell me more about this Mr. Bagot, this friend of yours, this clergyman."

"What is there to say? He holds the living of Lambton, we were at the university together, and I am paying him a visit. He is single, of modest means, the son of another clergyman who hopes to make more of his career than his father did."

"That is very much as I thought." Lady Redburn gave Mr. Warren a shrewd glance from her sharp black eyes. "An ambitious clergyman is all very well, but if his ambitions turn in the direction of making a fortunate marriage, then one must be wary. He seems very eager to ingratiate himself with Miss Bingley, and I assume that her fortune is what draws him to her."

George Warren was silent, feeling sure that Lady Redburn had not come to the end of what she wanted to say.

"Am I to take it that you think such a match would be suitable for your cousin?"

"Not at all," said Warren coolly. "She is not precisely my cousin, we are connected through my stepmother, but no, I would not choose to have Mr. Bagot connected to my family in any closer way than ties of moderate friendship."

"It seems to me that you have been encouraging the man to make advances towards Miss Bingley."

George Warren smiled. An unpleasant smile, with a glint of malice in it. "Miss Bingley is a very complacent young lady, and it is good for her to have to watch what she is about. She dislikes Mr. Bagot, and therefore I find it entertaining to encourage him to pursue her. She would never accept an offer from him, and I am sure that her parents, my dear aunt and uncle, would not countenance such a match even if she liked the fellow."

The look Lady Redburn gave him now was one almost of approval. "This was all done in a spirit of mischief, to stir up a little trouble, to tease Miss Bingley."

"Exactly so."

"You have clearly succeeded to admiration, and I dare say Mr. Bagot will have to learn to bear his disappointment. However, what you will not find so entertaining is the fact that Miss Bingley has met a man whom she does not dislike, and whose attentions she appears to welcome."

"You astonish me. Miss Bingley seems rather a Diana, impervious to her suitors. I should be surprised indeed to find that any man had caught her fancy. Do you refer to someone who lives in Derbyshire? I cannot think who it could be."

"If you kept your eyes open, you would have seen Miss Bingley today at Harlow Park, disporting herself on the lake in the company of Mr. Drummond. Do not mistake me, I think Mr. Drummond an estimable man, and I believe is very good at what he does. He, too, is the son of a vicar, but has no money."

All the amusement had left George Warren's face. "Mr. Drummond? The man who works for Mr. Darcy, digging up his gardens and putting up glasshouses? Marry Miss Bingley? You cannot be serious."

"It is not a matter of whether I am serious or not, Mr. Warren. It is a question of whether Miss Bingley is serious. I am not so old that I cannot see when there is an attraction between a man and a woman, and I assure you that it is the case with Mr. Drummond and Miss Bingley."

"The devil it is," exclaimed Mr. Warren, and then made a quick apology for his language. "That will not do at all, such a marriage would annoy my mother exceedingly. She has never forgiven her brother for marrying Jane Bennet, and I know has always hoped that Louisa, who I have to concede is good-looking, would marry well. Although," he added spitefully, "my stepmother's father, the late Mr. Bingley, made his money in trade. Perhaps his granddaughter is planning to carry on the tradition, by marrying a tradesman."

"I am glad to say that Miss Bingley's connection with the Darcys is a remote one, but even so, I would not care to see Darcy's niece married to a Mr. Drummond. It is true that Mr. Darcy married beneath him, but there is no need to make a family tradition of it."

"I shall write to my mother directly, to warn her of what is afoot. She can speak to her brother, and I'm sure she will be able to convince him that this must be put a stop to, before his daughter throws herself away on this penniless employee of Mr. Darcy's."

"Pray convey my good wishes to Lady Warren, and you have my permission to say that I am deeply concerned to see what trouble Miss Bingley may be getting into."

They had nearly come to the end of the walk, where it debouched into a wider way, a gravel walk lined with classical statues. Lady Redburn stopped beside a grinning Pan. "Perhaps you could enlighten me, before you return to your companion, just why you are in Derbyshire? I cannot believe that Mr. Bagot is such a draw that you would come all this way to see him."

"I needed to be in this part of the world upon an urgent matter of business, and it is more convenient for me to put up with Mr. Bagot rather than stay at an inn."

"More convenient, or more convincing, Mr. Warren?"

"Both," said Mr. Warren shortly.

"A family matter? An amorous affair?"

Lady Redburn's probing questions were impertinent, yet Warren was chary of cutting her short, as he would already have done with most people. She had a knowing look to her, and besides, he wanted to keep in her good books.

"It is private business, I have some loose ends to tie up. My visit relates to certain events that took place during the war years, and I assure you has nothing to do with any member of the Darcy family."

"I am glad to hear it."

Unbeknownst to Phoebe, she was hot on the heels of Louisa, who had reluctantly parted from Mr. Drummond when he finally brought the boat back to the edge of the lake. She knew that to spend the rest of the day in his company, as she longed to do, would arouse comment, and both of them were aware how careful they must be not to become the subject of gossip. Mr. Drummond went towards the house, while Louisa continued her search for Phoebe on that side of the lake. Several people claimed to have seen her, when she made enquiries, and it seemed to Louisa that Phoebe had been everywhere; what was she up to?

A chance remark from a stout woman who was fanning her red face with such energy that Louisa could hardly make out what she was saying directed Louisa towards the knot garden. There, Lady Maria told her that

Phoebe had left her only minutes before, and pointed the way she had gone.

Lady Maria watched in some amusement as the black shovel hat of Mr. Bagot rose from behind the hedge. "My dear Lady Maria, were those the dulcet tones of Miss Bingley I just heard?"

"You have missed her. You look exceedingly hot, Mr. Bagot, pray rest for a moment. There is a bench conveniently situated there under that tulip tree which will serve the purpose."

Mr. Bagot was having none of it. Not hot at all, mild, balmy day, had been sitting too long, would not take up any more of Lady Maria's time, he could see she was absorbed by the beautiful plants . . . and he was gone, leaving Lady Maria looking vastly amused amid the tight hedges and ebullient flowers.

Mr. Bagot had longer legs than Louisa, and he soon spied her walking towards the sunken garden. He increased his pace, calling out to her, and Louisa, who wanted nothing less than to be obliged to endure even five minutes of the wretched clergyman's company, plunged under the yew arch, barely aware that she was entering the famous maze.

She had been through the maze as a child, and had delighted in getting lost, but now she wished she had paid attention to the key. How did she get to the centre, and from there back to the entrance? First right, second left, third right? Or the other way about? In her agitated state, she couldn't remember.

It took some five minutes for her to be hopelessly lost, and at every turn she could hear Mr. Bagot's voice, now louder, now more faint, calling out to her.

Phoebe was puzzled by these fluting calls for Louisa, although only with part of her mind; the rest of her heard footsteps behind her, and she pressed on, certain that it was Mr. Stanhope.

Stop running away, stand still, and talk to him like a grown woman; tell him why you sent him that letter, ask him not to seek you out, make it clear you have nothing to say to him. She didn't trust herself. Face-to-face with him in this pastoral landscape, how could she be sure she would act as her reason told her? And if she didn't, if he once more pressed his suit, told her he loved her, if once again she melted into his kiss, how would her resolve stand up to that? If it didn't, if she succumbed, as her heart would urge her to, how many years of misery might she be bringing down upon herself? Consider how her mother had been affected by one lapse from the straight road of marital fidelity; how would it be if it happened over and over again?

Phoebe had not forgotten the key to the maze, and Louisa was mistaken in thinking it was a regular pattern, for it was more subtle than that. Phoebe could see the whole maze laid out in front of her, as though she were a bird soaring above it and looking down on its twists and turns and cunning undulations. It was a knack she had, and she was never more grateful for it than now, as she flew towards the centre of the maze. From there, she knew a short way out, and would emerge at the other side while her pursuer ran to and fro between the high hedges.

It was with astonishment that she took a turn and found herself running headlong into Louisa. "Good heavens, what are you doing in here, and why are you so distraught? Who is calling your name? Where is Mr. Drummond, why are you alone?"

"It is Mr. Bagot, I didn't want to talk to him —"

As she said these words, Mr. Stanhope stepped into the little clearing. He was, Phoebe noticed with resentment, perfectly cool and composed, as though he had just stepped out of his dressing room, not a wrinkle in his well-fitting coat, not a stain on his pantaloons, his frothy stock a miracle of white perfection. A dandy; a rake and a dandy, a snare for any woman weak enough to be taken in by him.

"Quite right," he was saying to Louisa. "The man is a bore. He approaches, we had best be on our way. Miss Hawkins, I fancy you should be our guide?"

Phoebe had a suspicion that he knew his way around the maze as well as she did, but this was no time to find out. Without another word, she led the way on to a narrow, wavering path, with hardly room for a person to pass, and they were out of sight by the time a panting Mr. Bagot arrived at the spot they had just left. He whirled round, then chose a broader, more inviting path and went on his eager way.

"He will find himself back at the entrance in a trice," said Phoebe, leaning back against the hedge and laughing. "How unwise for a clergyman to choose the broad path instead of the narrow one."

"Destruction instead of salvation," agreed Mr. Stanhope. "Are we nearly at the centre?"

A few more lefts and rights, and they were standing in the clear space at the heart of the maze. It was a charming place, with an antique statue of Aphrodite poised as though about to bathe, above a shell-shaped pool into which the water plashed from a conch shell held aloft by Cupid.

"Ah, Eros and his bows of desire," remarked Stanhope, looking appreciatively at Venus's naked beauty.

Louisa blushed, and Phoebe said tartly, "Love's darts is how the poets describe his weapons."

"Love, desire; Aphrodite rules over both."

"And a lot more besides. Louisa, shall we find our way out of the maze directly?"

"Yes, indeed, there is nothing I want more, what a horrid place it is, so hot and damp and confusing. Mr. Stanhope —"

"Mr. Stanhope may stay and feast his eyes upon the goddess's shapely form, or he may accompany us, it is up to him."

Phoebe felt bolder now that Louisa was at her side. The look she gave Mr. Stanhope was one of defiance, which didn't waver as he looked back at her.

They reached the small exit from the maze in a very few minutes, and there Phoebe, holding on to Louisa's hand, nodded a good-bye to Mr. Stanhope, and set off towards the house at great speed.

"Jack," she cried, hailing her friend with enthusiasm.

He was delighted to see her, had been looking for her, they were going to start the dancing, all informal, no lists, no lining up in order, free and easy was the rule today. Inside the great hall, a group of musicians was striking up a waltz. Jack's hand slid round Phoebe's slim waist, and he twirled her on to the floor.

Mr. Stanhope stood in the doorway, watching the dancers. Phoebe always danced well, for she was light and graceful on her feet and had an instinctive feel for the music. She was well-partnered, she and Jack danced wonderfully together. A man in a claret coat who was standing nearby had noticed it as well, and with a knowing nod of his head, said, "We shall see Mr. Jack and Miss Phoebe wed yet. Their wedding day will be a day to make merry, for they are a handsome couple, and nothing would please their families more than to see them man and wife."

Mr. Stanhope prided himself on keeping a cool head in whatever circumstances he might find himself, but nothing in his life previously had prepared him for the surge of jealousy that swept over him at the stranger's words.

By God, they would not dance and make merry at the wedding of Phoebe and Jack

Harlow, not if he had anything to do with
it.

CHAPTER TWENTY-EIGHT

The next days passed in a whirl of activity for Phoebe, who was too busy to notice Louisa's air of quiet happiness as she helped with the preparations for the ball and, unbeknownst to Phoebe, spent delighted half-hours in Mr. Drummond's company.

The day of the ball dawned. A faint mist hung over the river at Pemberley and curled softly up the lawns and meadows on either side. The sky was a clear pale blue, with the faint outline of the moon, nearly at its full, visible as dawn broke.

The great house was abuzz with activity soon after dawn, as all the servants in the house were up and about before their usual hour of six o'clock. They came yawning and stretching into the servants' hall, pink and sleepy, but already alive with the excitement of the day. M. Joules was in the kitchens, summoning his staff as a general might before a battle. They had been at work for days with the preparations for the day of the ball, and he had now only hours to get ready a dinner of several courses for thirty people, many of them of the highest rank, and a ball supper for four hundred.

In London, Mrs. Darcy would have employed Gunter's to see to the ball supper, but in the country the great houses had to provide all the food themselves. Although the household was large at Pemberley, there were not enough staff to deal with all this extra work, and help had been drafted in from all the villages and towns around.

The unpleasant job of cutting the ice blocks in the ice house, and bringing them up to the house, had fallen to two or three of the brawniest estate workers. It was hard work, hacking at the huge lump of ice, and a messy business, since the ice, cut from the lake in January and hauled up to the ice house to be covered in straw, was thoroughly dirty by this time of year. It would be needed in the kitchens to keep the fresh food cold, and to chill the ices and ice puddings that would be served in the evening.

The work was made harder by the fact that the ceiling of the ice house, plentifully provided with hooks, now had joints of meat, salmon, and turkeys hanging there to keep them fresh. All of these had to be brought up to the house, and more supplies were arriving every minute. Salmon and trout came from the local rivers, but the lobsters, which would be made into patties for the supper, had travelled overnight from the coast.

Mrs. Makepeace was nowhere to be seen. Her duties lay not in the kitchen, or the servants' hall, but upstairs, making sure that everyone staying in the house had everything they needed, and checking and preparing the rooms for the guests who would be arriving during the day.

Sally whisked into the kitchen, and announced that Miss Verney was demanding to know where the children's breakfasts were. "You would think on a morning like this, when everyone is so busy, she would have the courtesy to come down and get it herself. But, oh no, she is far too grand for that, far too much the lady. You know she is to be at the ball this evening, at least she is allowed to put on an evening dress and hover on the landing with the children so that they may see what is going on. I wouldn't be surprised if she didn't go down and mingle with the guests, she is fool enough to do that."

"You better keep your tongue still on that front, Sal," said a passing parlour maid.

"Mrs. Manningtree's maid, that Figgins, says that Lady Mordaunt thinks the world of Miss Verney, and won't hear a word against her. Figgins has no time for her, and nor, she says, do the rest of the staff in Paris. They dislike the way she gives herself such airs. And they say she cannot control the children, who are ill-behaved, and do not mind their manners."

M. Joules came in from the bakehouse, where he had been checking on the baking of a large batch of cheesecakes. With the day already hot, and bidding to become still hotter, the temperature in the bakehouse was not at all comfortable, and perspiration streamed down his forehead as he called for a jug of fresh lemonade to be brought into the kitchen.

Mr. Rutland put in a brief appearance in the servants' hall. He was on constant duty that day, and in his element. He reported on the new arrivals: the Earl and Countess of Earnshaw were come, as were Lord and Lady Rutherford, the Marquis and Marchioness of Lewisham and several other members of the nobility with lesser titles. "Lord and Lady Warren were asked, but declined," he said.

Sally snorted. "Mr. George Warren is quite enough of that family to have around. He waylaid Molly in the corridor just now, and complimented her on her pretty feet. She was that shocked, and set up screeching. She stopped soon enough when Mrs. Makepeace came on the scene and gave her a quick slap. I told her, never mind your feet, it's when the gentlemen start wanting to look at other parts of you that you have to worry."

"And we'll have no coarseness in here, Sally, thank you," said Mrs. Makepeace, coming into the servants' hall to take a quick breakfast. "You just keep your mind on young Colin, and don't go making remarks about Mr. Warren or any other of the guests."

The servants were pleased to see these members of the nobility arriving in their state, but their real pleasure was reserved for the members of the family. They had begun to arrive the day before, when Mr. and Mrs. Wytton with their infant daughter, Hermione, reached Pemberley at midday. Hot on their heels came Mrs. Wytton's younger sister, Alethea, and her husband, Titus Manningtree. Lady Mordaunt had come alone, as Sir Joshua had been too busy with business to attend, and she had, Mrs. Makepeace told the other servants, sat up half the night in her bedchamber talking to her twin sister, Belle. "Miss Alethea, Mrs. Manningtree, I should say, was up at the crack of dawn," she reported, "and is now seated at the pianoforte in the drawing-room, playing away as though she had never left the house at all. That only leaves Mrs. Barcombe, and Mrs. Wytton says that she will be here by this afternoon."

The outdoor gardeners had been up at dawn to cut and bring in the fruit and vegetables from the kitchen garden and the orchards, while the indoor men set about selecting the finest fruits from the glass-houses, and the flowers that had been brought into bloom especially for this day.

Phoebe had given particular directions as to just what flowers she would need, and how they must be cut for the arrangements she had planned. Miniver was put out to find that Phoebe had risen by six o'clock, saying that she would be too tired by the end of the day to enjoy the ball if she rose so early.

Even as she spoke, Miniver knew her words were in vain, and indeed Phoebe, full of energy and enthusiasm, did not look as though anything would tire her. Dressed in an old round gown, she hurried out to supervise the work of the indoor gardeners, and to make sure that the estate carpenters had finished laying the wooden flooring in the new glasshouse, completed only two days before and a gleaming glory which, busy as they were, every servant still stopped to gape at as he or she went past.

From there she went into the flower hothouses, fragrant with the heavy scent of summer flowers, gorgeous with glossy leaves and waxy blooms. The indoor gardeners, quiet and efficient in their big green aprons and gloves, were cutting and sorting and arranging the great armfuls of flowers which would be carried into the house and out to the glasshouse. Phoebe saw Mr. Grayling, and paused to have a word about the flowers for the dinner table before she went outside again to make sure that the roses were coming in from the rose garden.

Louisa found her there, still for a moment, with her face buried in a handful of rose petals. "To me, roses are the very essence of summer," Phoebe said.

Louisa rubbed one of the velvety petals between her fingers. "I like roses, too, but it saddens me the way they are so exquisite in their perfection and then in a moment they turn and fade. And some of the varieties of rose are too sumptuous for my taste. It would never do to have wildflowers in the house or on the tables, but I must say that I prefer the snowdrop or the bluebell to these voluptuous blooms."

"You would be hard done by to find snowdrops in June," said Phoebe drily. "Spring wildflowers are lovely in their way, yes, but I love the glory of hothouse flowers. They seem to suit a ball, which is after all a very artificial affair. The gentle little flowers of wayside and hedgerow can have no place in a ballroom."

They walked back to the house together, passing servants going to and fro, taking chairs from this part of the house to that part of the house, arranging tables on the terrace, maids hurrying past with piles of linen, garden boys making sure that the huge tubs on the terrace to the south of the house were in a state of perfection.

"I came to find you," said Louisa, "to tell you that our uncle and aunt have arrived. Aunt Elizabeth has brought with her armfuls of extraordinary plants, I believe that Mr. Grayling has been summoned to put them in some subtropical part of his glasshouses. Mr. Darcy is, of course, eager to see what has been done in the gardens, and in particular to look over the new glasshouse. Mr. Drummond was on his way there, in a very nervous state."

"It is so beautiful, it is such an extraordinary structure that Mr. Darcy must be pleased. I am sure there is nothing like it in the whole of England, and it will set quite a fashion."

"It will seem extraordinary to be dancing in there tonight. It is an original idea, and should be charming if the weather holds," said Louisa, her mind still on Mr. Drummond.

Both of them looked up into a cloudless blue sky. It was a perfect June day, with the slightest breezes ruffling the leaves and the grass. "Mr. Grayling swears it will hold fine, he says we are in for a spell of warm weather which will last for several days yet."

"So as long as the moon remembers to rise," said Phoebe gaily, "we shall do very well in the glasshouse."

Louisa looked over to the glasshouse, struck anew by how wonderful it was. "It is fortunate that it is not considered unlucky to gaze at the full moon through glass, as is the superstition with the new moon."

As the day went on, Phoebe had no time for any kind of superstition. She was far too busy, anxious that all her arrangements should work, and that her aunt and uncle would be pleased with what she had done.

Mr. Tetbury had arrived from London the previous day, and was at her shoulder with his lists and his practical advice and his considerable skill in organising large parties. She liked him immensely. He was a thin, nervous-looking young man who had been intended for the Church but, having no kind of religious inclination, had instead sought to make a living in this way.

Phoebe admired his prodigious memory, his clear mind, and his eye for details. At a glance, he could tell exactly how many candles would be needed at this time of year in the dining room, in the drawing-rooms, and on the terraces. "It was a stroke of genius, if I may say so, Miss Hawkins, to utilise the new glasshouse, with the ballroom in such disrepair after the storm. Mr. Drummond has spoken to Mr. Darcy about it, and they have agreed that this will be a good opportunity to remodel the ballroom in a more modern style. Mrs. Darcy felt that in any case it was looking rather shabby. The plan is to have doors opening into the orangery, which will be charming."

"Yes, and when the guests to Pemberley have become used to dancing under glass, as they will tonight," said Phoebe, "then they will be happy to find that next time they will be able to waltz among the orange trees. Which reminds me, I forgot that I wanted the men to take some of the orange plants from the orangery into the glasshouse. Now the flooring is down, it looks very beautiful but very empty, and apart from the flowers, I think it would look well to have some of the larger plants. Oranges, lemons, and perhaps some of the potted palms that are in the old glasshouses."

Mr. Tetbury pulled out a black notebook. "Let me attend to that for you. You have other things to do, I know, and you have also your social obligations to think of. I believe the lady and gentleman over there are wanting to attract your attention, I think they wish to speak to you. That is Mr. Portal, is it not?"

With an exclamation of pleasure, Phoebe turned round and went over to where Pagoda Portal and Mrs. Rowan were standing beneath the bust of a Roman gentleman with eyeless sockets and a large, beaky nose. They greeted her with their customary kindness, and Mrs. Rowan said, in her direct way, that she was glad to see Phoebe in looks once more.

"I am rather flushed just at present, for I have been very busy today. When did you arrive? Did you have a good journey? There are so many friends here, you will find yourselves in excellent company."

"Indeed we shall," said Pagoda Portal. "We have only just this minute left Cassandra, she and Horatio drove down from London with the Rutherfords. Now here are still more arrivals, I suspect they are another neighbouring family who have been invited to come early so that the gentlemen may enjoy some fishing."

"Will you be among their number, Mr. Portal?"

Mrs. Rowan gave Pagoda an affectionate look. "Alas, Mr. Portal is not a fisherman. He has been known to take out a rod, but I must say the results were disastrous, since he and the line and the fly and the fish all became entangled upon the bank. That kind of behaviour does not make you popular with your fellow fishermen, for those gentlemen take their fishing seriously, and since then he leaves others to their riparian sports."

"I'm not the only one who finds standing upon a river bank wrestling with a fish a dull way to spend an afternoon," observed Mr. Portal. "Here are the Martindales, and while I feel quite sure that Sir Henry will join the fishing party, I am equally sure that Mr. Stanhope will not."

Phoebe could not help starting at the

sound of his name, and Mrs. Rowan, quick to notice such things, gave her a sharp look. "I know that you are acquainted with Mr. Stanhope, for we had the pleasure of entertaining you both at one or two of my parties in London. Have you seen much of him while he has been in Derbyshire? It is extraordinary that he should be in this part of the world, for it is well-known that he dislikes the country."

What could Phoebe reply to the civil enquiry? How could she say that no, she had been at extreme pains to avoid his company, and that, as though to make her more miserable, he seemed determined to seek her out?

"He has dined here, and he was present at the Harlows' fête a few days ago, but otherwise we have been so busy with preparations for the ball that Louisa and I have not been very sociable."

"Unlike Lady Redburn, I notice," said Mrs. Rowan with a wry smile. "What on earth possessed her to ask Mr. Warren to stay, for I am sure that she did so? I cannot believe that either you, Phoebe, or Miss Bingley would have done so, although of course he is Louisa's cousin, and perhaps she likes him."

"I cannot think so ill of Miss Bingley,"

said Mr. Portal forthrightly. "I don't care whose cousin he is, the man is a scrub, with no morals or scruples that I was ever aware of. Why is he in Derbyshire? That is an even more interesting question than why Mr. Stanhope is here. After all, Stanhope's sister lives in these parts, I never heard that Warren had any relations up here."

"Mr. Warren has been staying with the vicar of Lambton, a Mr. Bagot."

"What? That must be Walter Bagot's son. His father was one of those pinching, parsimonious parsons. He spent some time in India, and we were all very relieved when the climate proved too much for him and he returned to bore people in England with his preaching. And so now his son has the living of Lambton, does he? Let us hope that he is a better man than his father."

"He is a lengthy preacher," said Phoebe. A twinkle came into her eyes. "He fancies he would like to make a match of it with Louisa Bingley. However, he will be unlucky, for she can't bear him."

"That'll be Warren up to his mischief again, although it seems a minor kind of intrigue for him, he usually hunts bigger game. He must have some ulterior purpose in coming here, perhaps I shall make it my business to find out what it is." He lifted a hand and called out, "Stanhope! Arthur, come over here, I have a question to ask you."

Phoebe at once started to move away, but Mrs. Rowan put out a hand to restrain her. She said in a quiet voice, "Phoebe, my dear, there has to be an end to running away, you know."

Phoebe turned her eyes to the ground, resolutely refusing to look at Mr. Stanhope. She was torn between the inexpressible pleasure of his presence, and the rage that rekindled in her when she thought of him and Mrs. Vereker. He was talking to Mr. Portal, but his eyes kept sliding towards Phoebe.

"Warren? I agree with you, Pagoda, he's up to something, and I begin to think that I have a very fair idea what it may be. If I am right, it is even more dastardly and despicable than anything he has done before, and I'm afraid it might well bring a considerable scandal upon his family."

Phoebe started at this. "I hope not," she exclaimed. "Louisa, Miss Bingley, that is, is a close connection of his, for her aunt is his stepmother. The Bingleys would not be happy at all were there to be a scandal in that direction."

"Pooh," said Mr. Portal. "Lord Warren has

been embroiled in a good few scandals of his own, there is much in his life that won't bear close investigation. I doubt if another one will bother the Warrens overmuch, Stanhope."

"This one will. I am trying to think of a way that will prevent it ever becoming publicly known, but it may be hard to do with the persons involved."

CHAPTER TWENTY-NINE

What was he talking about? His voice was grim, and very serious; she had never seen him look like that before. He was no longer looking at Phoebe, but had drawn Mr. Portal aside, and was talking to him in a low voice. Henrietta Rowan put her arm through Phoebe's and said, "Now, you will want to show me this miraculous glasshouse that everyone is talking about. If you can spare the time from your numerous duties, let us walk outside and you can take me there."

Phoebe did not know how to refuse, although she would rather have done so, since she had a very good idea that Mrs. Rowan was keen to broach the one subject that she did not want to discuss. Sure enough, as they went down the wide steps to the parterre, Mrs. Rowan began to talk about Mr. Stanhope. "I will be quite blunt with you, Phoebe, and you must not mind me, for it is my way. I know that you were very much attracted to Mr. Stanhope, and it is obvious to me, as it must be to many others, that he is head over heels in love with you. What are you playing at? What has happened for you to throw this wall up against him? He's not a man to play fast and loose with, surely you must see that."

Phoebe shook her head. "It is kind of you to be so concerned with my interests, Mrs. Rowan, but there is really nothing to tell you."

"If that is meant as a rebuke to me, I shall take no notice of it. I am not so easy to quell as that, Phoebe, nor am I such a fool as not to notice that you are still powerfully attracted to Mr. Stanhope, deny it as you may. Good heavens, what are you thinking of? Do you imagine that men like Arthur Stanhope grow on trees? The chances are that such a man will never come your way again. I never saw a pair more suited to one another, what is the matter with you?"

"My father cares neither for Mr. Stanhope nor for the idea of a match between us. Not that there is any question of a marriage, for I wouldn't marry Mr. Stanhope if he were the only man left single in England."

"That is a nonsensical thing to say, and you know it. Why, what has he done to cause you such deep offence?"

Phoebe wished the ground would open up and swallow her. Mrs. Rowan was too forceful, the question too direct. She felt unable to defend herself, and she knew it would be childish to give in to the impulse to shout at Mrs. Rowan, to stamp an angry foot and ask her to mind her own business, to say that Mrs. Rowan had no understanding at all of the situation, and then to turn tail and run. Instead, she increased her pace. "If we turn down this path here, then we come upon the glasshouse, as it were unexpectedly, and it is an excellent way to get a first view of it."

This tactic worked, and the sight of the extraordinary glasshouse struck Mrs. Rowan into silence. She stood and stared, and then, shaking her head, said, "I would not have believed it. I have never seen anything like it, it is beyond one's wildest imaginings. All that glass, those curves and that dome, gleaming in the sunlight, it is a glass palace from a fairy story. There needs to be a Cinderella with a glass slipper, and a Prince Charming, don't you think?"

Phoebe said, more prosaically, "After tonight, many of the more tender and exotic plants will be moved in there, and the gardeners will set about making the pineapple pits. Mr. Drummond, who is largely responsible for its construction, says that palm trees will grow to a considerable height. It will be a subtropical garden for my aunt."

They went into the glasshouse, and walked up and down its length, while Phoebe explained the principles of its construction and Mrs. Rowan gazed up through the glass panes.

"Observe the ironwork, so beautifully done, and so intricate. It is a remarkable feat to build a structure like this."

"The idea of a large glasshouse was Mr. Darcy's," said Phoebe. "But the design, and the understanding of how it must be built, is Mr. Drummond's."

"Is he still here? I must go and find Mr. Portal and bring him here to see this, and then I know he will wish to talk to Mr. Drummond. How I should like to have such a structure in our grounds at Richmond, although there, of course, it would have to be on a smaller scale. It needs a house as magnificent as Pemberley to provide a backdrop for a glasshouse like this."

As Phoebe had hoped, the marvel of the glasshouse had quite taken Mrs. Rowan's mind off the subject of Mr. Stanhope. She took the first opportunity she could to say that she had to go back into the house, as there were many things she had to see to. "If I see Mr. Portal, I shall direct him to the glasshouse."

"However, we haven't quite finished our conversation."

"I have nothing further to say on the subject of Mr. Stanhope," said Phoebe firmly. "I will allow that there was a time when I was inclined to" — she sought for the right word — "welcome Mr. Stanhope's attentions. That is no longer the case, and I beg that we do not talk about this subject any longer."

Mrs. Rowan, as though acknowledging defeat, smiled, and they walked back along the path. Phoebe saw two figures in the distance, deep in conversation. "That is Mr. Drummond there, with Louisa Bingley."

Mrs. Rowan had eyes as sharp as her understanding, and one glance told her how things were between Louisa and Mr. Drummond. "Good heavens," she said. "What will Mr. and Mrs. Bingley say to that?"

"Say to what?" said Phoebe.

"Well, if you can't see how things are between them, then you must be a greater fool than I took you for. Surely you cannot be so wound up in your own affairs that you do not notice another couple who find a great deal of pleasure in each other's company? What is his family, what is his fortune?"

Unaware that he was under scrutiny, Mr. Drummond was at that very moment proposing to Louisa Bingley. He took both her hands in his, and was looking deeply into her eyes. "It may seem very wrong, Miss Bingley, dearest Louisa, for me to ask you to be my wife. I do not have the position in society, nor the estate nor the fortune, that a young lady in your position has the right to expect. I cannot help myself, I am in love with you, and I cannot imagine life without you."

Louisa, a look in her eyes that answered him before she spoke a word in reply, put out a hand and touched his cheek. "Fortune and estates mean nothing to me. I can imagine no greater happiness than being your wife. I have money of my own, and I'm quite sure that you will make such a success of your profession that everyone will say how lucky I am, and what an excellent marriage I have made."

Mr. Drummond, suddenly aware in how public a place they were standing, bit his lip, and with his hand on her elbow, guided her into a more secluded part of the shrubbery.

Mrs. Rowan gave a little sigh of satisfaction. "If Louisa Bingley is to go kissing Mr. Drummond in the shrubbery, she must be very sure what she is about. She would not wish to see Mr. Drummond dismissed from Mr. Darcy's service, I feel sure. Do her parents have any idea of this romance?"

"Mr. and Mrs. Bingley have not yet arrived. Louisa met Mr. Drummond for the first time when she came to Pemberley, so there is no way they can be acquainted with him, and she will have been circumspect in her letters to them, she will hardly have mentioned him."

"She has had three seasons in London, has she not? It is astonishing that she has not married already, for she has much of her mother's beauty. Will her parents be able to persuade her out of the match, if they wish to do so?"

"Louisa is a gentle creature in many ways," said Phoebe, "but once she has given her heart and her word, I truly think nothing will sway her."

"Let us hope her parents have the sense to recognise that, and like Mr. Drummond for what he is, instead of regretting what he is not. Do you like him? Is he an honourable man, apart from being an excellent designer of glasshouses?"

"I like him very much indeed. He is a most amiable man, and just the kind of person to make Louisa a good husband. She will take a great interest in his profession, and he will take great care of her."

"It sounds rather an insipid arrangement to me," said Mrs. Rowan. "But I am not the person to talk about marriage, for I married an eccentric and a traveller, which was exactly what I needed and wanted. You would never be happy with such a man as Mr. Drummond, Phoebe. He is a capable man, it is true, and a man of character, but you need to marry a clever man who moves in a wider sphere. There are not so many of those in a world full of dull and stupid men, and you would do well to consider that."

Was there no way to get the talk away from Mr. Stanhope? It was with great relief that Phoebe saw Mr. Grayling bearing down on them, a frown upon his face, and a query as to the exact way in which she wanted the lilies arranged. With a word of apology and a curtsy, Phoebe took her leave of Mrs. Rowan, thankful to escape, and set about reassuring Mr. Grayling that what she had planned, although not quite in the usual style, would be very striking and just right for the surroundings.

Mr. Stanhope had expected Sir Henry to join the men who were going fishing, for he was extremely fond of the sport, and the river at Pemberley was a favourite with the fishermen. So it was with some surprise that he saw his brother-in-law detach himself from the group of gentlemen advancing over the lawn with fishing rods, and, with what appeared to be a rather furtive look around, head back into the house.

Mr. Stanhope followed him, wondering what he was up to. He felt pretty sure in his own mind that he knew exactly where Sir Henry would be going, which was to a part of the house that he had not seen when Louisa Bingley showed him round.

Sure enough, Sir Henry went up the main staircase, and then on up a further flight to the second floor. There after another look round, while Mr. Stanhope pressed himself into a doorway, Sir Henry went on up a steep flight of stairs to a higher floor. Mr. Stanhope was just setting off after him again, when a maid came out of the door and stopped, astonished at the sight of him. She gave a bob as she said, "I think you are lost, sir."

Not a jot abashed, Mr. Stanhope replied

that no, he wasn't lost, but merely wanted to make his way to the nurseries, as he thought that Mrs. Barcombe might be up there.

The maid looked at him doubtfully, and said that she didn't believe that Mrs. Barcombe was there, but if he wished to see for himself, then he should keep going up the stairs and turn right at the top. "Not to the left, sir, that's where the governess has her rooms."

Just as Mr. Stanhope had thought. He moved quickly up the stairs, and at the top he turned left. There was Henry, hovering outside a closed door, looking thoroughly ill at ease.

Mr. Stanhope felt it was time to make his presence known. "Henry," he called out in a loud, cheerful voice. Sir Henry jumped, and whipped round, alarm spreading across his face. "Arthur! What the devil are you doing here?"

"I might ask the same question of you."

Sir Henry tugged at the stock tied around his neck, as though it were choking him. "I — I think I took a wrong turning. I was intending to go to the, er, the library."

"Which is, if my recollection serves me correctly, on the first floor. Had you availed yourself of a tour around the house so kindly provided by Miss Bingley, you would have known where the library was. You will forgive me if I say that you were an exceedingly bad liar, Henry. I have a very good notion why you are here, and it has nothing to do with finding a book. Not that you are, as far as I know, much given to reading books."

Sir Henry shot him a look of intense dislike. "Arthur, I beg that you will go away. You do not know what harm you may do me by being here."

"I think, on the contrary, that it is time this whole business came to an end, Henry. You are making my sister miserable, and really there is no need for all this intrigue and pretence."

With these words he strode forward, and before Sir Henry could protest, he turned the handle of the door and pushed it open. The two men stood in the doorway, looking upon a scene which must be embarrassing for them, if not to the participants. Miss Verney lay on the bed in a state of considerable dishabille. One bare foot dangled over the end of a narrow bed, and George Warren, on his knees, had his lips pressed to the arch of this pretty foot.

"Good God, what is this?" said Sir Henry. He tried to pull Stanhope back from the door, but Stanhope shook him off. "This is no time for prudery, Henry." He shut the door behind them with a bang. By now, Warren had got to his feet, and flushed with anger, he glared at Stanhope and Sir Henry. "What the devil do you mean by bursting in like this?"

"If Miss Verney would care to arrange her clothing, I think we might all sit down and have an interesting discussion," said Mr. Stanhope in a cool voice.

Miss Verney did not seem in any way put out by being discovered in this state by the two men. She calmly pulled her dress up from her bare shoulder and reached out for a shawl. "Well, gentlemen? To what do we owe the honour of this visitation?"

"When I saw you here," said Mr. Stanhope, "I did not at first recognise you. Your face seemed familiar to me, but it was not until later that I recalled where I had seen you before. After Waterloo, I was sent to our embassy in Paris, with the Duke of Wellington. My particular responsibility was on the intelligence side, and one of my tasks was to find out where certain leaks of highly sensitive matters had come from. We knew that an Englishman was involved, and we found out that he had been working with a member of one of the French émigré families, who had settled in London after the revolution. While the popular view is that all these families detested Napoleon, the truth is that some of the younger members of this family chose to throw their lot in with Bonaparte. We assumed we were looking for a man, but from information that was laid before us, and some skilful investigative work, we discovered that it was a woman, not a man."

Miss Verney fiddled with a tassel on her shawl. Her eyes were pools of darkness, and the look she gave Mr. Stanhope was both amused and sensuous. "You cannot blame me, I was not the one who stole the secrets. You need to look closer to home for that, among your own kind, Mr. Stanhope."

Sir Henry gave a kind of howl, and Mr. Stanhope turned to him with some surprise.

"I beg, Arthur, that you do not go into this any further. I had no idea you knew so much. I have gone to great pains to cover up the involvement of my sister's son in this despicable episode, for I knew it would break my sister's heart were she ever to discover that Charles had betrayed his country."

"You're a perfect fool, Henry. Charles Harlow never betrayed anyone. A truer, more gallant soldier never existed. He served his country, and died for it."

"That's not the story that Miss Verney will tell," observed George Warren dispassionately. "You'll find that Sir Henry has been willing to pay a considerable price to have the shameful details kept from public knowledge."

"I do not care to ask just how much you have already paid to Miss Verney, Henry."

Sir Henry coloured, and muttered something inaudible.

"As it happens, you have spent your money unnecessarily. Yes, it was a so-called English gentleman who betrayed his country and sold its secrets, but the man who did this was not Charles Harlow, but the man you see standing before you now."

Sir Henry looked at Mr. Stanhope in complete disbelief. "But his father is Lord Warren, it is impossible. Besides, Warren was never in the army."

"I would think the better of him if he had been," was the laconic answer. "But Mr. Warren is not the kind of man to put his own life in danger. How he came by the secrets I do not know. Given his predilection for blackmail, one may only guess. However, once I was alerted to the presence of George Warren in the vicinity, and I saw him together with Miss Verney at the

Harlows' fête, my suspicions were aroused. A letter to London brought a speedy response, and I can tell you with certainty that Mr. Warren, and not Charles Harlow, was responsible for the breach in our security."

Even as he spoke, Miss Verney was sliding from her bed, and with swift grace began to put on a travelling dress. "I think it very unlikely that you will be able to prove anything," she told Mr. Stanhope in completely calm tones. "George, do not stand there with your mouth gaping, it will do no good. I think it is time for us to leave Derbyshire."

"You are mistaken," said Mr. Stanhope. "The time has come for Mr. Warren to leave England, and to leave England for good. I dare say you, Miss Verney, will go with him, and good riddance to both of you; you make a fine pair."

CHAPTER THIRTY

It was late in the afternoon when Miniver finally chivvied Phoebe back indoors to change for dinner and the ball. "There is everyone else gone upstairs to dress an hour ago, and guests will be arriving for dinner at any minute, and here you are looking like you've been dragged through a hedge backwards. Miss Louisa went upstairs quite half an hour ago, and she's not in anything like the state that you are. Although she looks completely moonstruck, I can't think what's come over her. Betsy was speaking to her and I don't think she heard a word she said. Got something on her mind, has Miss Louisa."

Three quarters of an hour later, Phoebe was ready to go down to dinner. She was dreading it, and her sense of apprehension was increased by the knowledge that her parents were at Pemberley, for Sarah had come bounding into her bedchamber to announce her arrival, and to tell her that she had a new dress to wear for the ball tonight of pale pink satin adorned with little knots of cornflowers. "What are you wearing, Phoebe? Oh, one of the dresses you had made in London. And roses for your hair. How pretty!"

Until the last minute, Phoebe had hoped against hope that her parents would not be able to come to the ball. When last she heard from her mother, it had seemed unlikely that they would make the journey from London, but here was Sarah, full of talk of her dances and parties and successes, and with a great deal to say about a young man called James. "He will be here tonight, and you will be able to meet him. He is staying with the Harlows, and he has asked me to keep the first dance for him. Who are you going to dance with? Have you many beaux in Derbyshire? Or has it been very quiet? I am sure all the eligible men must be in London."

She rattled on, while Miniver deftly dressed Phoebe's hair. She drew it back from her forehead, and set the wreath of fresh roses among the dark curls. "That is a very becoming style," observed Sarah, "but won't the roses wither and droop during the evening?"

"I have two more made up," said Miniver. "Fresh flowers are right for a summer ball in the country."

"And they match the clusters of roses on your lace hem," said Sarah approvingly.

Phoebe was dressed entirely in white, except for the dash of colour from the silk roses set into the flounces of her dress. Although her face was still inclined to be pale, the country air and sunshine had given colour to her cheeks, increased not by the excitement of the ball, but rather alarm as to what she feared was going to be a difficult evening. She felt sure that Mr. Stanhope would once again attempt to have a private conversation with her and she was determined not to give him the opportunity. Apart from not wanting to talk to him, what would be her parents' reaction, if they saw him with her?

Miniver told Sarah to run along. "One of your earrings is loose and you must fix it if you don't want to lose it." When she had gone, she told Phoebe that there was nothing wrong with Sarah's earring. "You take a few minutes to sit down and compose yourself. What a way to carry on before a ball, running around all day, like one of the servants."

"I prefer to be busy," said Phoebe. She

looked at her reflection in the glass and pulled a face.

"There's no need to go grimacing at yourself like that, Miss Phoebe. What's the point of my making all this effort to turn you out looking a beauty, if you're going to make faces like that?"

"I am grateful, Miniver, for all your trouble," said Phoebe. "Although, to be honest, I shall be very glad when this evening is over."

"Many a young lady has said that before you, and found out before the moon set that her life had changed," said Miniver cryptically.

Phoebe and Louisa went downstairs together. There was already quite a crowd assembled in the drawing-room, and Phoebe was greeted with affection by her family and by many old friends. She did everything she could to keep on the opposite side of the room to Mr. Stanhope, but was thwarted when the time came for her to go in to dinner. He was at her side and holding out an arm for her to take, and it would have been noticeable if she had drawn back.

She was acutely aware of her mother's pursed lips, and the grave look on her father's face as they saw her go into dinner with Mr. Stanhope. Good heavens, if only they knew how little she wanted to be beside him, and she was profoundly grateful to find that Mr. Portal was seated on her other side.

Dinner was served in the state dining room. It looked its best with the table gleaming with silver and crystal, and the ravishing display of flowers that tumbled from a deep silver dish in the centre of the table. At the head of the table was a tall silver chalice piled high with cherries and strawberries, and at the other end, a matching silver dish held a magnificent pineapple. M. Joules had surpassed himself, and Phoebe, who had expected to be able to eat nothing, was surprised to find how hungry she was. She had been so occupied during the whole long day that she had not paused to take any of the fruit and cold meats that had been laid out for lunch, and now she set to with a will. Asparagus was followed by salmon with cucumber. Chicken cream and fillet of beef à l'Espagnole came next, served with potatoes and spinach, and then turkey poults and ducks with green peas.

In the first half of the meal she talked resolutely to Mr. Portal, but then, as the guests turned to talk to the people on their other side, she was obliged to make conversation with Mr. Stanhope. She passed remarks about the weather, the number of guests, the works that had been done following the damage of the storm, until finally she ran out of words.

He seemed amused, smiling at her in a way that had made her heart turn over. How could he look at her like that, and mean nothing by it? That, of course, was what made a man into a rake. If he had no charm, no power to attract, then he would hardly enjoy the success among the opposite sex that would win him the reputation of being a rake.

She was further made uncomfortable by where she was sitting, which was directly opposite one of the great classical paintings of Pemberley. It depicted a pastoral scene, an Arcadian landscape. The god Apollo, wearing very little but looking extremely noble, was depicted in hot pursuit of Daphne, who was wearing even less, with her hair flowing behind her. It was an extremely sensuous painting, and when Phoebe saw that Mr. Stanhope had noticed it and his lips were twitching, she was furious to find that she was blushing.

"A fine painting, would you not agree, Miss Hawkins? A Poussin if I'm not mistaken."

Mr. Portal, whose neighbour on the other side was deep in conversation with Sir

Henry Martindale, joined in their conversation. "I never can remember these mythological stories; it comes from my being sent away to India at such an early age, which left me sadly ignorant of the classics. I am sure you, Miss Phoebe, who have studied Latin and know about such things, can tell me the story."

He looked at her expectantly, and Phoebe reluctantly explained that the god Apollo, having been pierced by an arrow from Cupid's bow, had fallen in love with the nymph Daphne. "She did not welcome his advances, and you may see that at the moment shown in this scene, in her desperate attempts to escape from him, she has called upon her father, a river god, to turn her into a tree. She will become a laurel tree, and as a token of the love felt for her, Apollo will take the laurel as his particular emblem."

"An admirable account," said Mr. Stanhope. "Some people question the advantages of education for women, but I myself think everyone in possession of their wits should have the benefit of some classical learning. I feel sorry for Daphne, do not you, Miss Hawkins? I think it might be rather painful to be turned into a tree, and I think she would have done far better to submit to Apollo. After all, the story tells us that she was his first love, and that he was no such philandering fellow as his sire Zeus was. I feel sorry for him, also, to be rejected in such a very forceful manner. One wonders what he had done to offend her."

"I do not think she was offended, I think she did not care for him, and no doubt had a very good idea that, like most of his kind, his love for her would not be lasting. Myself, I think she was better off as a tree."

With that, she tucked into an iced pudding, keeping her head down, and, gauche though she knew her behaviour was, refused to say another word to Mr. Stanhope, restricting her words to Mr. Portal.

Dinner finished at about ten o'clock, and the ladies withdrew. Soon, guests would be arriving for the ball, which was due to start at eleven. Back in the great drawing-room, Phoebe was called over by her mother, who was seated on a small sofa.

"I was very distressed to see you sitting next to Mr. Stanhope at dinner," Lady Hawkins began. "Your father asked him to have no contact with you, and indeed imposed the same restriction upon you."

"I assure you, Mama, it was not by any desire of mine that Mr. Stanhope was seated next to me. I have made every effort to avoid seeing him, and short of absolute rudeness, which might cause some comment, I cannot do more."

Across the drawing-room, Phoebe could see Louisa making urgent signs at her. She was only too ready to leave her mother, and took the opportunity to do so when Lady Redburn approached Lady Hawkins, saying in her loud, authoritative way, "Ah, Georgiana, a word or two with you."

Phoebe did not care to think what malicious words these might be; she was more concerned with Louisa, who looked extremely agitated. She drew her towards a window seat, where they could be private. "What ever is the matter?" Phoebe asked.

Louisa pressed her hands to her cheek as though to push back the blush that suffused her face. "I have not been completely frank with you, Phoebe. I did not tell you that Mr. Drummond has asked me to marry him, and I said I would. He planned to ask my father for his consent this evening, if he could find time to be alone with him. But I have learned from my mother that she and my father already knew about the attachment between myself and Mr. Drummond."

Phoebe stared at her. "How is this possible? You have been very secretive, you have not said a word of this to anyone, and although I noticed that you liked Mr.

Drummond more than a little, I have not breathed a word of it to anyone."

"I know just how my parents came to hear of it, for they told me. It was my Aunt Caroline who warned them. She called on my parents, not two days ago, to say that I was in danger of making a fool of myself, and should be got away from Pemberley as quickly as possible. She told them that the man in question must be considered wholly unacceptable, and she was sure that my father would put a stop to it as soon as he had all the details."

Phoebe made a sound of exasperation. "I do not wish to be critical of your Aunt Caroline, but it seems to me that she is meddling in something that is none of her business. She had it from Mr. Warren, of course, there is nothing in the world that that man likes better than to make trouble. But surely your father is a man of too much sense to listen to that kind of malicious gossip?"

"Thank goodness, he is. He listened to what Aunt Caroline had to say, and then discussed it with my mother, and both of them agreed that they would make no judgements until they had come to Pemberley themselves and ascertained what the situation was. They taxed me with it, and I made a clean breast of what had happened. And," she went on, her chin going up in a rare gesture of defiance, "I've told them that, whatever they may say, I intend to marry Mr. Drummond."

This was a Louisa that Phoebe had never seen before. Of course, Louisa was of age, and could marry whom she pleased, but the old Louisa would have thought long and hard before going against her parents' wishes. "It's amazing that you would contemplate defying your father," she said.

"It hasn't come to that, fortunately. My father told me just before we went into dinner that he had spoken to Mr. Darcy, who speaks so highly of Mr. Drummond, praising his character and his abilities, that my father is already well disposed to him."

"So Mr. Darcy would not disapprove of such a match?"

"Mr. Darcy says that it is none of his business, but that my Aunt Caroline's suggestion that once he heard what Mr. Drummond had been up to, he would instantly dismiss him, is far off the mark. I managed to snatch a moment with Mr. Drummond; he is resolute, and will speak to my father as soon as he can. I am sure it will work out all right, and that by the end of the evening, I will be able to proclaim myself an engaged woman, knowing that I am marrying the best man in the world. Oh, Phoebe, I only wish that you could be as happy as I am."

Phoebe was delighted at Louise's news, and her pleasure in her friend's happiness gave an extra glow to her own looks.

A glow that vanished as she walked a few minutes later into the ballroom, and saw Mr. Stanhope deep in conversation with Mrs. Vereker.

Her hand flew to her mouth, and she found it almost impossible to draw a breath. She reached out a hand to support herself, and found her arm firmly held by Mr. Portal. "Whatever is the matter? You are ill, let me fetch help."

"No," said Phoebe in a voice that seemed to come from very far away, "I am not ill. I have just had a shock. I shall be perfectly well in a minute or two, please do not concern yourself with me."

Mr. Portal guided her towards a little sofa. He made her sit down, and, spreading the tails of his coat, sat down beside her. It was a spindly piece of furniture, with gilt legs, and it creaked ominously as he settled himself. "I know exactly what has put you into this state," he said in the calmest of voices. "You have just noticed Arthur Stanhope talking to Lady Caltrop."

411

"Mr. Stanhope is not talking to Lady Caltrop, whoever she may be. He is talking to Mrs. Vereker. His long-time mistress," she added with contempt. "I cannot think what she is doing here, her name was most certainly not among those invited, for I wrote the invitations myself."

"I cannot believe that Lord and Lady Caltrop would be present at a ball at Pemberley had they not been invited."

Phoebe rested her head in her hands. "Yes, you are right, Lord and Lady Caltrop were on the list of those to be sent invitations. But that has nothing to do with Mrs. Vereker. I do not know why you are talking about the Caltrops, I do not know who they are, nor do I wish to."

"Mrs. Vereker, who is, as you may know, a widow, did Lord Caltrop the honour of becoming his wife a little while ago. They were married, to be precise, on the tenth of April. I know this, for I was present at the ceremony, which took place at St. George's Church."

The tenth of April was a date etched on Phoebe's heart, for that was the day that she had seen Mrs. Vereker leaving Mr. Stanhope's house, and the day that she had written the letter to Mr. Stanhope breaking off all contact with him. "It is impossible! I saw

Mr. Stanhope and Mrs. Vereker together on that very day, she was coming down the steps of his house."

"I dare say you did," said Mr. Portal. "He mentioned to me that she had called at his house that morning, for he had a wedding present for her. It was a particularly fine jewel that he wished to give her, as a token of the happiness she had brought him in the time that they had been together. You may be an unmarried young lady, Miss Hawkins, but you cannot shut your eyes to the realities of the world. Mr. Stanhope and Mrs. Vereker had a long-lasting liaison, which was generally known. It was frowned upon by sticklers, and accepted by everyone else. It ended amicably on both sides, as such affairs generally do, and I dare say they will always remain on good terms."

"So she had the chance to marry a nobleman, and, one may suppose, a rich one, and took it. It does not mean that his feelings for her have lessened, or, if she has moved out of his life, that he will not simply find another Mrs. Vereker, a new mistress."

"Don't be prudish, Miss Hawkins. It does not become you, and you are too intelligent to indulge in that kind of prosaic thinking. Whatever you may have heard, Mr. Stanhope is not a rake. All the time he was carrying on his affair with Mrs. Vereker, there was never any suggestion that he was also enjoying the favours of other women."

He patted her hand and got up. "There, you are looking a better colour. My advice to you, and please note that I rarely give advice, so it is worth taking when I do, is that you seek out Mr. Stanhope and have a proper conversation with him. I think it will clear up many misunderstandings, and you owe him no less, even if you do decide not to follow the instincts of your heart, but instead to separate yourself from him for good."

CHAPTER THIRTY-ONE

Phoebe sat for a long time on the sofa, thoughts buzzing through her head. At first, she was inclined to dismiss everything Mr. Portal had told her, but sense came to her rescue, and she had to accept that it was as he had said. At least, as far as Mrs. Vereker marrying Lord Caltrop was concerned. But how could he speak with such authority as to Mr. Stanhope's feelings? How could he know that the liaison between Mr. Stanhope and Mrs. Vereker had come to an end? Lord Caltrop might prove to be a complacent husband, and Mrs. Vereker an unfaithful wife, happy to continue her relationship with her former lover.

Masculine footsteps, and there, standing over her, was Mr. Darcy. He was looking as handsome as he had ever done, in his black evening coat and white satin breeches. He held out his hand. "Come, Phoebe, the ball is about to begin, and you must be there. I have to congratulate you on your excellent arrangements; the ball is already declared a success."

Guests were walking along the carpet laid down to mark the way from the house to the glasshouse. Flaming torches on either side gave the scene a fairy-tale quality, and the figures moving toward the glittering structure appeared to be characters out of an opera rather than the English gentry at a ball.

Most of the guests fell silent as they went into the vast space of the glasshouse, the thousands of panes glinting in the flickering light of the ring of torches around the outside, and the candelabra hung within it. Exclamations of delight and praise came from every quarter, and Phoebe, glancing at her uncle, saw a look of real gratification and pleasure on his face.

Mr. Darcy moved over to his niece's side. "When I had a dream for a new landscape at Pemberley, I could not have conceived anything as exquisite as this is tonight."

The musicians struck up, the dancers took up their places, and Mr. Darcy opened the Pemberley ball, dancing with the Marchioness of Lewisham. "Charlotte is an amazing beauty tonight, is she not?" said Eliza Bruton, watching her sister with great affection.

"You look distraught, Phoebe, is something amiss? Mr. Darcy told me how much he owes you for making all the arrangements for the ball, you have done a wonderful job, tonight will certainly be a night to remember."

Then Eliza's hand was claimed by a short man with a humorous mouth, and she went away to dance. Phoebe stood by herself, lurking behind one of the urns of lilies she had set up that morning. Her eyes were searching the company, looking again and again at the moving, shifting throng, at the dancers as they came past, looking for the one person she wanted to see.

Jack Harlow approached to ask her to dance. Even before the words left his mouth, he was thrust aside with a curt, "This dance is mine, Jack." Jack raised his eyebrows, shrugged, and with a wink at Phoebe, went off to find another partner.

Mr. Stanhope stood before her. Phoebe's heart was in her eyes, she could not say a word. Mr. Stanhope said, "Phoebe, we must talk," and without another word, took her arm and led her out of the glasshouse. In a moment they were out of the light and in the eerie shadows cast by the rising moon, just showing its brilliant face above the hill behind the house.

They walked in silence down the path which led to the river, and out on to the arched bridge. The water was dark and full of the soft sounds of the night; music from the ball floated out to them on the still air as Phoebe sought to find expression for what she felt.

There was no need for words; he looked down at her, and then with a sudden, urgent movement swept her into his arms, for a kiss so passionate that it shook Phoebe to her core. Finally, reluctantly, they drew apart, and as Phoebe opened her mouth to speak, he laid a finger across her lips.

"You misjudged me, and my affections, the strength of my feelings for you. No, listen. I was greatly honoured by Mrs. Vereker — do not wince at the name; it is time for us to be honest with one another. It is over between us, it was over some while ago, and since I met you, there has not been a thought of another woman. I'm not the philanderer your father takes me to be, although I can't deny that his other objection to me, that I come from a Whig family, is justified, and that I cannot change. I want to marry you, and if your feelings for me are what they were before that dreadful day when I saw your father, then we shall be married, however much your parents are opposed to the match."

Phoebe's head was against his shoulder, and she lifted her face to reply to him, laughter in her voice. "And what of your parents? Will they welcome me as a daughter-in-law?"

"They'll come round in time, and they won't have to see much of either of us, since we will be overseas for much of the time. My love, such a joy we shall have of it, and how busy you will be. I dare say you will outshine even my mother as a hostess, your parties will be the talk of Europe."

They stayed there for a long while, watching the silvery reflection of the moon rippling across the water, delighting in each other's company.

They had been missed. Sir Giles had been casting an anxious father's eye over the guests, looking in vain for Phoebe. His brother-in-law saw what he was at, and came over to him. "Giles, a word with you. It is about Phoebe and Arthur Stanhope. You may not want to hear what I have to say, but Phoebe's happiness means as much to me and to Elizabeth as it does to you and Georgiana. My aunt, Lady Redburn, has apprised me of the situation. I do not agree with her judgement on this, as on many other matters, and I think it is time that you and I put our heads together to work out what is best for Phoebe."

The musicians launched into a waltz, Arthur Stanhope circled Phoebe's waist with a strong arm, and as the beams of the moon filled the glasshouse with shimmering light, they went back into the glasshouse and began to dance.

TOUCHSTONE READING GROUP GUIDE

MR. DARCY'S DREAM

FOR DISCUSSION

1. Discuss the title of the novel. What is Mr. Darcy's dream? What are his wishes for his family and for the Pemberley estate?

2. "Nothing is constant, nothing can stay the same as it is year in and year out," according to Louisa (page 215). What changes are afoot in *Mr. Darcy's Dream?* Which characters embrace progress, and which characters resist it? What are their motivations for change or resistance?

3. Politics come between Phoebe and Stanhope: her Tory family and his Whig family are at odds. Do you think politics play as great a role in family relations and romance today? Why or why not?

4. Compare Miniver, Phoebe's maid, to Betsy, Louisa's maid. Who is more outspoken? Who has a better relationship with the woman she serves? What do these characters add to the novel?

5. Louisa tells Phoebe, "You are too rigorous in your judgements. You do not give time for people's virtues to grow on you, you are so quick to dismiss them that you never find out their true worth" (page 65). Is Louisa right about Phoebe's quick judgements? Who does Phoebe judge correctly, and who does she misjudge at first? Are her instincts unreliable?

6. Regarding unfaithful husbands, Phoebe wonders, "Was this the common lot of wives?" (page 278). How do female characters address marital infidelity in the novel? How would you answer Phoebe's question about husbands and wives?

7. Discussing women with Mr. Drummond, Phoebe says, "Our world is a smaller one than that of you men" (page 149). Do you think that the world is still a smaller place for women today?

8. Accepting Mr. Drummond's proposal,

Louisa says, "Fortune and estates mean nothing to me. I can imagine no greater happiness than being your wife" (page 390). Is Louisa naïve to dismiss money and social standing in her choice of a husband, or is she likely to find happiness with Mr. Drummond? What challenges might the couple face in the future?

9. Mr. Stanhope is a gentleman of the city, while Phoebe enjoys activities of the country, especially horseback riding. Where do you think the couple should make their home?

10. If you have read other works by Aston, how does *Mr. Darcy's Dream* compare to the other books in the series?

A CONVERSATION WITH
ELIZABETH ASTON

Mr. Darcy's Dream begins with heart-break: Sir Giles Hawkins forbids Phoebe to marry Arthur Stanhope. Why did you begin the novel in the middle of Phoebe and Stanhope's love story: after they fall in love at first sight, and at the beginning of their separation and misunderstanding?

Because this is a very dramatic point in their love story, and because the story is about how they come to know and understand each other better, so that, in contrast to some of the other marriages we see in the story, they can build a relationship which should make for a strong and lasting marriage.

The climax of Mr. Darcy's Dream takes place in the glasshouse that Mr. Darcy dreamed of and Hugh Drummond de-

signed. What inspired you to feature a glasshouse in the novel? What does it symbolize to you?

I found a picture of an extraordinary glass-house that was built at about this time in England. It was an amazing structure of curves and lightness and elegance — in fact you would think it was modern. It was the new iron technology that allowed people at this time to erect a glasshouse like that one. Glasshouses are about growth and light, just as the pineapples which grew in them are symbols of prosperity.

One could argue that *Mr. Darcy's Dream* — with its cat-and-mouse love story and rampant misunderstanding be-tween the two lovers — is the most similar of your books to *Pride and Preju-dice*. What do you think?

I don't think I would agree with that. The misunderstanding in *Pride and Prejudice* comes from exactly that, Darcy's pride and Elizabeth's prejudice. The misunderstand-ing in *Mr. Darcy's Dream* comes from Phoebe's mistaken belief that Mr. Stanhope is a rake. She is inclined to jump to this conclusion, without finding out if it is true

426

or not, because of her experience of infidelity in her own family, and her knowledge of the amorality of the Whig families such as the Stanhopes.

Servants play a substantial role in the novel, especially the two maids, Miniver and Betsy. Why are they given such a strong voice in the novel?

I wanted servants to have a voice in this novel because so much of it is set at Pemberley, a great house, and these households were very much a community, with the servants in their way as important to the well-being and well-running of the house as their masters and mistresses.

Relations between England and France are highlighted in the plot, from Stanhope's memories of the Battle of Waterloo to Hélène Verney's spying for France. Do you see this political and military background as a departure from Jane Austen? Why did you include this historical context in _Mr. Darcy's Dream_?

Jane Austen famously makes few references to the war with France that went on for most of her lifetime, even though several members of her family were caught up in the aftermath of the French Revolution and in the Napoleonic Wars. I'm not attempting to write a new Jane Austen novel, nor a sequel, and for me the historical and political context adds an extra dimension to the story.

George Warren resurfaces in *Mr. Darcy's Dream* as a villain; readers will remember his scheming ways from previous books in your series. Why did you revisit this conniving character?

George Warren has been the villain of all the previous books in this series, and so of course, I had to include him in *Mr. Darcy's Dream* and show him getting his final comeuppance!

A reader could easily enjoy *Mr. Darcy's Dream* without having read the earlier books in your series. Do you purposely craft each novel as a stand-alone experience? Do you recommend that new readers start at the beginning of the series?

It's always fun to follow a series through from its beginning, but since each book in this series has its own heroine and a stand-alone story, although with some characters from the other books playing a part or being mentioned, I don't think it much matters which book you being with — as long as you enjoy it.

From architecture to evening dress, the details of nineteenth-century England truly come alive in *Mr. Darcy's Dream*. What is your most reliable resource for researching this historical period?

There's no single reliable resource that I use for my research. It's partly knowledge and awareness of the period accumulated over many years, and partly having access to a good collection of books about the period and of that time.

Mr. Darcy's short speech about Phoebe's happiness closes the novel. Why does Darcy get the last word?

Mr. Darcy is only an unspeaking "presence" in the previous five books, as I deliberately decided not to use Jane Austen's main characters as characters in my stories. But I felt that he should have the last word in *Mr. Darcy's Dream*.

ABOUT THE AUTHOR

Elizabeth Aston is a Jane Austen enthusiast who studied with Austen biographer Lord David Cecil at Oxford. She is the author of *Mr. Darcy's Daughters, The Exploits & Adventures of Miss Althea Darcy, The True Darcy Spirit, The Second Mrs. Darcy,* and *The Darcy Connection.* She lives in England and Italy.